EPICUREAN
DELIGHTS

Visit us at www.boldstrokesbooks.com

EPICUREAN DELIGHTS

by

Renee Roman

2018

EPICUREAN DELIGHTS

ISBN 13: 978-1-63555-100-6

This Trade Paperback Original Is Published By
Bold Strokes Books, Inc.
P.O. Box 249
Valley Falls, NY 12185

First Edition: January 2018

Credits
Editors: Katia Noyes and Cindy Cresap
Production Design: Susan Ramundo
Cover Design By Tammy Seidick

Acknowledgments

Being a published author has been a long time dream. I'll spare you the details, but I owe more gratitude than I could ever express to Radclyffe. I would still be struggling to find my way if it were not for her tutelage and encouragement. Thank you, Rad, for the realization of a dream…my dream.

I also want to thank Sandy Lowe. You've taken the time to ask probing questions and make the stories I write come alive with your "whys" and "what-ifs." They kept me thinking and creating a deeper, richer novel.

Thank you to everyone in the BSB family, including the many authors who shared their friendship and answered my endless questions—I'm indebted. I need to thank my editor, Katia, whose patience and willingness to glean the best story from this fledgling wasn't always easy, and I'm glad you got me there. You were right. Sometimes less is more. To the production staff who are too many to name (and many I have yet to learn their names). Know that each of you has played an important part of my journey to fulfillment and I am appreciative of your dedication to the craft.

To my beta readers, Cathy and Jo. Thank you for giving me your hours and your honesty. And my cheerleaders—Kris and Maggie, who pushed me to "get the damn thing out the door." You were right. It was past time to let it go.

For the friends who understand my need to write even if it meant missing some of the good times. Evie, thanks for making your home a safe haven to write in and welcoming me to the "Yaddo." Dutch, thanks for the great author photo (I'll expect a few more!). To my family, many of whom only recently discovered this hidden talent I've harbored for years… Surprise! I do more than cook and bake.

And to my wife, Sue. You haven't always understood the way an author's mind works, but you never failed to encourage me to keep going. Thank you for putting up with my absence during the process and loving me anyway.

Readers—without you, authors like me would have little reason to write the next one. There will definitely be a next one.

To each and every person who has touched my life, whether mentioned by name or not, I live in gratitude for the amount of love you've shown. In return, I give you my heart and soul, written among the pages that bear my name.

Dedication

For Hudson,
and the memory of love that was hers
to give and take.

In a world of turmoil and tears,
she found peace.

Chapter One

Hudson grabbed her backpack from the seat and leaned against the car, smiling. Her time with her students gave her a reason to be happy. They were a special group of kids, and she'd been grateful for the opportunity to know them. She was going to miss them when they moved on to the more advanced class. She opened the driver door and retrieved a bouquet of flowers. They'd been a gift from Michelle, one of her older students, who was moving out of the area. The girl had been a clumsy, gangly youngster when they'd met. In just shy of a year, she'd turned into a disciplined swimmer, graceful in and out of the water. Michelle told her it was Hudson's belief in her abilities that had given her the confidence to do so well.

Hudson held the flowers and closed her eyes, inhaling deeply. When she opened them again, she looked up in gratitude. Clouds drifted across the pink-tinged sky. The earth was coming alive after the harsh winter. A cool breeze lifted the damp curls from her face as she watched two birds bathing in an abandoned pail. Although she wanted to stay outside longer, she headed inside the apartment. She was dreading spending another night with her younger roommates at their shared home. Though if she thought about it, it had never been *her* home and never would be. It was where she slept and sometimes ate, but there wasn't one thing in the apartment that felt like home. Home was hundreds of miles away. Where people knew and loved her. No one knew her in Albany. Certainly, no one loved her.

"I was just thinking about you." Jill pulled out a chair from the kitchen table. "We need to talk."

"Not now. I really need a shower." Hudson stepped into the laundry room, shoved the damp *gi* into her hamper, and strode toward the hallway but didn't get far.

"You look sexy even when you're sweaty. The shower can wait." Jill pointed to the chair.

Hudson didn't feel sexy. She'd always been physically active and her body was well toned. There were times her looks were a curse rather than a gift. And she'd never been one to fall for insincere compliments. Actions spoke louder than words. At least her breakup had taught her something useful.

"Okay, but I smell." Hudson lifted her arm, sniffed, and wrinkled her nose. She hoped Jill would let her escape, but when she glanced in her direction, Hudson knew it was time to have the inevitable conversation. She'd put if off long enough. Although her outward appearance was one of a confident, secure woman—inside, she was the exact opposite.

Jill sat across from her at the table and folded her hands. "Tell me what's going on."

"What do you mean?" Hudson tugged at a loose thread to avoid looking in her direction. The melancholy she'd been battling the last few weeks prevailed, but she hadn't wanted to admit to her roommates that it was time for a change.

"You know what I mean. What's wrong?" Jill wasn't serious often, but when they made eye contact it was obvious this was one of those times.

Hudson wanted to find the right words and figured she'd stalled as long as she could. "I'm grateful to you and Cathy for taking me in."

Jill pursed her lips. "You make it sound like you were a stray dog running amok in the streets." They both laughed, breaking the tension. Once Jill settled down, she waved a hand at Hudson. "I know what you're trying to do, handsome, and it's not working. Enough with going off subject. Spill it."

"Wow. You aren't going to let me get out of this are you!" Hudson blew out a breath. "How did I get here?" she asked.

Jill stared at her with confusion. "You answered the ad, silly woman."

Hudson sat back in a huff. "No, no. Not *here*." She pointed to the floor.

"Well, that's what you asked." Jill threw her hands in the air. "What then?"

"This past year hasn't been anything like I would have imagined."

Jill reached across the table and ran a thumb over Hudson's cheek. "Life isn't predictable. What *did* you imagine it would be?"

Hudson's heart ached. She'd quit her job and moved hundreds of miles from everyone and everything she knew to get away from her ex—the woman who'd ended their five-year relationship without batting an eye. It was time for her to make a change, too. But this wasn't how she'd planned on breaking the impending news.

"World travel. Women falling at my feet. Winning the lottery." She grinned. "You know—the same thing every sexy butch with a fantastic personality wants."

"Sounds wonderful, except for the women thing 'cause, you know, I'm into guys."

"Eww." Hudson wrinkled her nose.

"Hey! I can't help it if I like…" Color rose in her cheeks. "Never mind. See. Here we go again. Will you please just tell me what's bugging you so much?"

"I want…" Hudson paused, shaking her head. "I *need* to live alone and figure that out."

Jill's face turned wistful. "That's what I thought. Cathy and I are young and—" Jill's already pink face turned red before she rushed on. "Not that you aren't, but…"

"Oh, so now you think I'm an old lady?" Jill shrunk in her chair.

Laughing, Hudson slapped Jill's arm. "I know what you meant, but yeah, at thirty-six I'm not into all-nighters anymore." The conversation hadn't been as bad as she thought it would be. "Although, if I suddenly become rich, who knows." Hudson hoped Cathy would be okay with the news, too. She'd been very lucky to find such a sweet duo as roommates, even if they were a bit wild at times.

"I told Cathy you weren't going to be here much longer. You're an amazing woman and a good friend." Jill stood and squeezed her hand. "We're all going to be fine."

Three hours later, Hudson was frustrated. Her newspaper was a mess of crossed out listings. There weren't any apartments she could afford in her neighborhood; all the studios were downtown, not anywhere near where she wanted to be, and a decent one-bedroom in her current area was well over her budget. With all the rental properties in Albany, there had to be one that was right for her. All she had to do was find it.

Disheartened, she packed her gym bag. The dojo was the one place she found refuge. A good workout would bring her life into perspective.

Master Jin moved across the padded surface, watching her. The precision of his movements, along with the certificates hanging on the wall, suggested he was well into his seventies, although his real age was anyone's guess. He was often mistaken as lacking real power, but new members learned how wrong that assumption could be. She was still in awe of the physical control he showed. Even now, as he scrutinized his students, his face remained composed.

Hudson was sure he could tell how stiff her body was. The uninterrupted flow of energy was missing in the repetitive movements she'd performed thousands of times. When she'd asked to join eight months ago, he'd made it clear he only admitted students who were serious in dedication, form, and technique. Up until today, she hadn't disappointed him. She struggled to finish the sequence, out of breath and perspiring.

"Again." His stern voice filled the room as he waved his hand, indicating his displeasure. "Focus."

He stepped beside her as she performed the opening movements, leading her through the motion and projecting his calm energy. While she could feel his aura pressed against her skin, her inner turmoil formed a barrier. Again, she faltered.

"Stop. You need to meditate. You cannot be one with the world if you are not one with yourself."

If only it were that easy.

Hudson knelt on a corner of the mat, closed her eyes, and focused on her breathing. She struggled. Panic choked her. The dojo was the only place she was ever able to escape the uncertainty of her life. The hopelessness threatened to overtake her if she let her guard down. She searched for the calm, centered space that allowed her energy to flow. Distantly, she heard Master Jin's voice. *Search inside yourself for the way.* She could do this. She had to.

Forty-five minutes later, she opened her eyes and stood waiting for Master Jin to acknowledge her. She'd concentrated on the good in her life. Teaching youngsters to swim at the Y always lifted her spirits, and she looked forward to her next class with renewed anticipation. Their innocence and enthusiasm were infectious, and Hudson loved being around them, hoping someday there would be children of her own.

Master Jin faced her. "Much better, Hudson. Shall we begin again?"

Chapter Two

A ri parked at the far end of the lot and slowed her racing heart. *This is it.* Even though she wanted to run inside to find out how soon she'd receive her loan check, she took her time to enjoy the fresh air and sunshine. The day had turned warm, and a breeze rustled the leaves on the trees and lifted hair away from her face. She'd picked out a favorite skirt and silk blouse from her limited wardrobe hoping to project a professional image.

The extra steps helped settle her nerves, and she strode into the National Trust Bank with confidence. She gave her name to the office receptionist and reviewed a mental list. She had written a solid business plan and completed the application. This was the last piece of the puzzle she needed in order to get her catering business off the ground, and she was encouraged when she received a call to set up an appointment to talk with a loan officer. It all pointed to an approval for the money. Now, sitting across the desk, she knew how wrong she'd been.

She stared at the loan officer in disbelief. "I don't understand. Are you sure you have the right application?"

The man handed her a piece of paper. "Is that yours, Ms. Marks?"

Ari looked over the form. There was no doubt it was her application. The sinking feeling in her gut wasn't her only reaction. She stared a minute longer and forced the tears back, unwilling to show how upset she felt. Nodding, she handed it back.

"Can you tell me why I was denied?" Somehow, she managed to keep the disappointment from her voice.

"It's nothing personal." The agent appeared to regret being the bearer of bad news. "The bank has tightened its financial belt, so to speak, with the economy being what it is. You don't have any collateral, so there's no guarantee of repayment."

She wanted to scream! How could they expect someone asking for a loan to have collateral in the first place? "I see. I appreciate your time." Standing on shaky legs, she stuck out her hand. "Thank you."

"I'm very sorry. I wish I had better news."

"So do I," Ari said before ending the handshake. She turned and hurried to the exit. Her mind raced. She'd asked her boss at the restaurant where she worked and friends who owned businesses what her best options were to obtain the funds she still needed to open her business. Their advice was to go to the branch office right in Albany because they would be more motivated to invest in the local economy. Perhaps she'd been wrong to trust anyone else with such an important decision. *Too late for second-guessing.* She had no choice. She'd think of some other way to get things up and running. She had to. After spending the last six years focused on her formal training and saving every cent she could, she wasn't about to give up.

The trip home to her one-bedroom apartment took less than twenty minutes, but it felt more like an hour. Her hands shook as the disappointment set in. *Now what the hell am I going to do?* The answer was simple. She'd do the same thing she always did when life fell short of her expectations. She tossed her purse and keys on the table, curled up in the corner of the couch, and tucked her feet under her while she waited for her best friend, Kara, to answer the phone. All she needed right now was to hear a friendly voice.

"Hello?"

"Hi, Kara. How are things in the big city?" She tried to sound casual.

"Good. How are things in the little city?" Kara lived in New York City; any other town couldn't compare in her eyes.

"They're okay." Despite her best effort, her voice cracked. They'd been friends since the second grade and grew up in a rural neighborhood in the northern region of New York. It wasn't long before they became inseparable. Even during high school, if there was a pep rally, dance, or party, they always went together. They also didn't have any secrets between them. She still remembered the night she'd told Kara she liked girls and had been shocked when Kara said, "I was wondering when you were going to figure that out."

When Kara had been accepted at Pace University in the city, Ari had been left to decide whether to follow her dream of being a chef or settle for a career of her parents' choosing. Her mother had taught her how to cook and bake, but Ari longed to cultivate a finer palate and sharpen her skills, inspired by TV cooking shows. Kara had been gone a whole semester before she applied to the Culinary Institute of America. Her parents didn't have any idea. They were convinced she was filling out applications for nursing school and business colleges, which she did if nothing more than to buy herself some time. Ari was convinced, if she were accepted at the CIA in Hyde Park, they would give in and support her. Every day, she raced to the mailbox in hope of finding an acceptance letter.

And when it finally arrived, she couldn't contain her excitement. Her parents, however, didn't share her joy. In the end, she wasn't given a choice. She left her parents' house and moved in with Kara, where she stayed until she earned her degree. Moving upstate to the Capital District had been one of the hardest decisions she'd ever made. Kara told her it was about time she got out from under her wing and even helped her move, assuring her living in the twenty-first century meant they could visit each other often.

"Tell me what's wrong, and we'll figure it out."

She held her head in her hand. "The damn bank turned me down." Clattering noises over the phone meant Kara was on the move.

"I'm coming for a visit."

Kara always knew what to say to make her feel loved. "You don't have to do that. I can figure this out." Spending time with Kara was enticing, but with working in the medical billing office and hosting at the restaurant nights, she couldn't afford to take time off. Especially now.

A growl came through the phone. "I know I don't *have* to and I know you can figure out what to do. It'll just happen quicker and be a lot more fun if we do it together."

"You know I'd love to see you. Are you sure you can get away?"

"They owe me. I got them out of a big jam, and they'd do just about anything to keep me happy. No worries."

"I won't be able to take much time off." She tried to remember her schedule at the restaurant for the coming week.

"Whatever time you have will be great. You can show off your village."

"Hey! I'll have you know, it's a real city. A very pretty one, I might add." Ari picked up old newspapers and empty food containers as she moved around her small apartment. She'd been working so much she hadn't had the energy to clean, but she didn't want Kara to think she'd turned into a slob. Thinking of her impending visit, she felt the corners of her mouth lift. The future, at least her immediate one, looked a little brighter.

Chapter Three

Ari pulled Kara into a bear hug. "God, it's great to see you."

Holding her tight and smiling, Kara spun her around before letting go. "I've missed you, too." She picked up her discarded suitcase.

"I'm parked right outside."

They hooked elbows, turned from the crowd of train passengers, and headed toward the exit to take the quickest route back to Ari's place. Less than twenty minutes later, Kara plunked on the sofa and got comfortable.

Ari needed a drink if she was going to relive the events of the last six months. She handed Kara a glass of wine and paced as she talked. The worn carpet under her feet reminded her of all she'd gone without since earning her degree. Even with two jobs she never spent money unless she absolutely had to, and those times could be counted on one hand. Like when the zipper broke on her well-worn black pants. Or the pair of living room curtains she'd found in a bargain bin. The apartment was filled with mix-matched items. Not that it mattered. Kara was the first person to visit her apartment. She didn't have much energy left at the end of a day for a social life either.

"You know how hard I've been working to save enough money to open my own business." Ari thought about the long hours she spent developing flavors while she'd been at CIA. Every imaginable ingredient had been at her disposal. Her instructors marveled at her drive and told her it had been a long time since they'd seen a student with such passion for cooking, encouraging her to embrace the feeling. "I've even been making all these different recipes and bringing them to My Fare, where I'm a hostess, for the customers to try." Ari grabbed a stack of papers in protective sleeves. Some of the recipes were fairly common. Others she'd developed along the way, tweaking the flavors until she was happy.

Kara flipped through the top few. "This one looks good. Will you make it for me?"

Ari promised before continuing, telling her everything she'd done, including writing a woman-owned, start-up grant proposal and a small business loan application. By the time she finished talking, she felt better than she had in weeks. Sharing with someone who cared eased her fears.

"There must be something more you can do."

Ari shook her head. "I've tried everything. The only thing *more* left is to keep saving and hope for the best." She hated sounding resigned. She'd worked so hard for so long, and now her dream seemed even further away.

Kara held her hand. "Hey, I didn't come here for you to give up so easy. We'll think of something. Okay?" She pulled Ari in for another hug and rubbed her back. A loud grumble made them both laugh.

"I can't think when I'm hungry." Kara rubbed her stomach.

"Everything is close by," Ari said. "We can walk the neighborhood and get something to eat."

Ari took Kara's bag to her bedroom. "This is it. You can either bunk with me, or I can sleep on the couch." She turned. "Either way, I'm glad you're here."

"Me, too. Let me change out of these grungy clothes, and we'll take that walk."

Ari pointed out some of her favorite shops along Carriage Way. Two of her favorites were Fancy Pants, a vintage clothing boutique, and I'll Be Dangled, a funky handmade jewelry store with a window display of whimsical scarves and hats. She was happy to have Kara by her side while they pawed items, just like when they shopped together as teens. It was good to hear Kara's folks were doing well. They had been more supportive over the years than her parents ever were.

She'd forgotten about the easy rapport she shared with Kara. They talked as they strolled along the edge of the park, soaking up the last few hours of the June sun. Kara pointed to a shop and they ducked inside. Ari picked up a pair of particularly interesting earrings several times before finally putting them down. At least her frugal ways didn't take away from enjoying Kara's company.

In the next block, they checked out a pottery shop. Kara purchased a small bowl with pale blues and greens as a gift for her mother, who was coming to visit her in a few weeks. Kara said her dad was a bit harder to buy for and decided to keep looking.

"Are you shopped out yet?" Ari asked.

She looked at Ari in disbelief. "You know that's not possible, but I am famished."

They stepped through the door of Lacey's Bistro and were greeted by the scent of pine. A smooth, polished bar ran the entire length of the building with an impressive display of wine in floor-to-ceiling racks. Ambient lighting and warm colors filled the long, open space. Candles on every table and in many of the nooks and crannies added to the overall atmosphere.

"This okay?" Ari asked, pointing to one of the small cocktail tables with padded seats.

Kara turned in a slow circle. "It's beautiful." A painting displaying a semi-nude woman hung on the wall. "Is this a lesbian bar?"

Ari leaned close and whispered, "I think so, but don't tell the owners."

Kara wrinkled her nose. "Funny," she said.

"Actually, it's owned by a lesbian couple, but the patrons are mixed. Eclectic, like the decor. Every dish is an original creation. Sarah invited me to cook with her one afternoon, and I learned some of the finer points of fusion cuisine."

Kara raised her glass. "I've missed the shit out of you. Whatever the problems are, I know you can figure them out. I love you."

"I love you, too," Ari said.

Ari's friend Rae approached their table.

"Hello, Ari." She kissed Ari on the cheek.

"Rae! It's been a long time. Where have you been?" Ari turned in her seat and gave her a hug.

"Running a business isn't all it's cracked up to be at times, but I wouldn't have it any other way. I've had to change my gym time to evenings. Are you still going?" Rae asked.

"It's been a while."

"I'm going for a swim at the Y on Saturday if you want to join me."

Ari hesitated. "Okay." She wasn't enthused with the idea.

"Good." Rae glanced at Kara. "And who is this lovely woman?" Rae asked.

Ari made introductions. Rae asked where things stood with the plans for opening her business. Ari shared the disappointing news.

"I'm sorry to hear that," Rae said before her eyes brightened. "Have you considered buying a house?"

"What?" Ari leaned closer.

"Buy a house. It will give you collateral, and if you find the right one, you can run the business from it and write it off as an expense. Win-win."

"Oh, Rae, I don't know."

"Rae's right," said Kara. "It's worth considering." She looked at Rae. "What could it hurt?"

"Just promise me you'll think about it," Rae said.

Ari sighed in resignation. "Fine. I'll think about it."

"Great. My job here is done. Kara, it was a pleasure to meet you." Rae took Ari's hand and brushed her lips over the back, then she winked over her shoulder as she strode out the door.

Kara picked up her glass before motioning to Ari to do the same. "To a great solution from a sizzling hot woman."

"So, how do you know the looker?" Kara asked.

"She owns her own business in town. And she's a regular at the restaurant where I work. I've picked her brain a time or two for ideas."

"Uh-huh. I'm sure you have," Kara said. "How regular?"

Ari pursed her lips and picked up a menu. "Let's order. I'm starved."

Tugging at the shirring of her one-piece suit, Ari tried not to let her discomfort show. It had been a long time since she'd been swimming, and the bathing suit felt too snug. People milled about nearby, but they didn't seem to notice her fidgeting. A group of children splashed around at the far end of the pool, their cheers and laughter echoing off the tiled walls. Rae had texted saying she was running a little late and to start without her. Ari sat on a bench and waited for adult swim time, taking it all in.

A head broke the surface, and a tall figure emerged from the shallow water. The woman gathered the children around her and demonstrated a stroke. Clearly defined muscles flexed in her shoulders and arms, highlighted by the water's reflection. Wet tendrils of dark, wavy hair clung to her face and neck. A feeling stirred deep in Ari's center, one she'd all but forgotten. Her heartbeat quickened as she continued to stare, mesmerized by the dark-haired woman, and forgetting all about her discomfort.

The shrill sound of a whistle made her jump. The children scrambled out of the pool shaking off water as they went. The woman followed them toward the locker room, heading in Ari's direction.

Their eyes met and the woman smiled. Ari was mortified at having been caught. Heat rose up her neck. She broke their connection by turning away, looking anywhere but in her direction. When she was sure the coast was clear, she glanced at the doorway. The heat in her face began to subside. *If swimming instructors looked like that when I was a youngster, I'd have a gold medal by now.*

Ari handed Kara a glass of Riesling.

"How was your swim?" Kara lounged at one end of the couch, a cooking magazine open on her lap.

"It was fine until I tried to do an underwater flip and ended up swallowing half the damn pool." She flopped on the other end of the couch, looking forward to a much-deserved break. The rest of the morning had her running errands, including the dreaded grocery store. Unless she was shopping for ingredients for a new recipe, she rarely stocked her refrigerator. Kara's arrival meant she needed to have food in the apartment, and wine was always on the list. She also picked up the items to make the recipe she'd promised Kara.

"It did have an upside though."

"What was that?" Kara asked.

"There was a very attractive swim instructor." Ari envisioned the toned body. She pressed her thighs together and tried to ignore the unexpected throbbing.

"Well, as I live and breathe! You haven't mentioned a woman that way in ages. A little eye candy for your swim? Did you talk to her?"

"Of course not." She drained her glass. "She had a group of kids with her, and they left the pool right after I got there." Ari waved her hand dismissively.

Kara tossed the magazine on the table. "Shit. You're going to have to go for another swim." She waggled her eyebrows, making Ari laugh.

"Maybe. I'll be pretty busy house hunting and working." She stared into her empty goblet. The prospect of buying a home scared her to death. Even with a decent down payment, the mortgage would most likely prove to be too much for her to handle.

Kara scooted closer and put an arm over her shoulder. "Don't you dare be sad. I know you can find the perfect place. Then you can tell the bank to go fuck themselves." Kara always did have a way with words. "As long as I've known you, you've never backed down from a challenge, including the really big ones. You're going to make this work, you hear me?"

Kara was right. There'd been many challenges in her life, and she'd conquered each one. This was just one more.

"I'll drink to that. Hell, this isn't nearly as scary as that time we went careening down the hill and crashed into that car." She laughed at the memory. They'd been insane to try the daredevil stunt, but they'd been kids and the element of danger was exciting to them back then.

"Tell me about it." Kara giggled. "I still have the scars to prove riding on your handlebars wasn't as cool as we thought!"

The newsstand held dozens of papers from the region, as well as an array of free house hunting guides and open house flyers. Ari stacked them in her arm and kept searching, not wanting to miss any. She had an appointment the next afternoon with Sally, a Realtor that Rae had recommended who wanted to have an idea of what she was looking for and how much she could spend. Sally told her it was a buyer's market, meaning she could negotiate a better price if she found a house she liked. The news was encouraging. She hoped a sizeable chunk of her savings would be left for the business. She was going to need it.

Ari spotted more magazines on the bottom shelf, and when she leaned over, the precarious stack slipped and shot across the floor.

"Damn it."

A pair of black western boots stepped into view and the person wearing them handed her a couple of magazines that had slid out of her reach.

"Thanks," Ari said before looking up. *Oh, my God. It's her.* She stared into the captivating eyes of the instructor from the Y. It took a minute to realize the woman was offering her outstretched hand to help her up. The muscles in her arm flexed, just like they had in the pool. Ari swallowed hard. The fire low in her stomach smoldered to a slow burn.

"You're welcome." The woman looked around. "I think that's all of them." She smiled, displaying dimples. She tapped the stack Ari had finally managed to straighten. "Looks like you're going to be busy."

Off-kilter from the sudden rush of attraction, all Ari could do was nod before finally finding her voice. "Yes. Looks like you are, too." She pointed to the renter's guide in the woman's hand.

"Yeah. Time to find someplace I can call my own. Good luck." The woman turned and headed for the door.

"Wait!" Ari's sudden outburst drew stares. The woman looked back, and her friendly features turned to confusion.

She fumbled, knowing she needed to come up with a reason for calling after the woman. "Can I buy you a cup of coffee?" *Now what do I say?* "As a thank you?"

"That's very nice of you, but it was just a couple of magazines."

"Still," Ari said, "one good deed deserves another."

CHAPTER FOUR

Sitting so close to the woman was unnerving. Ari didn't know where the sudden impulse to pursue the woman had come from, but staying mute would make her look more foolish than she already felt. While one part of her brain was glad the woman accepted her invitation, another wondered what the hell was wrong with her.

She stuck out her hand. "I'm Ari. And thank you again."

The woman clasped her hand and gave a gentle squeeze. The warmth against Ari's cool skin sent a shiver up her spine. The light sweater she wore didn't ward off the reaction.

"My pleasure. I'm Hudson." She blew across her steaming coffee before taking a tentative sip.

Ari watched her soft looking lips, unable to stop staring at them until Hudson spoke, then she pretended a sudden interest in the contents of her cup.

"Are you looking to move into the area?"

Ari shook her head. "I already live in the southwestern part of town. I moved up from NYC a couple of years ago." She sipped on her latte. "I'm looking to buy a home in my neighborhood."

"You have a little whipped cream on your lip." Hudson pointed to her own mouth.

Ari quickly dabbed her lips with a napkin. "Smooth, aren't I? So much for making a good first impression."

"Is that what you're doing? Trying to impress me?"

"No! I…" Of course that's what she was doing, although she couldn't imagine why. She'd been with any number of women in dozens of situations, but none had thrown her into such a tailspin.

Hudson laughed and touched her hand. The heat she left in its wake should have scorched her skin. *What in the hell is wrong with me?*

"I was only teasing you. You're doing fine. So that's the reason for all the flyers and magazines?" Hudson glanced at the renter's guide on the table before turning her attention back to Ari.

"Well, I'm actually looking for a multipurpose place. One I can live in and run a business from."

"What kind of business?" Hudson sat back, looking like she had all the time in the world.

Ari wondered if telling Hudson about her personal life was going too far. After all, they'd only just met. She considered how much she should share, knowing once she got started it would be harder to stop, but she couldn't come up with a good reason not to. If Hudson was like her parents, she'd see it as nothing but a foolish venture. *Here goes nothing.*

"Catering. I have a master's in culinary arts, and I'd like to start using it, but so far it hasn't gone quite the way I planned." The truth wasn't far off the mark, and she felt better for not lying about her goals.

"I know what you mean about things not going as planned."

Hudson took a breath as though she was going to say more, but nothing came out, and Ari picked up the conversation. "What about you?" Ari asked. She drained her mug, remembering to lick her upper lip clean. No need to embarrass herself any more than she already had.

"I live with a couple of roommates. Not the ideal situation." Hudson glanced at her watch. "Thanks for the coffee and the chat, but I've got a class to teach soon."

Ari took the opportunity to find out more. "You teach swimming at the Y, right?" Hudson's face became wary, so Ari went on. "I think I saw you there a couple of weeks ago right before the adult swim."

Hudson's features relaxed. "That's it! I thought you looked familiar, but I couldn't remember from where. You were near the locker room entrance."

Ari perked up and nodded. *She remembers me.* "That was me."

Hudson stood. "Maybe we'll run into each other again."

Ari hoped so, but she couldn't tell Hudson her body hummed, and she wanted more time together. A lot more. Hudson's mouth and full lips begged to be kissed, and she didn't want to stop there. Ari's gaze moved along her strong jawline and continued to the indentation at her neck, traveling over the wide shoulders before ending at the bulging bicep flexing as Hudson shoved her hand in her jeans. Hudson cleared her throat, ending her fantasy.

"I'd like that, without me being on the ground." *I'd much rather be in bed.* Ari feigned interest in the slow-moving traffic to hide her nervousness before saying good-bye.

Thoughts of Hudson came at the most inappropriate times and this was definitely one. The papers Ari held would soon bear her signature. She had to concentrate to keep her hands from shaking. Hope swelled inside and her lofty dreams felt closer. She'd run out of patience and given in to Rae's suggestion.

Sally Huron sat across the table waiting for her to sign the contract.

Ari had done her research. The commission rate was fair and the language concise. She signed the paper and the deal was done.

"I know you're worried about finding just the right house. All I ask is for you to keep an open mind when we look at properties."

Kara had told her the same thing.

"It might not be your idea of perfect, but it might be perfect for you."

Ari nodded, shaking Sally's hand. "I will. I don't want to be one of those clients." Sally's head tipped to one side. Ari bit her lip. "The kind that must drive you crazy with unreasonable expectations." She didn't want to be a pain in the ass, but she couldn't help feeling pressured to make the right choice for her business—and her life. If Sally's expression was meant to put Ari at ease, it worked.

"Somehow, I don't think you'd ever fall into that category, but I'll keep it in mind."

When Ari got back to her car, her nerves were still on edge. There was no way she could drive. She pressed the speed dial number. When the familiar voice said, "Hi," she took a deep breath.

"I did it."

"I left too soon. This calls for a celebration," Kara yelled through the receiver.

"Don't you think that's a little premature? All I did was sign the contract."

"Come on. You haven't let loose in so long, I'll bet your undies are in a bunch."

"They are not!" She hated to admit it, but she hadn't really had time to relax since she'd made the move almost two years ago. There was always something to worry over, or plan, or calculate. She'd squirreled away every penny. Treating herself was a luxury.

"Stop."

"What?" Ari asked.

"Stop worrying about money. At least for tonight. Okay?"

"How do you know what I was thinking?"

"Unless you've been replaced by an alien, I know you, Ms. Marks," Kara stated matter-of-factly.

Kara was right. She hadn't changed her ways in years. *Maybe that was part of the problem.*

❖

Hudson stared at the ledgers spread in front of her. A cursory glance told her they weren't as much of a mystery as they were a mess. As an independent financial auditor and accountant, she liked that she could set her own hours. But there wasn't a guaranteed paycheck, and she'd taken a second job for its steady income. She hung her blazer over the back of the chair, then rolled up her sleeves. It took her an hour to get through the first few pages of incomprehensible numbers and untraceable entries. A couple of hours later, she pushed away from the desk and rubbed her eyes. She was desperate for a cup of coffee.

Can I buy you a cup of coffee? Ari's voice. Soft as velvet. She hadn't wanted to accept until she'd seen the silent plea in her eyes. Sitting and talking had been enjoyable. No expectations. No flirting. Just two people having a casual conversation. The same way she and Pam had started. Goose bumps prickled her skin. It was a good thing they hadn't exchanged numbers. She didn't want a repeat of that fiasco.

Determined not to linger on thoughts of Ari, she stood and stretched her back. She'd promised Jill and Cathy she'd join them for dinner and drinks. She was already running late. She could be at the bar in less than twenty minutes and dialed Jill's cell to let her know. The loud music almost drowned out the voice on the other end.

"Hi, Hudson."

"I'm leaving work now. Where are you?"

"We're a few doors from Cagney's. We were in the mood for greasy pizza. You want to meet us here?" Jill yelled over the noise.

"No, that's okay. I'll catch up with you later. I need a little down time."

"Okay. Later." Jill ended the call.

Her anger flared. *It was just like them to change their minds.* She took a breath. *I did the same thing when I was their age.* She turned the key and then backed out of the lot. She was looking forward to a quiet dinner. At least she hoped it would be quiet.

❖

Hudson walked through the door and braced for pounding music to hit her. When it didn't come, she took a seat at the bar and let the quiet jazz soothe her earlier irritation away. This wasn't the type of place her roommates were known to frequent. Now she understood why they had backed out.

"What can I get you?" the bartender asked.

"A good glass of red wine with some dark fruit and spice flavors."

"The Franck Balthazar Cornas Cuvee 2007 is our best, but it's only sold by the bottle."

What the hell. I deserve it. "I'll take it."

The rich burgundy liquid coated the glass as she swirled it. The first sip made her taste buds come alive. She ordered food and was pleasantly surprised by how well it paired with the perfectly cooked lamb chops. She pushed her empty plate away as her cell phone vibrated.

"Hello?"

Giggling and shushing came through the phone. "Hudson, it's Jill. I don't think we're going to make it. There's a big group of our college friends here, and no one wants to leave. Do you want to join us?"

"I think I'll pass. I'm going to finish my drink and head home. Have fun."

Just as well. I'm pretty beat. The half bottle of wine was more than she should have had, but it was too good to go to waste. Maybe she could take it with her. She was about to ask the bartender when a beautiful butch with dark blue eyes and curly dark hair caught her eye. The response of her rapidly beating pulse startled her right before her inner voice yelled, "No." She'd reacted to Pam in much the same way. A flood of angst made her shiver. Beads of moisture formed on her upper lip. The visceral reaction to the woman made her stomach flip. She needed to get out of there. Quick. She abruptly pushed her chair back, which caught the bartender's attention.

"I have to leave. Can you give the rest of this to the woman in the white shirt?" She pushed the bottle toward him.

"Sure. Everything okay?"

Hudson swallowed the bile rising in her throat. "Yes. Just an urgent matter." She forced a smile. "Thanks." She settled her check and hurried out.

When the cool air hit her she was able to breathe. She hurried to her car. Frustrated, she banged both hands on the steering wheel. *What the hell is wrong with me?* She had no control over the irrational panic, and it scared her to death.

Ari plopped on the loveseat with a grunt. She enjoyed interacting with the restaurant's customers, but the long hours and little sleep were taking their toll. Her head pounded and her feet screamed to be free of the confines of her fashionable yet well-worn shoes. She needed a new pair and dreaded spending so much money on comfort. She could wait another few weeks until they went on sale. Every penny counted. She'd prove to her father she wasn't a failure. She didn't want to ever have to admit he was right. Not like that time in grade school.

Her sixth-grade class had performed a short production of *Alice in Wonderland,* and she'd been chosen to play the Cheshire Cat. Her mother had quietly encouraged her and even snuck in moments here and there to help her memorize her lines. Her father had pissed and moaned during the days leading up to the play. He had better things to do than spend an evening with a bunch of misfits. On the ride to school, he glanced in the mirror and growled at her. "I hope you don't embarrass your mom and me, or there'll be hell to pay."

Ari had done okay until she made the mistake of looking at the audience like the teacher had instructed them during rehearsals. The first and only person she saw was her father. He wore a snarl on his weathered face, and she froze when it came to remembering her next line. All she could think of was the promise her father had made if she embarrassed him. And that's exactly what she was doing. Luckily, her friend was standing next to her and nudged her into action, whispering her line. After that, she didn't dare look anywhere but at the other cast members. When it was over, she found her mother in the crowd. Her father wasn't with her.

"Where's Father?" she asked.

Her mother's face was tense as she helped her get her coat on. "He's in the car. It's best if you don't say anything to him."

Ari knew she would most likely be punished. She slid into the backseat and kept her eyes lowered.

Her father pulled out of the parking lot and slammed his hand on the steering wheel. "I knew damn well you'd screw up." His eyes were full of fire as he stared at her in the rearview mirror. "You'll never amount to anything. Don't ever ask me to come to school again, you hear me?" he yelled.

All she could do was nod. She was trembling so much that she didn't trust her voice, but she wouldn't cry. She never let him see her cry. That night she had buried her face in her pillow and sobbed until the hurt dulled. His words cut her deeper than any spanking ever could, although she was glad he had never touched her. Ari believed he didn't want to soil his hands. He had never wanted children. And he had let her know every chance he got.

It had taken a lot of encouragement from Ari's friends to survive his verbal abuse. Her mother hadn't been much help. She'd cowered under his hard stare, always the dutiful wife who did what she was told. This was her chance to show him she could excel despite his discouragement. But still, there was always the ingrained doubt. What if she couldn't find a house she liked? What if the zoning laws wouldn't let her run a business from her home? What if? Her life was full of what-ifs right now. Crunching the numbers didn't help with her anxiety level. There were too many pieces to fit into the financial puzzle. Student loans took a fair chunk of her income—thanks to her parents' lack of support.

Exhaustion took over and she fell into bed. Her brain was fried. As she drifted off, all she remembered was remarkable gray eyes. Hudson's eyes. She wished they'd exchanged numbers. Not that she had time to call. Or date. Or have sex. But still…

Chapter Five

Hudson flipped through the want ad magazine. She really wanted her own kayak, but she needed a place to live first. Students milled around outside the entrance to the YWCA as she searched. She was fortunate in having such a great group of kids. Her time with them was a pleasure and reminded her of when she was an eager student with a group of enthusiastic teammates. She tossed the magazine aside and headed in their direction.

"Hi, Hudson! Can we do the butterfly today?" Jocelyn, the one with potential, always asked what stroke they'd be practicing. Hudson had been the same at her age.

She tried to school her reaction as she ruffled Jocelyn's hair. "I don't know. Does everyone else want to do the butterfly?" The entire group cheered. "Okay. Okay. The butterfly it is," she said. "Now everyone go inside and suit up. I want to see some good stretching before we hit the water."

When her students had completed two warm-up laps, she blew the whistle.

"Okay, everyone gather around." She slid into the pool. "Butterfly time." Hudson spread her arms like wings and pretended to be a butterfly. The kids cheered and splashed each other before settling down.

"Who wants to show the group how it's done?"

Hands flew in the air. "I do. I do!"

Patrick stood off to the side. He was new to the group, having joined a few weeks ago. He had talent but remained quiet. Hudson hoped he'd come out of his shell with some encouragement.

"Patrick?"

The lanky boy looked up. "Yes, Ms. Frost?"

Hudson admired his good manners. She motioned him to stand beside her. "Call me Hudson. Okay?" He nodded shyly. "How about you show us your butterfly?" She looked at the group.

Timmy spoke up first. "Yeah, Patrick. You're good at it." Soon more voices followed, cheering Patrick on.

She put her arm around Patrick's shoulder. "What do you say? Want to give it a go?" Even though his cheeks turned rosy, she could tell when his eyes met hers, he was excited to lead the group.

"Okay." Patrick took off and swam to the other side of the pool. He returned and stood with his teammates. They congratulated him with excited praise. He was beaming.

Hudson put them through a rigorous routine before her final whistle signaled everyone should get out of the pool and head for the locker room.

Becka rounded the lockers a few minutes later, but she didn't look at Hudson.

"Hi, Becka. Do you have a question?" Hudson sat on the bench so they were eye level.

Becka bit her lower lip as she looked up. "How come you aren't afraid to let girls see your body?"

"Well, we're all girls for one thing. Every girl's body has the same parts; they just look different at certain times as we grow. No one should be ashamed of the way they look."

"Yeah." Becka nodded. "Are you ever mad you don't have big boobies?"

"No." Hudson suppressed any urge to laugh. "I try to take care of the body I have."

"You sure do that. My momma says she'd pay good money to have a body like yours. Bye." Becka skipped out the door.

Hudson shook her head. She couldn't help but grin and wondered how many of the other mothers made her the topic of conversation.

❖

"Hud, what's up, girl? Haven't seen you in a while."

"Hey, George. I've been here and there, keeping busy." George leaned on the counter, ignoring the tall stool nearby. Hudson suspected he was trying to give his back a break but was too proud or too stubborn to use the stool. She rounded the counter, pulled the stool closer, and handed him a cup of his favorite specialty coffee. She and George had developed a fondness for each other. She felt guilty for not stopping in more often. Hudson wandered the short aisles and picked out a couple of items. When she returned to the counter, George looked like he had something to say.

George tipped his head in her direction. "Maybe I could ask a favor?"

"Sure."

Grinning with a few missing teeth, he tipped his chin to the narrow hallway leading to the back. "There's a box in the kitchen. I can't get it no farther. My back…" He gestured behind him.

"No problem, George."

"You be careful. She's a heavy one," he called after her.

Hudson hefted the box loaded with books. George stood next to the counter when she returned. "Where do you want it, George?"

"Here, here. Put her down, girl." George pushed an old chair toward Hudson and pointed. "Appreciate it."

"Where's it going?"

"That church down the street. I've read them all a few times. Almost know 'em by heart by now." George chuckled before sipping from the cup, a satisfied sigh escaping his cracked lips.

"I'll toss it in my car and drop it off."

"You're busy. No need me adding to it." George put her goods in a bag. "Eight dollars," he said and slid the bag toward her.

She placed a ten-dollar bill on the counter, tossed the bag on the box, and winked at him.

"Least I can do for a friend."

❖

Ari looked at her workload. The medical billing office paid well and provided health insurance, which was the main reason she stayed. The thought of having to pay for her own coverage when she quit was another thing she tried not to think about.

"Want to do lunch?" Rhonda edged a full hip onto the corner of her desk. Her curvy friend wore silk better than anyone she knew. It hugged Rhonda's body in all the right places, and they often joked about the unwanted attention she received because of it. Her husband was the jealous type, and Rhonda discouraged the men in the office from overstepping friendly boundaries. She also wasn't about to hide under ill-fitting clothes. "I have a right to show off what God gave me. It doesn't mean I have to put up with being pawed," she'd said after someone tried to get a little too friendly. She and Ari had soon developed an easy camaraderie. She picked up a stack of papers. It would be easy to get lost in the sincerity of Rhonda's companionship and turn her attention away from her financial worries to the more pleasant topics she and Rhonda talked about.

Hudson was a pleasant distraction, too, able to divert her attention to more intimate thoughts, along with turning her center to liquid fire. Heat rose to her cheeks. She was grateful Rhonda didn't know what she was thinking.

"I'd love to, but I have to leave early and wasn't planning on taking a lunch." Ari saw Rhonda's disappointment. "Can I have a rain check for next week?"

Rhonda's eyes rolled in exasperation. "Girl, you work too much. Do you ever have fun?"

Ari couldn't remember the last time she'd relaxed and had fun before Kara's visit. She knew she couldn't continue to ignore being good to herself and enjoy life more. She didn't want to drive herself into an early grave.

Rhonda patted her hand and stood. "It's okay, honey. Next week is fine." She turned to leave and paused. "Don't run yourself ragged. Everyone deserves a break, including you."

Ari didn't understand her disappointment. There wasn't room in her life for a relationship. It made no sense to look for Hudson. *Then why do I keep doing it?* She stepped into the water after deciding all she wanted was a friend. *Everyone needs friends, and Kara isn't here anymore.* She swam lap after lap and tried to concentrate on her strokes. Every time she found her rhythm, Hudson's warm smile filled her vision.

A few minutes later, she gave up, knowing she was only kidding herself by thinking the only reason she was there was for the exercise. Ari rounded the lockers, her head down, and collided into someone. Arms shot out to steady her.

"Oh, my God," she gasped. "I'm so sorry." Gray eyes locked with hers, a mischievous expression quirking one corner of Hudson's mouth.

"We really need to stop meeting like this." Hudson's hands slid down the length of her arms before breaking contact and taking her warmth with her.

So much for making a good second impression. "I seem to have a knack for making a fool of myself." Ari wrapped her towel around herself, self-conscious of her outdated suit and less than perfect body. Hudson didn't have an ounce of fat on her, and she imagined how the ripple of Hudson's muscles would feel under her hands.

"I don't think you're a fool. I'd wager you're anything but."

Hudson raised an eyebrow when Ari looked up, as though waiting for Ari to respond. Her legs turned to spaghetti under the intensity of Hudson's gaze.

"Sorry," Ari mumbled and brushed by. All she wanted to do was grab her stuff and run.

Hudson caught her hand. "I have a class in ten minutes, but I'd like to reciprocate that cup of coffee sometime."

Warning signals went off in Ari's head. She didn't have time for someone new. Especially for someone who caused such a primitive reaction. Maybe Hudson would think twice if she gave her a reason to recant the offer.

"You're not afraid I might knock you down next time?"

"I'm pretty tough. I'll take my chances."

Against her better judgment, Ari gave in. "Okay, but don't say I didn't warn you." She went to her locker and Hudson followed. She was too close and the space around her felt thick and cloying.

"Do you have a cell phone or a pen? I seem to be without either." Hudson gestured at her one-piece suit.

"Uh, sure." Ari unclipped the key from her strap and fought to get it in the lock. Closing her eyes, she took a steadying breath and prayed it would open. She almost shouted when she heard the click. She rummaged in her bag and finally produced her phone and shoved it at Hudson.

Hudson stared at her. "If you'd rather not…"

"No. I mean yes. Coffee. Coffee would be great." Ari leaned against the lockers, hoping the awkward moment would end soon. Hudson handed her phone back.

"Call me whenever. For coffee." A brilliant smile lit up her face.

"I will. I work a couple of jobs and I'm house hunting so it may be a few days." It sounded like a brush-off even to her. Maybe that was okay.

Hudson raised her hands in surrender. "No pressure."

Ari saw the disappointment, but it didn't linger. *Why am I being rude?* Hudson hadn't done anything to deserve being snubbed. She chewed her lower lip.

"Hey."

"Yeah?"

"Would Wednesday be good for you?" Ari asked.

"Call me. We'll figure it out."

Hudson walked to the edge of the pool and dove in. Her long strokes allowed her to cover the length in a matter of seconds. Confusion reigned over her emotions. She could have sworn Ari wanted to spend more time with her. Now she wasn't so sure. Maybe Ari was like all the others. Women who were drawn to her looks and didn't bother to find out about her as a person. She had always wanted someone who would love her for the things they couldn't see. The things that mattered most in a relationship, such as strength of character and honesty. Making a "cute couple" only went so far. She longed for the depth of love her parents shared. They'd found it, so why couldn't she? She needed to talk to them. Find out what were some key elements in their loving, supportive relationship. Pam had been a mistake. She'd read the cover and the blurb, but the inside pages had missed the mark.

Was Ari another Pam? Maybe she'd misread Ari's intentions. It was a stupid move on her part. She should know better. If the past had proven anything, it had shown she couldn't trust her instincts. Maybe Ari wouldn't call, and she'd save herself from worrying about more heartache. There wasn't any way in hell she was ready for another relationship.

She broke the water's surface and found her students lined up at the edge of the shallow end. Some yelled greetings and others were stretching to warm up. How long had they been waiting? There'd be time for deep thinking later. She had a job to do. She stood and put the whistle to her lips, blowing a short, strident blast. What followed was a mass of uncoordinated arms and legs, splashing and spraying water in their attempts to be first at her side.

Well, that wasn't unpleasant at all. Not. Ari flipped off the water and shook her head. She'd sent so many mixed messages that she was convinced Hudson had no idea if she'd ever call. One minute Ari wanted to know her better, the next she was convinced there was no room in her life for a relationship. Which was it? She needed to address things one at a time. Someday there'd be room for a special woman in her life. It wasn't tomorrow. Still, it would be nice to have a friend to talk with about important things, but building a close rapport took time. Time was the one thing she didn't have a lot of. And Hudson, with her perfect body and handsome features, was a big distraction. One she couldn't afford right now.

CHAPTER SIX

Ari double-checked the address and pulled up to a large Victorian on a quiet street. An old-growth lilac bush out front was in full bloom and could benefit from a pruning. An elderly couple sat in rocking chairs on their porch a few doors down and stared in curiosity. She wondered how long the house had been on the market and if the owners still lived there. Sally's enthusiasm gave her hope this might be the one. Kara had been calling every few days to lend moral support. Excitement fluttered in Ari's stomach.

Sally waved from the front steps, and Ari took a deep breath. Nervous energy coursed through her body. Every house she'd looked at so far had left her crestfallen. The kitchen was too small, the house, tiny. The neighborhood was wrong. It needed a total renovation.

Sally hooked arms with Ari and led her up the front stairs. "I just know you're going to love this one," she said. "It's been on the market for a while, but…well, see for yourself." She entered the code on the lockbox, retrieved the key, and unlocked the front door.

"So, as you can see," Sally began, "there's a good-sized living room, a lovely dining room, and the best part of all is the partially renovated kitchen."

Ari gawked at the spacious kitchen with stainless steel appliances, including a Wolf five-burner stove with a double oven. The owners had invested a small fortune in them. Upper and lower wooden cabinets lined three of the walls and provided plenty of counter space, but they would need refinishing. The huge center island screamed "use me," and she imagined the surface covered with trays of delectable treats. Closing her eyes, she could smell the aromas swirling around her, tempting the neighbors to her door. Continuing the tour, she opened another door that led to a walk-in pantry and pictured all the equipment and goods she would be able to stow inside. Whoever owned this house loved to cook.

"I hope the rest of the house is this impressive."

"Come with me." Sally pointed out a small but functional bathroom, two modest bedrooms, and the master suite. Aside from needing some patchwork and painting, it was in good shape. Walking back to the kitchen, Sally pointed to a thick oak door with a double deadbolt.

"That leads to the upstairs apartment over the garages in back. There's a separate entrance on the side." She opened the door, flicked the light switch, and led the way.

Another door at the top opened into the apartment. The living room was a decent size. It also had a well appointed, eat-in kitchen, full bath, and a large bedroom. The closets were spacious with a stacked washer/dryer tucked behind louvered doors. A small covered porch faced the postage-sized yard. The grass was sparse and could use attention, but it was cute. It had everything she wanted. The one caveat—it had to be way out of her price range. Her earlier optimism began to fade.

Her heart hammered in her chest. "How much do you think I could rent this for?"

"I looked up comparable apartments and you can get as much as nine hundred a month, if you included one of the garages."

She started crunching the numbers.

"Let's head back downstairs." Sally locked the door.

"What's the asking price?"

Sally gestured to the table and opened a folder. "The asking price is two hundred eighteen thousand, but they're motivated to sell. I think they'd accept a lower offer." She leaned forward as if sharing a well-guarded secret. "I found out they're paying three mortgages and they want out in a hurry."

Red flags went up. "What's wrong with the house?"

"As far as I can tell, it's in great shape." Sally shrugged. "Not many people want to be landlords these days."

"Can I run my business from here?"

"As long as you don't hold events on the property, you can have a home-based business." Sally handed her an official-looking printout entitled, "Zoning Laws in Albany County."

Ari picked up the house flyer and stared at it for a long time.

"Do you want to make an offer?" Sally asked.

"Hell, yes! And we're going to shoot low and hope for the best."

"Great. I'll send them an offer. They may counter, but I have a feeling they'll take what they can get."

Ari paced behind the hostess station, unable to focus on the dinner customers waiting for their table to be cleared. The house she'd looked at earlier was foremost in her mind. She'd dared to go as far as picturing a scene in the kitchen—every space occupied by dishes prepared for her first catering order.

"Ari?" Ralph, the owner, called out to get her attention. He pointed to the table in the corner.

She grabbed menus and turned to the patrons. "Sorry for the wait. Right this way." On her way back to her station, she mouthed an apology to Ralph and refocused. Sally told her it might be as long as a week before she heard if the sellers would accept her offer. One that was fifteen thousand below the asking price. It was a risk, but one they both hoped would pay off. Now she wondered if it had been a wise move. She loved the house, and the extra income from the apartment would go a long way to putting her mind at ease about being able to afford it. As long as she could find a reliable tenant.

A group of six patrons walked in. It was going to be a long night.

❖

Two days later, Ari rushed out the back door. Sally had delivered the signed contract at the start of her shift, so this was her first chance to take a break.

I'm going to be a homeowner.

"Hello?" Kara barked into the phone.

"I know it's that time, but I had to share the news." Kara would be binge watching *CSI*. "I got it."

"You got what?"

"The house. They accepted my offer."

"Holy shit! For real?"

Ari laughed. "Yes, for real. They were so happy to unload it they agreed to pay for the inspection *and* my closing costs."

"That's fantastic. When's moving day?"

"I have no clue, but I should close in a few weeks."

"You know I have a million questions, right?" Kara laughed.

"Yes. So do I." She took a breath before asking, "Do you want to move here and rent the apartment?"

"Honey, you know I'd love to, but I love my job and being in New York City."

"I know. It was silly of me to ask." It had been wishful thinking on her part.

"You must know someone there who's looking for an apartment."

A scene flashed in her mind. It was crazy. "I might."

"Good."

"Hey, Kara?"

"Yeah?"

"I love you. Thanks for letting me interrupt your show."

"Anything for you. I love you, too. Call soon, okay?"

"Will do. Bye." She headed inside, glad she had a short shift tonight. She prayed the next two hours would fly by.

When she got home, Ari sat on the edge of the couch holding the contract in her hand. She scrolled through her contact list. There it was. Hudson Frost. Biting her lower lip, she looked at the clock and wondered if it was too late to call. She wouldn't sleep a wink if she waited. If Hudson didn't answer, maybe she'd call again tomorrow. For some strange reason, she didn't want to leave a message. *Here goes nothing.*

Hudson watched the flash of screens as she flicked through channels. Bored, she debated going out for a drink, but it was getting late, and she had to work in the morning. The vibration of her phone caught her off guard, displaying a number she didn't recognize. She almost let it go to voice mail before swiping the screen.

"Hello?"

"Hi. Is this Hudson?"

"Speaking." The voice sounded familiar, but she couldn't place it.

"It's Ari." Ari paused before saying more. "The woman who has a habit of running into you. Literally."

Hudson sat up. It had been almost a week since she'd seen her, and she expected to never hear from her again. "Glad you clarified. I know so many Aris." She was being a smartass, but Ari seemed like the type who wouldn't mind some good-hearted ribbing.

"Ha ha. You're funny." Ari's voice dripped with sarcasm.

"Sorry." Maybe she'd been wrong about Ari's sense of humor.

"Gotcha." Ari giggled into the phone.

"Now who's the smart aleck?" She settled back against the couch.

"I was calling to see if you were free tomorrow for our coffee date?"

A date. Hudson's heart skipped a beat. She didn't want this to be a date, did she? That was why she was surprised when she said yes. *What the hell am I doing?* Too late now. If she changed her mind, she'd sound like a confused teenager, which was exactly how she felt.

"Tomorrow works."

"Great. How about six o'clock at the Dark Side Bistro on Main?"

Hudson ignored the voices running amok in her head. "I know where that is. You're serious about your coffee."

"Uh, if you—"

"Ari?"

"Yes?"

"I'll see you there." Hudson pressed end. Whether she'd meant for coffee to be a date or not, it certainly felt like one. She picked up the remote and resumed her search for something that could hold her interest.

Ari certainly did. She laughed out loud thinking about the times Ari had tried to appear calm without success. Like their first meeting when Ari had whipped cream at the corner of her mouth and Hudson had resisted wiping it with her finger. And when she'd literally run into her and Hudson had held her for too long. And then at the locker, when she'd closed the distance between them and could see Ari's hand tremble.

Yes. Ari had her attention. Now she needed to decide what to do with it.

Ari had agonized over the location. She hadn't wanted Hudson to think they were on a date-date, but she wanted to be able to have a serious conversation without the din of a college coffee bar. The Dark Side had a sophisticated atmosphere and was a little more expensive, meaning the students tended to be few.

"This is weird," Ari said as they stood outside the Bistro.

Hudson's head cocked. "What do you mean?"

"I haven't dropped anything or run into you. I'm not sure what to do." She shoved her hands deep into the pockets of her jeans. This wasn't how she planned to start the conversation. Whether or not Hudson even wanted to hear about the apartment was just the tip of the iceberg. She couldn't imagine talking about rent, boundaries, or all the other things she'd thought about since last night. Hudson's easy nature helped her relax a bit.

"How about we start with coffee, and if we survive that, we'll see what comes next?"

Ari ignored the heat in her face and looked at the selection, including specialty drinks. There were so many to choose from she had no idea what she wanted and decided to have whatever Hudson was having.

"What's your pleasure?"

Hudson's eyebrow shot up. "It's a little soon to be asking for details, don't you think?"

Ari slapped Hudson's arm. "I meant coffee. What kind of coffee?" She dropped her gaze and shoved her hands back in her jeans. Flirting wasn't something she was comfortable with, especially when she kept telling herself she wasn't going to go there with Hudson. *Then why* do *I keep going there?*

Hudson hadn't meant to insinuate there'd be more than a casual friendship between them, but the color rising from Ari's neckline made her wonder if the idea wasn't as farfetched as she thought. She stifled the sigh that almost escaped. She was getting way ahead of herself. It was only coffee. Nothing more. At least that's what she kept telling herself.

They sat across from each other at one of the small outdoor tables. Hudson eyed Ari as she fidgeted with the lid on her coffee, nearly spilling the hot beverage onto both of them. Ari was nervous, and she wasn't sure why. She decided to try to put her at ease.

"So what do you do besides swim and have coffee with strangers?"

Ari snorted. The lopsided grin let her know Ari got the joke. "I work at a medical billing office and I also hostess at a local restaurant." She inhaled the rich aroma of her mocha latte and sipped.

Hudson admired Ari's long eyelashes and creamy, smooth complexion. "We have something in common." Ari's gaze met hers. "Aside from the Y, I'm an independent accountant."

Ari sat up with renewed interest. "Really? So you do bookkeeping and such?"

"Among other things, like audits and filing taxes."

"What do you do for fun?"

The question seemed innocent enough, but she wasn't sure she wanted to share more than the usual pleasantries expressed among virtual strangers. "A little of this and a little of that." Hudson took the lid off her coffee cup and sprinkled in a little cinnamon. "Any secrets you care to share?"

Ari fidgeted and looked down the brick path to the street.

"I didn't mean to pry." She reached across the short space and gently covered Ari's hand with her own. "Are you okay?"

Ari took a deep breath. "That obvious?" She leaned back and met her gaze. "I have an ulterior motive for calling you."

Hudson panicked. All her fears about seeing Ari again rose to the surface, threatening her idea of being just friends.

Alarm showed on Ari's face. "It's not what you think."

"How do you know what I'm thinking?"

Ari jerked back as though she'd been slapped, then stood. "This was a bad idea."

Hudson couldn't let her go. Not like this. She grasped Ari's arm, and Ari yanked it away before facing her.

"I don't know why I reacted like that," Hudson said. Would she ever be able to have a normal relationship? Did she even know what normal would feel like? And why was she worrying about any of that now? She hadn't intended to lash out. "Please give me another chance."

Ari pointed to their abandoned cups. "Let's finish our coffee."

After they sat, Hudson spoke first. "Ghosts of Christmas past."

"What?"

"It's a long story for another time. So…what motive *did* you have for calling?"

"Are you still looking for an apartment?"

"Yes. Why?"

"I have one. Well, I'll have one to rent soon. When I saw it, I thought of you and figured you were probably the handy type."

It was Hudson's turn to have a little fun. "You mean you didn't call me because of my charming ways?" Ari nearly choked on a mouthful of coffee. While she tried to recover, Hudson pushed the envelope. "And just what type is a handy type?"

"You know."

Hudson shook her head. "No."

Ari groaned in frustration. "You're going to make me say it, aren't you?"

Hudson remained silent, and Ari sighed.

"Butch." Ari picked up her cup and studied the contents, determined to look anywhere but in Hudson's direction.

Hudson broke out in laughter.

"That's not funny," Ari said before she broke down and joined her. For a few minutes, she couldn't stop laughing. Tears ran down her face. She wiped her eyes.

Hudson forced herself to concentrate so she wouldn't start laughing again. "Why me?" She needed to know if Ari had a secret agenda. The kind she was desperate to avoid. It all came down to a matter of trust.

"You seem trustworthy. Someone I won't have to worry about being on the property. That's what I need. Lord knows I've enough to think about. You said you needed a place to live. I think you said, 'A space of your own' or something along those lines. You can have it, if you want."

A myriad of emotions churned behind the carefully constructed calm veneer Hudson tried to display. Her jaw muscles tightened.

She struggled over what should have been an easy answer. Yes or no. But the demons got in the way. It was a monumental moment. One Hudson didn't want to make a rash decision about. It was true she was desperate to have her own place. Somewhere to call home. Did that mean she should jump on Ari's offer? She believed they shared a mutual attraction that bubbled under the surface. It could erupt. Then what? Move again? Run away because...*Stop. I'm overthinking this.* Still, she needed to give the idea careful consideration. If she said yes it would be a commitment, and she needed to be sure if she were ever going to make another one. She stood and tossed her empty cup.

"Would you mind taking a walk?"

Ari hesitated. "Okay."

"I think better when I'm moving."

Ari picked up her cup. "Lead the way."

After walking and weighing the pros and cons, Hudson pointed to a bench. "First, I really appreciate you thinking of me." Nothing she was about to tell Ari was easy. "The past year has been rough. I'm not sure I'm the best person to count on."

"It was presumptuous of me…" Ari began.

Hudson placed the tips of her fingers against Ari's mouth. "Let me finish. Please. I need to see the space and go over details with you. I think we need to be sure the arrangement will work for both of us."

"Of course. That's a great idea." Ari sounded excited. "The house is in a great neighborhood, and there's plenty of room. You'll see." Ari waved her hand. It hit the rim of her cup, and the last of her coffee flew through the air, showering them both with brown droplets.

Hudson looked down at their clothes. Shock was the best way to describe Ari's face. That, along with the color blooming on her cheeks, indicated how embarrassed she was. How could Hudson be upset?

"I give up," Ari cried out, close to tears. "All I've wanted to do was put my best foot forward, and I've done nothing but show you what a total klutz I am." She searched her pockets and came up with a couple of crumpled napkins.

Ari dabbed at the spots on Hudson's white shirt, looking mortified the entire time. When it came to the spots on her chest, she couldn't help but laugh as Ari froze in mid-air, not daring to go any further. Ari shoved the napkins forward.

"Here. I've made such a mess." Ari tossed the empty cup in the trash. "Maybe you *should* fear for your life."

Hudson couldn't stand seeing her so upset. "Hey, it's okay. I've been getting out coffee stains for years."

"If I keep this up, you'll never want to see me again."

Despite all the mishaps, it was the last thing Hudson wanted, and the knowledge squeezed the air from her lungs. She hardly knew Ari—aside from her being accident prone, ambitious, and beautiful. What else was it about Ari that kept drawing her in? Everything inside screamed "run," but she couldn't. "Don't worry. You can't get rid of me that easily. So when can I see the place?"

"I should have the keys in a few weeks. Maybe sooner."

Hudson nodded. She could start packing and get some of her things from storage, not that there was much. Most of what she owned was still with Pam.

Ari stood next to her car. "Thanks for meeting me," she said, then pointed to the drying blotches on Hudson's shirt. "Let me know if the leopard spots don't come out."

"I'm not as concerned about them as you are. Call me when I can see the apartment. Unless you'd rather knock me down to tell me."

Ari's head dropped as she studied the ground. She looked mortified.

"I'm joking." Hudson held her hands. "It was a pleasure seeing you again, and thanks for thinking of me."

Chapter Seven

A ri tossed her towel on a bench and stepped down the ladder in the deep end. The pool was empty except for a class of four seniors exercising in the shallow end. The water was balmy because the pool was kept at a therapeutic temperature, and she floated along the surface. She closed her eyes, letting the stress ebb away. The smell of chlorine tickled her nose.

She flipped over and swam in her choppy style. It wasn't long before the women left and she had the pool to herself. She decided to try a more vigorous swim and increase the speed and force of her strokes. She fell into an even rhythm and reached the deep end. A cramp seized her calf muscle. She flailed her arms to keep afloat but went under. The pain was so intense that panic set in. She bobbed to the surface and gasped for air as the searing spasm spun her around. The edge of the pool seemed miles away as she dipped below the surface yet again. *I don't want to die. Not like this. Not now.* Her lungs were on fire. She tried to ignore the rock-hard muscle in her leg. She begged for relief. From the pain. The fear.

The water churned and bubbles floated past her face. Arms slid under her shoulders and pulled her upward. She took a gulp of air and coughed hard.

"Just breathe and try to relax. I've got you."

Hudson. Ari held her throbbing calf as Hudson took her to the shallow end. Her savior maneuvered her onto the steps.

"Hold on to the railing and let me take care of your leg."

Hudson's strong hands worked the muscles and flexed her foot toward her body, relieving the pressure she hadn't been able to.

Ari coughed and water spewed from her mouth, but at least she was able to breathe. Relief washed over her. "I thought I was a goner." Her heart did that trip-hammer thing again as Hudson massaged away the soreness. Her body pulsed with every stroke of Hudson's fingers, and as her fear left, she imagined being stroked in other places.

How many times was Hudson going to save her? She hated being vulnerable, even more so in front of someone she didn't know well. Vulnerability led to being open to all sorts of other emotions, and she had no intention of letting her body rule her head. Just thinking about giving in and letting go of control made her stomach churn.

"You look pale. Take some slow breaths."

Hudson's concern touched her deeper than the ministrations to her leg ever could. What could she say? *I never wanted you to see a weakness in me? I keep telling myself not to feel. That I don't have time for a "someone" in my life? That no matter what I do to avoid it, I find a way to be around you? Yes, to all of those, but not to anything I will ever tell you.* Ari pushed down every iota of attraction and made her voice stronger than she felt.

"I'm good. I'm not used to being rescued."

Hudson gently set her leg down. "I'm glad I was here." Hudson looked around at the deserted area. "I wish I'd gotten here sooner." She pointed to the video camera in the corner near the ceiling. "When I came out of the staff restroom, I saw you go under and knew you were in trouble." Disappointment marred her otherwise handsome face.

Ari knew she should say or do something to show her gratitude, but the only thought crowding her mind was the knowledge that Hudson was becoming a fatal attraction. An attraction that would lead to the death of her independence.

"Yes, well, you got here," she said brusquely before forcing a smile that felt as phony as she was sure it looked. She didn't miss the hurt in Hudson's eyes or the way she visibly jerked from the comment. She wished she could take it back. She wished she'd never given Hudson the opportunity to rescue her. But what she really wanted to do was throw her arms around Hudson and kiss her until neither of them could breathe. It was too late for a lame apology. She needed to gather what little self-respect she had left and get out of there.

"The truth is I hate seeming helpless. I thought I was going to die."

"That's why there are lifeguards. It happens." Hudson didn't look at her and kept talking in a matter-of-fact way. "It's my job. And it wasn't your fault. Everybody gets cramps. You're not weak." Hudson's gaze finally met hers. "Ari."

There it was again. The way Hudson said her name. "Thank you." The words came out in a whisper. She was lost. Ari loved those eyes. Along with the way Hudson touched her leg, the strength of her fingers. The depth of emotion Ari heard in her voice. *If only I could—No!* Not with Hudson. Hudson made her feel, and feelings were dangerous. They brought disappointment, and she had no time to nurse wounds. It was one reason she'd never let her father see how much his words affected her. She'd schooled herself to not react. And now she had other priorities. She was better off not even thinking of getting involved. Even as one part of her brain said she was being unreasonable, she couldn't fight the things she'd dreaded her entire life. *Time to get back to focusing on the business.* Ari walked gingerly up the steps.

Hudson stayed in the water and stared at her with questioning eyes. "Can I help you back to the locker room?"

"You've done enough. I can make it on my own." Ari ignored the reason she'd come to the pool in the first place. She mustered enough strength to face her. "If you're still interested, I should have the keys next week."

"All right." The pain still showing on Hudson's face and the questioning eyes were more than Ari could stand.

"I'll call you." Ari gathered what was left of her dignity, held her head up, and limped away.

Hudson stormed into the staff locker room and slammed her towel into the laundry basket. *What is it with that woman? She turns on and off like a damn light switch.* First, Ari gave the impression of being attracted to her, and then Ari was giving her the cold shoulder. As if she couldn't be bothered with Hudson at all. Maybe she should rethink renting from her. The precarious situation might turn into a total disaster. Worse than the *Titanic.* This ship was sinking long before it even sailed. Maybe she'd thought about getting on board at one point, but the idea was turning cold. There was always the possibility Ari was unstable, although she didn't think so. It was more plausible Ari was fickle and playing with Hudson's gullible side. A side she should have known better than to expose, and one she'd much rather avoid if at all possible. Maybe when Ari called, she'd tell her she changed her mind. And maybe, just maybe, she'd tell her to go fuck herself.

She didn't need mixed signals and confusing messages.

Nevertheless, the idea of cutting ties with Ari felt like a vise on her windpipe. She'd been naïve in thinking they could be friends. She knew her anger stemmed from being given the cold shoulder. Self-preservation had kicked in. She wasn't going to be at the mercy of another woman's whims. She'd learned her lesson. It was time she spoke up. She'd tell Ari she was no longer interested in renting from her and be done with it. Tomorrow she would hit the papers again. She had to take control of her life and needed to get on with it.

"Congratulations. It's official. You're a homeowner." Sally handed her a set of keys and slid a folder of paperwork across the table.

Ari looked at the key ring in disbelief. It had been one month since she'd first walked through the door on Huntington Drive. The next time she did it would be *her* home.

"I can't believe it's mine."

"Believe it, Ari. Now you can make it yours. I'll bet you can't wait." Sally closed her briefcase and stood, signaling her part in the deal was over.

"There's a lot I need to figure out." She bit her lower lip. The inspection had gone well, and except for a few minor repairs, the house was in good shape. She didn't know anyone who could do the patching, painting, and decorating. She'd have to hire someone. *Tomorrow is another day. I'll think about it tomorrow.* She needed to call Kara.

"Woot, woot! So tell me, do you feel any different?"

"What I feel is scared to death. For the next couple of months, I'll have a mortgage on top of rent, not to mention everything else," Ari said. She fought back the tears. Scared didn't begin to describe how she felt.

"Aww, don't worry. I'm sure Hudson will say yes, and even if she isn't handy, that's one less thing you'll have to think about. You said she was anxious to move, right?"

Little did Kara know it was no longer that simple. "Uh... well," she began.

"What happened?"

Her voice wavered as she told Kara about the scene at the pool and how horribly she'd reacted when her body wanted to give in to Hudson's touch. She held her head in her hand, wishing she could take back everything she'd said that day.

"Okay, don't cry."

"Kara, I might have ruined any chance of having a great tenant. I know she was hurt by the things I said. I could see it. I couldn't help myself."

"What couldn't you help, honey?" Kara asked.

She blew out a frustrated breath. "When she was rubbing my leg, I liked it. A lot. She's hot. With bedroom eyes and a perfect mouth. Then my body reacted to how great her hands felt and I started to fantasize about having her touch me."

"What's so bad about that?"

"I panicked. I don't want to get involved. I don't." She knew it was crazy to think one touch and a couple of coffees were the beginning of a lasting relationship, but wasn't that how things happened? Innocuous little moments that lead to more serious moments and before you knew it you were living together?

"Ari?"

"Yeah?"

"Stop it. Stop reading more into what was a perfectly natural reaction. Lord knows how you survive on the amount of intimacy you do is beyond me," Kara stated matter-of-factly.

"I have sex," Ari rebutted.

"Right. You have quick, unemotional sex every once in a blue moon. Like it or not, you're horny. So why not give in and live a little?"

"I do not want to have sex with Hudson," Ari said defiantly. But when she thought of how warm and strong Hudson's hands were and how easily she'd carried her to safety, the muscles in Hudson's arms and legs bulging and flexing with her movements, she wasn't so sure.

"Huh. You could have fooled me. It sure sounds like you wanted to have sex with her. But, okay. Even if she doesn't want to have sex with you, you could still rent to her." Kara had a knack for making practical solutions out of the worst situations. Her words were a wake-up call.

What if Hudson *didn't* want her in a sexual way? The thought was a little depressing. She hoped Hudson found her attractive. *What does it matter either way? I'm not going to sleep with her.* "You're wrong, but even if I *did* want to jump her bones, I haven't got the time or the energy to get into a relationship. There's just way too much on my plate."

"I'm still not convinced, but fine, you aren't interested in Hudson that way. All you want is someone you can trust to share your house with. There's no need to go down the relationship road unless you want to."

Kara was giving her a way out. A way to rationalize all the conflicting emotions she'd been fighting. Kara was right. Asking Hudson to be a tenant didn't mean she was in a commitment. It was more of a contract of sorts. In fact, maybe that was the best approach. Have Hudson sign a lease to let her know it was a business arrangement and nothing more.

"You're absolutely right. All I want is a tenant." Ari let out a long breath. She could handle this. Now, if she could only be sure Hudson wasn't so upset with her that she'd changed her mind.

"There's one more thing you need to do."

"What?"

"Apologize," Kara said in a motherly tone.

"I will not."

"Yes, you will. You know it's the right thing to do."

Sunlight filtered through the sheer curtains and fell across Ari's face. She hadn't slept well and didn't want to think about what she had to do. Snuggling deeper into the warm covers, she hoped to erase the unpleasant memory of the last time she'd seen Hudson. After talking with Kara, she'd picked up her phone time after time, knowing she should apologize. But she couldn't. Apologizing meant she'd been wrong. That she'd made a mistake, and Ari never made mistakes. Every important decision in her life had been carefully weighed out and planned. That's what was causing her angst. Her pursuit of Hudson, of seeking her out, was uncharacteristic. She didn't chase women. Ever. And she certainly didn't offer them a place to stay. What had changed? What had driven her to be impulsive? Going out of her way to look for Hudson, only to push her away when her body reacted to her touch? This was more than a simple physical attraction. Maybe it was the beginnings of love.

Her eyes popped open, and she squinted against the bright room. She was being ridiculous. What she felt toward Hudson couldn't possibly be love. Could it? Not that she would know what love felt like, since she'd never been in a relationship that lasted more than a month or two, and even then, it felt more like friends with benefits. There'd been no emotional investment on her part. Maybe that was why they'd ended. A date here or there. A nice time in bed. And she'd never pursued any of them for more.

Groaning, she tossed the covers aside and sat up. She'd closed on the house yesterday. The first thing she had to do was find out if she had a potential tenant or not. She prayed all the rest would fall into place.

Ari counted the rings. After four she began to lose her nerve and hoped voice mail would kick in. No such luck.

"Hi." Hudson sounded distant.

"I owe you an apology for the other day. I acted like a jerk and I'm sorry." When her confession was met by silence she closed her eyes and prayed she hadn't blown things between them. A bevy of possible responses from Hudson played in her head, each one more cutting than the previous.

"Apology accepted."

Ari looked at her phone. She didn't expect it to be that simple. Nothing in life was simple, and interpersonal relationships were anything but. Is that what this was—a relationship? It could hardly be considered as such since it consisted mostly of accidental collisions, but it was certainly turning into something more. Of what, she just wasn't sure.

"Thank you." She forged on. "I have the keys to the house. I can show you the apartment today if you're still interested." There was a long pause on the other end, and she feared the worse.

"You know you're not under any obligation."

"I know. I don't know what came over me. Nerves, I guess."

"Okay, I'd like to have the grand tour."

Hudson's consideration for her feelings took her by surprise once again. How she ever doubted Hudson's sincerity was beyond her, but she was going to do her best not to destroy the growing friendship between them.

"I'm glad you haven't changed your mind." Ari glanced at the clock. "How does one o'clock sound?"

"Give me the address, and I'll meet you there."

Hudson shook her head in wonder. What happened with not putting up with having her feelings hurt? When she'd read Ari's name displayed on her phone, she'd been determined to let the call go to voice mail. She was glad she'd changed her mind. Ari's immediate apology wiped away the anger and hurt that had plagued her since yesterday. Pam never apologized for her behavior, even under the worst circumstances. She was wrong to compare Ari to her ex. They were nothing alike, and she knew Ari was under a lot of stress that day at the pool. She'd acted totally out of character from their earlier interactions.

Maybe this will work out after all. She hoped it would, for both their sakes. The longer she stayed with the girls, the more she felt stuck—unable or unwilling to take the plunge and move forward with her life. It had been more than six years since she'd lived alone. She almost couldn't remember how it felt to come and go as she pleased without thinking about another person's feelings.

She pulled her gym bag from the closet and threw on a pair of jeans and a polo shirt. She had a couple of hours to kill. Nervous energy coursed through her. She thought about what Master Jin had said about focus and clarity. Meditation would help. As would some physical exertion. It was important she remain objective when she made her final decision about whether or not to rent Ari's apartment.

Chapter Eight

Huntington Drive was a short stroll from Ari's apartment, and she used the time to clear her head. Her anticipation grew as she rounded the corner. She'd only been at the house twice, and both times were before she owned it. Clutching the bag that contained a tape measure, pad, and pen, she paused at the bottom of the stairs. The house appeared much larger than when she'd last seen it.

"It's a monster," Ari said out loud before checking to see if anyone heard her.

She wasn't looking forward to rambling around in the vacant building. Standing at the front door, she squared her shoulders. Her hand shook when she raised the key. The tumble of the heavy mechanism sounded reassuring. The worry melted away when Ari stepped inside. This was hers. *All hers.* She could do whatever she wanted and no one was there to tell her it wouldn't work. Her father would most likely never step foot in her home and that was fine. She didn't need his approval.

The air was thick with built-up heat. She opened the nearest windows, picked up a pad and pen, and clipped the tape measure to her belt. Standing in the middle of the huge kitchen, Ari imagined the space she'd always dreamt of. A thin layer of dust covered every surface, sparkling in the slanted sunlight that filtered through the blinds. The original wide-board oak floors needed refinishing. She began making a list.

The apartment needed some TLC, but she was thankful it was mostly cosmetic. The first floor would need a bit more work, and she didn't want to move anything in without the floors being done. She hoped all the projects could be completed in a couple of months. Less if she found the right people at the right price. Maybe Rae could give her the names of reliable tradespeople. An hour later, her phone alarm sounded. Hudson would arrive soon.

Ari sat on the top step, inhaling the fresh air. Someone was cutting grass. The scent brought back fond memories of long-ago summers. The old growth maple trees surrounding the house provided lots of shade from the heat of the summer sun. In winter, they'd be bare and the house would reap the benefits. Dappled sunlight fell across the porch. The pattern shifted with the breeze. The atmosphere felt peaceful. She hoped Hudson would feel it, too.

Ari tried not to stare. Hudson's broad shoulders, strong arms, and narrow waist made her mouth water; add in Hudson's deep, sultry voice and those mesmerizing gray eyes, and her libido skyrocketed. Hudson turned around, and she snapped back to attention.

"It's a great apartment. Exactly what I want." Hudson hesitated for a minute too long.

Leaning against the counter, Ari crossed her arms in front of her, trying to hide her nipples as they poked against her shirt. "I hear a 'but' in there."

Hudson's frown made her stomach tense.

"I'm sorry, Ari. I'm just not sure I can afford it. I told myself I'd take on another job if I found the perfect place, but it would mean never being home, and home is where I'd want to be if I lived here." Hudson looked around the kitchen, running her hand over the granite countertop. "If it's any consolation I think you'd make a great landlord. Or is it landlady?" Hudson smiled.

"We could make a deal."

Hudson's eyebrow shot up. "What kind of deal?"

"That didn't come out the way I wanted at all. Again. What I meant was I could really use the help of a knowledgeable bookkeeper for my catering business. In exchange, I'd lower your rent to say…six hundred a month?" Sally had suggested eight fifty. Hiring a bookkeeper would cost her a couple hundred a month or more.

Hudson mulled it over.

"It's a very appealing offer, but what do I do before you start up the business? It could be a few months before you need me."

Ari grinned sheepishly. "Do you paint?"

"I've done my fair share."

"You could start up here and then, if you have time, I could really use your help downstairs." Ari rambled on. "I'm not very good at the bu—" She was about to say butch, but Hudson's glare stopped her short of being embarrassed by using a label. It was wrong and she needed to stop thinking of Hudson in those terms. "Buying paint?"

"Nice cover." Hudson's smile reached her eyes. Sliding her hands in the back pocket of her jeans, she looked around one more time. The posture accentuated her shoulder width and pressed her small, perfectly shaped breasts against her light blue tank top.

"Can you show me downstairs before I jump in headfirst?"

"Sure!" Ari headed for the staircase leading to the door that separated their two spaces. She wasn't sure how to say what she wanted to without offending, but she needed their arrangement to be clear up front. "This is another way out of your apartment in an emergency."

Hudson placed a hand on her arm. "I would never use it, Ari. Not unless I didn't have another choice. I think it's important we respect each other's privacy."

Relief washed over her. "Thank you for understanding." *I'm so glad I called her.*

After the tour, they sat at the vintage kitchen table the previous owners left behind. Ari did her best not to let her anxiety show.

"So, what do you think?"

Hudson leaned forward. Ari watched deep concentration etch lines on Hudson's otherwise smooth face.

"I say yes with some conditions. I'll paint your place first, but the rooms need to be empty. I'll set up your accounting and be your bookkeeper for the first year. Then you can decide if you want me to stay on or hire someone else. I have a busy schedule with two jobs, and I practice martial arts. But I promise you'll get your money's worth."

Nodding her agreement, Hudson went on. "You pay for all the materials. I'll let you know if something's broken. If I can fix it I will. If I can't, or you prefer I don't and you want to hire someone, that's fine. I'll pay you on the first of every month by check, and I'd like a receipt. If you want me to sign a lease I will. I don't have wild parties and I don't do drugs, unless you consider alcohol a drug. I can give you names for references if you like, and I can show you my bank account if you want to make sure I have enough money to make good on my promises."

Ari couldn't ignore the pain lying beneath the controlled façade Hudson showed her.

"Who hurt you so much?"

Hudson's face contorted and her cheeks flushed. "That obvious, huh?"

Ari's heart ached. "I can't begin to imagine what happened, but I want you to listen to me. Whatever it was—before this minute, right here, right now—is history." She hoped Hudson understood what she meant. "Even though we got off to a rocky start," Ari raised her hand in the air and waved it, "and that would be my fault, I think we can help each other."

Hudson leaned her head back and looked at the ceiling. "For all the fancy appliances in here, you think someone could have painted the ceiling?"

Ari looked up, too. The color that had probably started out as white was now more like a dingy gray. "Yuck."

Hudson laughed. "First thing, we check to make sure that vent works. I'm assuming this was a pre-reno throwback."

"I hope so." Ari checked Hudson's face once more. She touched Hudson's arm and asked, "You okay?"

"Never better," Hudson said. Ari scowled.

"Okay, that's not true, but I'm fine." Hudson leaned forward. "So does this mean you accept?"

"You drive a hard bargain. I like that, so it's a yes. I'll have another set of keys made." She chewed her bottom lip. There were still a ton of decisions to make and she didn't know where to start.

"I see the wheels turning. What are you thinking about?" Hudson asked.

"It's a little overwhelming. To be honest, I'm no interior designer and I suck at color schemes. I don't want to hold you up from getting started." She fumbled with the pad to avoid Hudson's intense stare.

"Would you like to grab a bite to eat and talk about what you have in mind?"

The offer didn't sound like a date, but the flutter in her stomach didn't agree. She should decline and go home.

"I'd like that."

❖

Hudson stood looking at the grand house. The Victorian had been pristine in its day and with a little TLC it would be again. The wide wraparound porch with its spindled railings needed scraping and a fresh coat of paint, as did the six columns supporting the overhang. The wooden bead board ceiling looked new, but needed a coat or two of varnish. The flared front steps were a feature she hadn't seen in many Victorians, but she liked the way they led up to the heavy oak door with the beveled glass side panels. And while the windows weren't modern vinyl, they were in very good shape. She made a mental note to test how easy they opened from the inside. The overhead light was modern rather than vintage. It didn't fit in with the age of the home. She'd have to ask Ari about replacing it. She had a feeling some of her ideas weren't going to fly. Ari had a stubborn streak. It was one of the many traits Hudson found appealing about her. She liked her feisty nature. Her biggest hurdle would be getting Ari to agree on the major design ideas she had for the home.

Home. That's what it felt like the minute she stepped inside. Finally. Having a hand in turning it into a place Ari would be proud of gave her another reason to be happy. *Am I happy?* She hadn't been happy for a long time. Looking back, even before the breakup, there'd been something fundamentally off with her relationship. Ari's ability to see into her soul touched her. She hadn't let anyone that far inside her psyche since before college. Letting her guard down might be a sign of her readiness to let go of the past and move forward. Moving forward meant leaving behind the self-pity she'd wallowed in for the last year. In the near future, she'd have a place to call her own and, if she weren't mistaken, a new friend she could rely on.

Things were looking up.

Hudson set the bags down and took off her jacket before straddling the chair across from her roommate.

Jill looked up from the Sunday paper. Her eyebrows knit together in surprise. "And just where have you been so early? I thought you were still in bed."

"I had an errand to run and decided to stop at the bakery." Hudson grabbed a napkin and picked out a glazed donut from her bag, then peeled the lid off her coffee.

"What was so important you were out before daybreak?" Jill asked. "Or maybe you're just getting in from a late night?" Jill leaned forward, eyebrows raised.

Hudson shook her head. She'd never felt comfortable bringing a woman back to the apartment. Not with the girls being so unpredictable in their behavior. Sometimes they'd make so much noise she couldn't sleep. The truth was she'd only had sex a couple of times since moving in with them, and chose to go to her hookup's place. She needed to tell Jill the real reason she'd been to the home improvement store.

"I found an apartment and I'm going to help with painting and stuff." She shrugged as though the news wasn't a big deal.

The look on Jill's face told a different story. The pools shimmering in her eyes made Hudson wish things were different, but it was time. Past time.

"Don't make this harder than it already is. You said yourself you knew I wouldn't be here forever."

Jill slumped back. "I just didn't think it would be so soon." She blinked several times and sighed before reaching into a bag and pulling out a cinnamon bun. "So, when are you leaving?"

Hudson laughed. "Oh, so now you can't wait to get rid of me?" She shoved Jill's arm, almost knocking her off the chair.

They were in fits of laughter when a sleepy-eyed Cathy emerged from her bedroom. "Hey, what's going on? I just got to bed and you two are already having breakfast?"

Hudson gestured to a chair and handed her a donut before she told her the news. Cathy looked sadder than she'd ever seen her.

CHAPTER NINE

The sky lightened and cast a myriad of colors across the glass-like reflection making it easy to see the gathering of water bugs. The sun welcomed Hudson with its heat as it burned the mist off the river's surface. Peace surrounded her. She sat and watched the fish swimming lazily alongside the kayak. *Her* kayak. It had taken a while to find one. Today was the first of many days she would be spending on one of the nearby lakes, rivers, and streams.

Aside from the dojo, kayaking was her second love. Her paddle cut through the water with a slow, steady rhythm and her mind wandered to the past few days. She and Ari had agreed on the preparations for the main floor and the idea of having something to occupy her otherwise solitary hours excited her. The awkwardness between them disappeared once they focused their attention on the house. She couldn't ignore her growing attraction and was determined to keep it at bay. There wasn't any reason to complicate an already strained friendship. Besides, she wasn't even sure Ari wanted more than her help with her business and respect for their living arrangements. She hoped it would be her last move in Albany for a long time.

❖

Hudson's footfalls echoed in the empty space, reminding her of the hollow feeling in her heart. "This isn't the same, so stop," Hudson said, talking to herself.

"What isn't the same?" Ari leaned against the doorway, concern creasing her forehead.

Ari's voice surprised her. Hudson looked down and toed a clump of dried dirt loose. "Nothing."

Ari moved over and stood in front of her, forcing Hudson to meet her gaze. "It didn't sound like nothing."

She attempted a reassuring grin. "Just a ghost from the past, but it's gone now."

Ari nodded. "Okay. Just for the record, I'm a good listener if you want to talk."

The lump in her throat threatened to choke her. She didn't want to use Ari's concern as a crutch or another excuse to feel sorry for herself. "Thanks."

Ari dropped the bags she'd brought on the counter and rubbed her hands together. "What's today's game plan?"

Hudson wondered if Ari would be excited once she got dirty. She didn't appear to be a woman who had experience tackling home projects on a regular basis. "Spackling, scraping, and a little demo. I went to the home improvement store this morning and picked up a few sample paints along with a bunch of charts I'd like you to look at."

Ari balked. "Ugh…I told you I haven't got an artistic…"

Hudson held up her hand. "You need to be involved in the color choices for your home. I need your help." She crossed her arms over her chest, making it clear she wasn't giving in to Ari's pouting, no matter how cute she looked.

"Fine. Show me."

She pulled three small containers from a bag. "The master bedroom needs the least amount of work, so we'll start there." She painted a sample of each color on the wall and turned to Ari whose mouth was open as she stared at the choices. She looked between the wall and Ari.

"What?"

"How am I supposed to pick? They're all so different." Ari put her hands on her hips and moved in for a closer look. "Are you sure you want my input?"

"Depends," Hudson said.

"On what?"

"On how many times you're going to make that face." She made a circular motion at Ari with her finger, indicating the pursed lips and rolling eyes.

"Are you always this smooth?" Ari asked.

"Only when I want to make a point."

"And what point is that?"

"That you can't get out of making some decisions," Hudson said.

"I don't see why you can't just do whatever. You said you were so good at design," Ari huffed in response.

"Well, I'm sure as hell not going to pick your bedroom color for you." Hudson didn't mean to sound frustrated, but if this was an example of what she was in store for, getting the house ready would take a lot longer than she first thought.

"Please don't raise your voice," Ari said.

Sighing and shaking her head, she leaned against the wall, determined to come to an agreement on the color. "I'm sorry. It was—never mind." She glanced at the choices again. "Okay, tell me what one you don't like."

"I'm not fond of any shade of purple." Ari pointed to the middle one.

"That's not purple. It's gray." Hudson leaned next to the sample and blinked. "Like my eyes."

"Funny, but it still looks purple to me."

They weren't making much headway, so she conceded. "Okay. No purple. Do you like one more than the other?" The left sample was a honey tone and the right a deep sage.

Chewing her lip, Ari shrugged. "I suck at this." She didn't sound upset, just resigned. "I like them both."

"So you want me to paint stripes?"

"God, no! That would be hideous," Ari gasped.

Hudson hadn't been serious, but Ari wasn't getting the hint that they needed to move on and decided to try a different approach. "How do you want your bedroom to feel?"

Ari rested her hands on her hips. "That's ridiculous. A room doesn't have hands."

She pulled her hand down over her face. This process was taxing her nerves. "No, no. I mean do you want it calming, energized, fun?

"Unless you plan on putting a merry-go-round in there, I don't think it can be fun, do you?"

Hudson had all she could do to refrain from giving her a sarcastic remark. Yes, she did think a bedroom could be fun, depending on what she was doing and with whom. Instead, she rolled her eyes. "What color is your bedding?"

"Yellow and white flowers on a tan background."

"Perfect. Then the green will work."

Ari uncrossed her arms and then tapped her chin with a finger. "Problem?"

"Just trying to visualize."

Hudson wished she had a box of crayons so she could draw it for Ari. Maybe Ari didn't see her sense of humor. Maybe Ari didn't know she was attempting to be funny and silently sighed.

"Do you want to stop?"

Ari dropped her hands to her side. "No."

"Good. The master bathroom's next." The samples were already on the wall and she was glad she'd only picked two. Ari could only stall for so long in choosing one. She waved at the wall. With only a small window in the room, she wanted to keep it light. The white tiles helped.

"Left. I really like the left one," Ari said with enthusiasm, pointing to a lighter shade of the honey she'd seen as a bedroom color option.

"Nice choice. You can connect the two rooms by adding green accessories in here like towels and rugs."

Ari's face beamed and Hudson's earlier frustration faded away. She needed to remember this was Ari's first home. She had to be patient. Ari wasn't deliberately difficult. True to her word of wanting to help, Ari spackled holes and scraped loose paint while Hudson put two coats on the master bedroom and bathroom ceilings. When she finally took a break, Ari had a spread of food waiting in the kitchen. Her stomach rumbled in response. All she'd had for breakfast was juice and a power bar.

"I didn't know what you'd like, so I got a bunch of stuff." Ari waved at the items on the table. "I cleaned the refrigerator the other day and stocked it with drinks. I'm going to replace it with a bigger one, but since it's new, I may put it in the garage for extra storage." She sat and handed Hudson a paper plate. "Dig in."

Hudson took a small portion of each salad and made a sandwich, then went to the fridge. She grabbed a bottle of water and looked over her shoulder, catching Ari's pointed stare.

"Want anything?"

She knew Ari had been watching her backside from the way she blushed.

"Iced tea." Ari focused on her plate and began to scoop without paying attention.

Hudson set down the tea and looked at Ari's plate. "Wow. You must have really worked up an appetite."

Ari's plate was heaped with piles of potato salad and macaroni and cheese. She confessed. "I wasn't paying attention."

Leaning back, Hudson waited until Ari looked up. "Do I make you nervous?"

Ari froze with her fork poised in the air. "Not nervous." She took a breath and met Hudson's questioning stare. "I feel different around you." She laughed. "And clumsy."

Hudson chortled. "No offense, but I have to agree with you there."

"None taken."

"Do I have food on my face?" Hudson wiped at the corners of her mouth, where Ari had been staring.

"No, no. You're fine."

They ate in companionable silence until she was full. Hudson pushed away her plate and took a drink. "Where did you go? It looked like you were a million miles away."

Ari stared at her food, no longer eating. "I was just thinking about everything we've planned to get done in such a short time."

Hudson took Ari's hand in hers. "You can count on me to help you get there. You know that, right?"

Ari seemed to be daydreaming again. "I…" she rasped. "I do know and I'm grateful, but the onus is still on me." She slipped her hand from under Hudson's.

"Just so it's clear I'm not going to bail on you." Hudson tossed their plates in the garbage and began picking up containers.

Ari jumped up. "Here. Let me do this. You go start whatever's next, and I'll join you in a few." She practically pushed her out of the way.

Hudson snapped the lid on the salad container and stood back. "Okay."

Ari kept her eyes downcast. "Now shoo."

Hudson headed down the hall and called over her shoulder. "Thanks for lunch. It was delicious."

Hudson moved the drop cloth, poured paint into a plastic cup, and tried to make sense of the last half hour. Ari was nervous around her. Had been since their first meeting. Today it was even more evident. Ari had been staring at her and blushed when she'd been caught. Maybe Hudson wasn't the only one fantasizing. *Ego get in the way much?* They'd agreed to be friends and nothing more. *Then why do I get the feeling there's more to the story?*

She didn't want to think about other possibilities. She remembered the panic attack she had when she'd looked that way at another woman. Maybe that's what was so disconcerting. Ari didn't make her panic. She made her feel—good. It was time to focus her attention away from Ari, at least for the time being.

Light streamed into the room through the wavy panes of original glass, adding to the existing charm. The molding and doorframes were also original, and she admired them all the more for having been left unpainted. Ari had told her the house was built in the early 1920s, although the exact date seemed to be sketchy. She had a good feeling about the integrity of the structure. It had solid bones, built on a solid foundation. Just like the start of any good relationship. *Jesus. I really need to get back to reality.* She shook her head and looked up.

Hudson checked the ceilings and formed a game plan. She wanted to finish both today and hoped Ari would stick around long enough to talk about the biggest project—the kitchen. She didn't know if she could take it on solo, but since they hadn't discussed the details she wasn't sure what it would entail. In the meantime, she had plenty of other rooms to occupy her time.

CHAPTER TEN

With her roommates in class, Hudson didn't have to share the contents of the care package she'd received from her mothers. She blew across her spoon and savored the flavor of the rich broth and tender meat. She missed home-cooked meals almost as much as she missed them, and thought about her earlier phone call.

"Hello."

The voice on the other end always made her happy. "Hi, Momma. How are you?"

"Hudson! I thought you'd been kidnapped or something. Between you and your brother, I'm at my wits end most of the time."

Momma G. loved to tease. It was an old game they played. "It hasn't been *that* long. I didn't mean to make you worry."

"How are you doing?"

"I'm okay," she said. "I wanted to let you know I found an apartment."

"Oh, honey, that's great news. When do you move?"

"It's kind of complicated. I'm helping with the painting and stuff, so it will be a month or two."

"With everything else on your plate, do you have time for that?"

Hudson thought of how much Ari depended on her. It was an honor to have her trust and she wouldn't take it lightly. "It's doable. The landlord and I have worked out a deal on the rent. It's exactly what I was looking for. I'll finally have a place to call my own."

She heard her mother puttering in the kitchen. It was another familiar sound that brought comfort she hadn't realized she needed. Or maybe she did and was the real reason behind her call. She missed her parents.

"You'll work it out. You always do." Momma G. paused for a beat. "There's something else going on."

"How do you do that?"

"Do what?"

"Know something's up even when you can't see my face," Hudson said.

"I'm your mother. I sure as hell better know when something is going on in my daughter's life. Talk to me, honey."

Hudson leaned back on the couch, not sure where to begin. "How do you and Mom manage to be so…happy? After all these years, how does it still work?" No, that wasn't quite it. "How did you find love?" She heard the wooden chair scrape across the floor.

"I don't think love is something you find, baby girl. I think love finds *you*. When I first met Dale, I thought she was the most stubborn woman alive. Still do. But I also couldn't stay away. Something deep inside gnawed at me whenever I was around her. That, and the fact she just didn't take no for an answer had a lot to do with it." She chuckled. "I finally gave in and we went on our first date. And then there was another, and another. I could feel the heat between us, despite her little quirks that made me crazy. I couldn't stay away because there were so many times Dale amazed me. Not just by what she said, but what she did."

The gentle tone of her mother's voice told her everything she needed to hear. Mom D. had found a place in Momma G.'s heart and there wasn't anything she could do but go with it. It sounded familiar, but it still scared the shit out of her.

"Hudson?"

"Hmm?"

"You'll know, honey. There won't be a doubt in your mind because no matter what your head tells you, you won't be able to convince your heart it isn't love."

"Thanks, Momma."

"I hope I helped a little. Love isn't easy to explain and it never fits in a box, but it's definitely a gift."

"I'll try to remember that." Despite the turmoil she was feeling about Ari, at least now she could try to let things between them work itself out.

"You take care of you. Okay?"

"Yes, Momma, I will. Is Mom home?" She couldn't talk to one and not the other without landing in a world of trouble.

"No. She's running around delivering vegetables to friends. Why she insists on planting so much I'll never know. We can't eat half of what's grown before it rots. I told her I'm not spending another weekend canning. You know her. She smiles and nods, saying 'Okay, okay,' just to keep the peace. I love her most of the time, but every once in a while…"

"You want to strangle her?" Hudson asked.

"Yep. You might get an early inheritance if she keeps this up."

"Momma!"

Her mother's infectious laughter closed the distance between them. "You wait and see. Anywho, I'll tell her you called and fill her in. Don't make it so long next time."

"Okay, Momma, I promise. I love you both."

"I love you, too. Ta-ta."

Ari's master suite was finished, and while the rest of the flat was in disarray, at least she could bring some of her things home. Hudson had put in long hours over the last week. Ari was off on Thursday and wanted to see how much progress had been made.

She would text Hudson to ask what projects she could do on her own. At nine o'clock there was little activity in the neighborhood aside from the occasional walkers. She pulled into the driveway and found lights blazing inside. Parking beside Hudson's vehicle, she shook her head. *Doesn't this woman ever sleep?*

"Hudson?" she called out.

"In the living room."

Ari crossed her arms over her chest and leaned against the archway. Hudson stood on the stepladder. She watched the steady flex and contraction of her muscles as she painted the trim near the ceiling. The masterpiece of Hudson in action was a sight to behold. She ignored the ensuing throb even though she craved more.

"What are you doing?" she asked.

Hudson stepped down and beamed mischievously at her. "Painting."

She pushed off and shook her head. "I can see that. What are you doing here so late?"

"What time is it?" Hudson asked.

Ari checked her watch. "After nine."

"Oh." Hudson shrugged. "It's not that late. I wanted to get this done so I can do the walls tomorrow night." She moved the drop cloth and ladder before pouring more paint.

"You can't keep this pace up," she said. Hudson was in good physical shape, but even athletes had their limits, and she worried she was pushing herself beyond her breaking point.

Hudson crossed the room. "I appreciate your concern, but I'm fine." She picked up a water bottle and took a long drink. "We made a deal and I intend to keep my end of it."

"And killing yourself in the process won't do either of us any good. Not only would I have an unfinished home, but I'd have to find a new tenant." She took a step closer meaning to take the rag from Hudson's hand to wipe paint from her cheek. Her line of vision fell to her glistening lips, full and flush with color. The breath froze in her chest. *I want to kiss those lips.* She faltered, afraid if she went with her gut the consequences would be devastating for them both. Blinking hard, she looked into Hudson's eyes. They were full of emotion, their swirling depths unreadable. She lost herself and forgot everything else. A gentle shake brought her back.

"Are you okay?" Hudson asked. Her brow furrowed in concern. She grabbed a chair and guided Ari to it. "Sit down."

Ari let out a shaky breath. "I'm fine. I might have forgotten to eat dinner." Hudson shoved a bottle of juice in her hand.

"Seriously? And you're worried about me?" Hudson fisted her hands on her hips. "You stay right there and drink that. I need to finish and then we're getting food."

"That's not…" Ari began. Hudson's fingertips pressed against her lips.

"Yes, it is. No argument. Okay?"

The simple touch sent an electric current through her and landed low in her belly. Hudson's determination made her sexier than she thought possible. *Stop it. You're going to make yourself crazy if you keep this up.* She sat back and put up her hand in a show of surrender.

"Fine, but I'm buying."

The diner was a fifties throwback and a popular spot for locals. It was after ten by the time they arrived and only a few booths were occupied.

"Do you trust me?" Hudson asked as she munched on fries.

Ari's head snapped up. "What?"

She relaxed against the booth. "You heard me. Do you trust me?"

"I don't really see how that has anything to do with my eating habits." Ari moved the food around on her plate before looking up again. "Yes. I trust you. Why?"

"Then why are you checking up on me?"

"It has nothing to do with trust. I'm off Thursday and you need a break. I haven't contributed much and I'm feeling guilty."

The realization Ari felt she was lacking hit Hudson head on. Forgetting to eat was a sure sign she had a lot on her mind. Hudson knew her limits. Ari was just discovering hers.

"I can handle the workload."

Ari folded her hands on the table. "I've got so much happening in my head and…" She sucked in air when her voice cracked.

If they were home, Hudson would have hugged Ari, reassuring her she didn't have anything to feel guilty about. Instead, she reached across the table and touched her arm.

"Everything will work out. We're in this together." The contact felt right. *No*, her inner voice screamed a warning. *Not again.* Reluctantly, she pulled her hand back.

"We should both take the day off."

Ari met her gaze. "There isn't time."

"Sure there is. You could use a break and so could my shoulders." Ari looked doubtful.

"I've got a proposition for you."

Ari laughed. "I'm sure you do." She set her elbows on the table and rested her chin in her hands. "Let me hear it."

CHAPTER ELEVEN

Ari stood in front of her meager closet. *What the hell am I supposed to wear?* Hudson told her to dress in comfortable shorts and a T-shirt, and to bring a change of clothes. She tossed a pair of capris, a sleeveless blouse, and a sweater into a canvas bag. Did she need toiletries or a brush? *Stop overthinking.* This wasn't like a date. Was it? No. Hudson made it clear they were going to do something fun and relaxing, and that it wouldn't cost her a penny. She checked her clothes in the mirror before looking at her feet. Sandals would be better with capris than athletic shoes. She added them to the bag before grabbing her keys and phone. Hudson would be there any minute. *Yeah, it feels like a date.* The thought of an actual date made her pulse race. She'd come so close to kissing Hudson and didn't know how much longer she could resist the temptation. Her lips looked so inviting. Full and sensuous. Closing her eyes, she pictured when their faces came closer and closer, until finally…

The doorbell startled her. Ari laughed at her foolishness and rushed to open it.

"Hi." Hudson stood awkwardly and looked over Ari's shoulder at the inside of her apartment. This was the first time Hudson was seeing where she lived.

"Ready to go?" Hudson asked.

"Give me a minute. I have to use the restroom." Hudson stood at the threshold and shifted her feet. *Where are my manners?*

"Come on in." She backed away, afraid to get too close, then hurried to the bathroom. *Geez, get a grip before she thinks you're a total psycho.* She leaned on the sink and took a couple of deep breaths.

"You can do this," she whispered at her reflection.

The morning air held the promise of a hot summer day, and although it was in the low seventies, the humidity was already building. A few wispy clouds lightened the azure expanse. Hudson turned the key and the engine roared to life.

"So where are we going?" Ari settled in the seat and turned to face her.

"It's a surprise. Do you like surprises?"

Ari opened her mouth before closing it again and staring straight ahead.

Hudson thought she wasn't going to answer.

"I don't know. The only surprises I've ever had weren't very nice." Ari glanced in her direction.

She saw sadness contort Ari's face into a painful mask. "I hope you think this is a nice one."

Ari nodded and turned back to the window.

It seemed as though Ari was lost in a memory. Hudson didn't mind the silence. There were times in her life when she needed to process her feelings, and that's what Ari looked like she was doing.

The bumpy road dipped and climbed as it wound around a sloping hillside. There was barely room for two cars to pass each other, and it forced vehicles to go slow. The destination was well worth the risk. She loved the area for having so much natural beauty close to where she lived. Hudson Cove had become one of her favorites; after all, it shared her name. Her parents had traveled along the Hudson River during a vacation before she'd been born. They'd loved the beauty of the area so much they thought it would be a perfect name for their child. She was glad it was a short drive and was looking forward to sharing the special location with Ari. She guessed Ari hadn't been there before, making the trip even more memorable. After taking a sharp right, she maneuvered the SUV down a short, steep road before it leveled out. She caught Ari sitting forward, her eyes wide with wonder, and pulled into a shaded parking space.

"Here we are." Hudson gazed out over the picnic area to the river.

"It's beautiful." Ari got out without waiting for her.

Hudson leaned a hip against the vehicle and slid her sunglasses up on her head. "This is one of my favorite places to kayak." She pointed to the boat launch area.

"I've never kayaked." Uncertainty tinged Ari's voice.

"We aren't kayaking today, but if you'd like to we can plan it for another time." Hudson tried to put Ari at ease. "I reserved a canoe for a few hours. Bring whatever you need and we'll head down." She grabbed a small cooler and a backpack from the hatch, locked the doors, and tucked her keys into a waterproof pocket. Ari put on a baseball cap, her long ponytail pulled through the back. She looked adorable.

"All set?"

"I guess. I'm probably going to crisp up out there."

"I've got sunscreen. Let's put it on here." Hudson smeared some on her face, arms, and legs, then handed it to Ari.

Ari slathered what she could reach, but she missed some of her back and the backs of her arms.

"Let me help." Hudson held her hand out for some lotion, and Ari held up her ponytail as she rubbed it on the unprotected areas. The feel of Ari's skin, smooth and soft, made her ache for more. She was grateful her sunglasses hid her eyes.

"Okay."

"You missed a couple of spots," Ari said.

Ari's fingertips were slightly rough, sending Hudson's senses into overload. She longed to feel Ari's caresses elsewhere.

"Okay. I think you're good." Ari handed back the tube.

Hudson led the way to a dark green shack that served as the rental booth, evident by the quirky hand-painted sign hanging above the only window. A faded life jacket hung from the side door and a cracked wooden oar posted the prices.

"Hey, Sam. How's business today?" She took three twenties out of her pocket and handed them through the window.

"Busy on a beautiful day like today." Sam looked around her to where Ari stood. "I see you brought company. Wondered why you were canoeing."

Hudson stepped back. "Sam, I'd like you to meet Ari. Ari, this is Sam."

"Nice to meet ya, Miss. Water's been the calmest I've seen it in a while. Probably means a storm's brewing." Sam chuckled, then opened the door and handed out paddles and life vests. "You two enjoy it out there."

"We will," Ari said. She took the paddles and followed Hudson down to the beach where several canoes and a few kayaks leaned against the rocks.

"He seems nice."

She picked out a canoe, flipped it over, and hefted it overhead. "I met him shortly after I moved here." She set it down at the edge of the water and took the paddles, sliding them inside. "Here, give me your hand." Once Ari was settled, Hudson handed her the supplies and pushed the canoe into the shallow water before climbing in. The canoe drifted around while she put on a baseball cap.

"Ready to paddle?"

Ari looked over the edge of the canoe. "I guess."

She laughed at Ari's apprehension. "Just relax and enjoy the scenery." She dug her paddle in and pushed them away from the shore.

❖

Once Hudson had reassured her the chances of capsizing were slim, Ari began to enjoy the idea of a canoe outing. She turned her face to the sun, basking in its warmth. *This must be how it feels to relax.* She saw a lizard sunning on a rock. It probably felt much the same as she did, without a care in the world. Hudson shared some of the river's history. She was a wonderful guide and pointed out a majestic bald eagle perched on deadfall near the river's edge. Baby ducks trailed behind an alert parent.

A fish jumped so closely to the canoe she almost dropped her paddle.

Hudson laughed at her reaction and a beautiful smile beamed from under the brim of her cap. Perspiration trickled down Hudson's face and fell on her yellow ribbed tank top. The spot continued to grow and threatened to darken the area surrounding her nipple. Ari cleared her throat several times to shake off the effects.

Hudson pulled in her paddle and turned on the seat to face Ari like she'd done it a million times. The canoe barely rocked. She reached into the cooler and pulled out a bottle of water, handed it to Ari, then grabbed another.

Ari cracked the seal. The noise disturbed the quiet. The cold liquid bathed her parched throat, giving relief. She pressed the bottle to the bare skin of her neck and closed her eyes. Her mind wandered. She fantasized about Hudson's mouth bathing her neck in soft, wet kisses and licking Ari's sensitive spots with her tongue. Hudson's voice whispered in her ear.

"Ari?"

She inhaled the heat against her cheek. The tingle tightened her skin and her nipples reacted. "Mmm," she moaned.

"Ari?"

Hudson's voice became louder and the fantasy ended. She opened her eyes to find Hudson staring at her, concern wrinkling her forehead.

"Are you okay?" Hudson asked.

She pulled her cap lower to hide her eyes and her embarrassment. "Sorry," she mumbled before taking another swallow. Her imagination had gotten the best of her.

"I think we should head back."

Ari raised her gaze to meet beguiling eyes. "No!"

"I don't want you to get heat exhaustion."

"I'm okay. I was just thirsty. I should have gotten this sooner." She held up the bottle of water before finishing it off. She was going to ask Hudson to tell her more about the river, but another trickle of perspiration traveled along the contours of Hudson's neck before it disappeared. Their eyes met. This time Hudson's mouth quirked into a one-sided grin. *Christ. Busted. Again.*

Hudson slowly raised her bottle to her full lips and turned her face away. Ari was fascinated by the contraction and release of muscles in her neck and throat as she drank. She never knew swallowing could be such a turn-on. The moisture gathered between her thighs was joined by liquid heat spilling from her clenched center.

Ari pointed to a cluster of river birch trees with branches hanging over the water. "Can we head into the shade for a few minutes?"

"That's a great idea."

They reached the area and Hudson pulled out two square pink envelopes from the backpack. She emptied the powder from one into another bottle and shook it vigorously. Hudson's breasts moved with the motion, and Ari fought to control her raging libido.

"Here you go."

Ari wrinkled her nose. "What is it?"

"Electrolyte replacement," Hudson said as she fixed one for herself. "It's pink lemonade flavored." She took a drink and rummaged again. "Do you like peanut butter?"

She took a sip. It wasn't too bad. "Sure. Who doesn't?"

Hudson handed her a pack of crackers with peanut butter. "Protein." She looked down the river in the direction they'd started from. "We've got another hour of paddling to get back.

We could probably make it faster, but I'm not a fan of muscle fatigue." She held up her crackers as she tucked the water bottle between her thighs and tore open the package.

The stories those thighs could tell. They ate in comfortable silence.

"Are you relaxed?"

Why does she keep asking me things? "Absolutely. This was a great idea." Ari placed her empty wrapper in Hudson's outstretched hand. Their fingers brushed. Their eyes locked. The heat in her cheeks had nothing to do with the sun.

"In case I forget to tell you later, I've had a wonderful time."

Their time together was over too soon. Ari's chest tightened as they neared the shore.

Hudson looked over her shoulder. "We can come again. If we stayed any longer, we'd both be lobsters."

She glanced at the sun, guessing they'd been on the water three or four hours. "Okay." Ari paddled along. She'd been surprised how fast she caught on to canoeing. Given Hudson's paddling lesson, she understood why the children at the Y were so enthusiastic.

Earlier in the day, Hudson had set her paddle in the hull and moved to the center seat. The boat rocked a little, and Ari had gasped, holding on to the sides.

"I promise you won't get wet," Hudson had said.

Too late. Ari had nodded, unsure if she should believe her.

"Take my hand."

She reached and kept her eyes locked with Hudson's.

"Now, stay low and swing around to sit here." Hudson patted the space she'd created on her seat.

Ari's forehead tightened and she glanced over the side. "I don't think I can."

"Sure, you can. Look at me and don't think about what you're doing. Just do it," Hudson assured her.

She definitely wanted to do it. *God help me. Here goes nothing.* Ari listened to Hudson's voice. Before she knew it, she was leaning back against Hudson's body with her arms wrapped around Ari's trembling waist.

"See. That wasn't so bad, was it?"

Hudson's body was a mixture of hard muscle and subtle curves, and it took her breath away. She couldn't talk.

Hudson picked up a paddle and held it in front of them.

"The timing of our strokes needs to be the same even though they're happening on opposite sides."

Ari bit her lip to stifle a groan. *Does she have any clue what she's doing to me?*

Hudson wrapped her hands around Ari's. "Lift when you breathe in, dip when you breathe out." Ari savored the physical contact. Hudson's breasts pressed against her back, her hard nipples drawing patterns against her skin as they moved together. She'd never been this intimate with anyone without having sex. Hudson reminded her to breathe.

"Ready to give it another try?" Hudson had asked.

"Okay."

They'd moved back to their original positions.

Hudson lifted her paddle. "All set to go?"

Ari watched the smooth, prominent muscles along Hudson's back. "Yes." *I'd go anywhere you lead.*

The canoe ran aground.

Hudson jumped out and pulled the front of the canoe farther onto the shore. "Are you hungry?"

Ari hadn't thought about it, but her stomach rumbled in response. Breakfast had been a cup of yogurt, and the crackers hadn't done much to fill her. "Yes."

"Good."

"Does that mean you're going to feed me, too?" Ari handed off their gear and stepped on the sandy beach. They dragged the craft up to the rocks and flipped it over.

Hudson pulled off her sunglasses, wiped the sweat from her brow, and met her gaze. The gray hue shifted to a deep slate. Ari thought she saw a flash of desire before Hudson slid the sunglasses back in place. She'd seen the same thing in a few of her previous sex partners' eyes, although she never really understood how just looking at someone could cause the reaction until now.

"Maybe it's another surprise." Hudson slung the backpack over her shoulder, then picked up the life vests and cooler before starting up the incline.

Ari hurried to catch up. "I don't know if my heart can take another surprise."

Hudson turned around. "I think your heart is fine." For a brief instant, she thought Hudson was going to kiss her, then the moment was gone and Hudson kept going.

Her heart pounded from the almost kiss. Maybe she'd been wrong, but she didn't think so. *Now who's sending mixed signals?* Hudson disappeared around the tall mound of ornamental grass.

"Hudson!" Ari's tone was laced with annoyance. "Why are you running?"

Hudson stood waiting. "I just wanted to see if your heart could take it."

Ari held the paddles in one hand, the other on her hip. "You think you're so funny."

"You said it, not me." Hudson snorted and headed for the shack.

Hudson rummaged in the back of the car and emerged with Ari's bag and a canvas tote.

"Where are we going?"

Hudson pointed to a large block building. "That's the shower house. We can clean up and change before we eat."

"I don't have a towel or toiletries."

"I brought enough for both of us." Hudson winked at her and held up the tote.

"How much stuff do you have in there?" Ari looked in the cargo area.

She closed the hatch. "You'll just have to wait to see."

Ari put her clean clothes on one of the wooden benches and looked around. "There's no curtains," she said, her hands on her hips.

Hudson looked around. "There's no one else here."

Ari pursed her lips. "There might be."

She threw her hands up and strode to the other end. "Not a soul." She moved next to Ari. "Believe me now?"

"It's not that I didn't believe you before."

Hudson didn't understand what the big deal was. Locker rooms were second homes for her. Regardless if Ari showered or not, she was a sweaty mess. There was muck from the shore between her toes, and sand and bits of grass drying on her hands and legs. She couldn't wait to get her clothes off.

Hudson undressed, revealing her sports bra and hi-cut briefs. Moisture coated her neck and arms. Ari's gaze moved lower. *She's got a fucking six-pack.*

Even knowing Hudson was fit didn't prepare her for the barely covered body she was seeing. The tank top she'd shed had hidden the beauty beneath. When she moved, her back was a symphony of flowing muscles and tendons. Her thighs were solid, bulging and flexing in the most delicious way, and she imagined her head between them. Hudson looked good enough to eat and she wanted to savor the taste of her. She wanted to know if Hudson's bronzed skin was as smooth as it looked. She didn't trust her legs to move away.

Hudson stepped closer, her fingertips trailing Ari's arm as she spoke. "I didn't know you'd be uncomfortable with me here. I can stand outside."

She shook her head. "It's not you. It's just..." She glanced back at the door.

"Did something happen?"

Ari stood taller and squared her shoulders. She was acting like a child. She gave a short laugh to relieve the tension she felt. "Nothing aside from some locker room teasing in high school. I was rather chubby."

Hudson picked up her hand and guided her in a slow spin. "Looking at you now I'd find that hard to believe."

Her cheeks felt warm. The sincerity in Hudson's voice gave her a boost of confidence.

"Thank you."

"You go shower and I'll stand guard."

Relief washed over her. "You don't mind?" She grabbed the tote and rushed to the last stall. "Thank you, thank you," she called over her shoulder.

Hudson sat waiting for her turn. Ari's discomfort bothered her. The water came on and Ari poked her head out.

"I'll be quick," she said before disappearing into the cubical.

Hudson snorted. She'd been naked in locker rooms for so long she never gave it a thought. She rested her chin in her hands. It had been a good day so far.

"Hudson?"

"All clear."

"I forgot my clothes," Ari called out. "Would you bring them to me?"

She really is shy. I wonder if she's that shy in the bedroom. Shaking her head at her wayward thoughts, Hudson picked up the folded stack from the bench.

"Here you go." She tried not to stare at Ari's long, lean legs and the edge of the towel that barely covered her chest. Even with it snugged around Ari's body, she could tell the breasts beneath would more than fill her hand. Her vision traveled upward to admire the slender neck and plump, pouty lips. Kissable lips. Ari cleared her throat, and Hudson remembered the clothes in her hands before she set them on a shelf next to the shower.

"Thank you. I don't know what I was thinking."

"How fast you could shower before someone else came in would be my guess." Hudson smiled.

"Ha, ha." Ari held out the bag and the tucked edge of the towel slipped. She caught it just before it opened all the way and their eyes met. Hudson got a glance of a creamy hip. Ari flushed a lovely shade of pink.

Ari sat in the passenger seat and wished their time together wasn't ending. "Thank you for a wonderful day."

Hudson turned sideways. "You're welcome. It was nice to take a break from the house." She reached across the console and took Ari's hand in hers. The gesture felt natural. "I enjoyed spending it with you."

Neither had mentioned the word date. They'd sat at a picnic table and shared a quiet meal, while enjoying the shaded warmth under river birch and box elders. Hudson had packed an array of fruits, cheeses, meats, and a baguette, along with a crisp and fruity bottle of white wine. She hadn't been too keen on the shower, but she'd needed it. The day had been otherwise perfect.

"I'm sorry I made such a fuss over the shower thing." They laced fingers, Hudson's larger hand covering hers.

"Hey. It's okay. You don't have to apologize for anything." She gave Ari's hand a squeeze. "Not everyone is comfortable in public settings."

Ari met her gaze. One side of her mouth lifted. "You mean strutting around without a care like you do?"

"Yeah, something like that," Hudson said.

"Well, I guess I should head in." Her line of vision dropped to Hudson's lips before meeting her questioning eyes. If she sat there any longer she'd do something she'd regret.

Hudson pulled away from the curb. She had the feeling Ari had been stalling and almost suggested they go for drinks. *You know how that would end. Nothing good can come from pining over someone who isn't looking for a relationship.* No. It was better to keep things casual. They'd had fun and relaxed, which was the whole purpose of their day together. There was no need to complicate the relationship. After all, they were working on building a friendship. She could do with a few more friends and it sounded like Ari could, too.

But then, there was her body's reaction to seeing Ari nearly naked. It didn't mean she wanted to sleep with her, though. Ari was attractive and she would have thought something wrong if she hadn't felt a pang of desire. If she didn't know better, she'd have bet Ari was fighting feelings of her own, but it was likely just the stress of the house and business. She was more determined than ever to do everything she could to help Ari realize her potential.

CHAPTER TWELVE

Ari dropped to the couch in a heap. Between the sun and the fresh air, she was exhausted. The day had been better than she could have imagined. Hudson was right in challenging her to try something new. She wondered if Hudson pushed herself in the same way when it came to trying other experiences. Ari closed her eyes, sinking deeper into the couch. She envisioned Hudson's body, reliving the effect it had on her and the times she'd felt the heat between them. Moments she thought they were going to kiss. *So much for anticipation.* Obviously, she'd mistaken Hudson's intentions. One thing was clear, Hudson was a caring, warm person, and she enjoyed every time they were together. Whenever Hudson turned sideways as she paddled, Ari had caught a glimpse of her sexy smile. She liked how they teased each other, too. She couldn't remember a time when she'd been with another woman and felt so relaxed—or turned on.

Except for when she'd panicked at the shower house. The thought of being naked in front of Hudson had set her on edge. When Ari almost dropped her towel, the look in Hudson's eyes showed longing. The thought of them being naked together sent electricity coursing through her. She wanted Hudson's skin pressed against hers.

In the past, Ari had only thought of a woman's body when she'd needed physical release. She'd also been indifferent about dating because she wasn't interested in a long-term relationship. No ties. No repeats. Keeping things simple was the best way to maintain her independence. Sex was a bothersome necessity. Except when she was around Hudson. Her immediate attraction had taken her by surprise and thrown her off stride, but she hoped it went much deeper than Hudson's outer beauty. She sensed a compassionate, loving soul resided inside.

"If only," she mumbled. As much as she liked Hudson and couldn't deny her feelings, she had to step back. This was her time to shine, an important opportunity to prove to her father she was capable of being a successful chef. Even if she never spoke to him again, she'd be sure he knew she'd made it without his support. As for her mom, well, she'd never stood up for what she believed in, and there was no reason to think her mother would ever change. No. If she were going to prove her worthiness, it wasn't going to be through another person. It was something she had to do on her own. Once the house was done, she and Hudson wouldn't spend as much time together, and the temptation would fade to the background. Although she wasn't sure that's where she wanted Hudson to be.

Ari stood back and admired the freshly painted kitchen. Hudson had been right. The melon color worked. Even in the fading daylight, it felt warm and inviting. Hudson had recently arranged for a final buffing and polishing of the hardwood floors. With the white trim and cabinets already done, the only thing left in the kitchen was the wall plates and lighting fixtures.

The guest bathroom was last on their list. She was going to paint it by herself as a surprise for Hudson. The woman needed a break. She'd been painting and doing repairs every free minute since the project had started more than a month ago. Ari hadn't been there to help as much as she would have liked, but she did what she could. She'd also made a trip to the city and emptied out her storage unit, hoping Hudson could incorporate some of what she already owned into the design. She pressed the speed number.

"Hey, Ari. I'm on my way to the dojo. What's up?"

"Don't bother to come to the house tomorrow." Ari cringed at her word choice. Why did she have such a hard time saying what she meant in a kinder way? Maybe it was the rush of adrenaline she felt when she heard the deep timbre of Hudson's voice.

"Are you firing me for taking a night off?"

The teasing tone coming through the phone made her laugh. "Hardly. I mean, I've got things covered tomorrow."

"There's not a lot left to do. Are you sure?"

"I'll see you Friday." She hurried to add, "And remember to have some fun."

Ari picked up the paint can labeled *GB* and carried some supplies down the hall. Hudson was methodical, labeling every can of paint, piece of furniture, and accessory. She knew the real reason. There'd been a near mishap when Ari had picked up what she thought was ceiling white that turned out to be trim white. Hudson pointed out the difference. It didn't seem like a big deal at the time, but having a glossy ceiling would have been horrible.

"Yeah, she's a keeper," she said aloud, glad Hudson hadn't been there to hear the comment.

Hudson looked around admiring the bathroom. "You do nice work."

"Thank you. I'm not sure if I'm as neat as you, but whatever mess I made I cleaned up," Ari laughed.

She took Ari's hand and gave a squeeze. Their eyes locked. Ari's pupils dilated. The irises swirled into a kaleidoscope of colors whenever she looked at Ari with more emotion than friends would. Hudson's sex pulsed with need. She wanted to pull her closer, touch her lips. Kiss her like she'd dreamt of doing. Ignoring the fire hadn't been easy. But she couldn't trust her instincts. They'd been wrong before and she'd paid too dear a price.

"Thank you for the break. I didn't realize how much I needed it."

"You're welcome." Ari returned to the kitchen. "When do you think you'll be done in here?"

"I can do the lighting and electrical plates tomorrow. That's all that's left. Once you move in, I can touch up whatever needs attention. Just let me know."

"I have to work both jobs Monday, then the restaurant Tuesday night, and both again on Wednesday." Ari looked miserable. "I guess I'll finish packing this weekend."

"I don't mind lending a hand with the packing," Hudson offered.

"No, no. You've done enough." Ari chewed her bottom lip, something she probably wasn't aware of. Hudson found it irresistible.

"Once you're settled in, I'll concentrate on upstairs." She was more than ready to be settled in, too. Her roommates had become sullen and needy. She didn't want to have to deal with their moods much longer. There were times she could barely deal with her own.

Ari stood close and put a hand on her shoulder. It felt warm and gentle on her bare flesh. Her pulse quickened. "Please don't wait on my account. I can get settled by myself." She sucked on her bottom lip. "Uh, that is, if you don't mind lending a hand with a couple of things."

"See, you do need me."

If she didn't know Hudson was teasing, the comment would have pissed her off. It brought back unpleasant memories of her father.

Ari had signed up for a few cooking lessons offered through the high school enrichment program the summer after she graduated. They didn't make anything elaborate, but she felt confident when she was in the kitchen. At the same time, she found her passion. She went home and shared the news with her parents, excited at the prospect of finding a career she knew she could excel in. Her father's total lack of support had hurt.

"You're supposed to find a way to earn a living. Plan a future with a husband and children." He raised his voice, making her flinch. "You can't do anything right and you certainly can't manage on your own."

She became angry and blurted she wasn't looking for a husband because she was looking for a woman.

"I'm through with you. I will not have you embarrassing your mother and me any longer. Don't count on any money, and don't bother to come home unless you come to your senses. And you damned well better not bring any women with you!" He had slammed his fists on the table and stormed out of the house without giving her a chance to rationalize with him.

Later that night, her father had quietly knocked on her bedroom door, and she had hope of making amends. "I want you out before I get home from work tomorrow."

He closed the door and walked out of her life. She and Kara had borrowed a truck and called a few friends. She took everything that was hers and moved in with Kara, who had already found an apartment in New York City. She had nowhere else to go, and Kara hadn't even asked her what she wanted to do. It had been the saddest day of her life.

She still felt her heart shatter at the memory. She'd vowed she would show him. He'd refused to give her any financial support because she had insisted she could make a living being a chef. To make matters worse, she'd also revealed she was a lesbian. She'd proven then she didn't need him and she didn't need anyone now. What she *did* need was help. She'd softened her independence over the years. Asking for help didn't mean she wasn't self-sufficient, it meant she was human. Now was one of those times. She pushed down the old habit of denial and swallowed her pride. She couldn't lift some of the furniture by herself or carry it up the front stairs and she did indeed need help.

Ari's gaze fell to her hand where it rested on Hudson's wide, strong-looking shoulder. She felt the muscle twitch and wished she hadn't. Ari took a step back and hoped Hudson missed the tremble of her hand.

"Ari?" Hudson asked "For you, I'll make time."

Hudson was captivating. *Stop. She doesn't want you. You'll just make a fool of yourself.* She nodded, willing the demons in her head to leave her alone. For the first time in her life it felt good to need another person. The fact that she was gorgeous didn't hurt either.

"That's the last of it," Hudson said and grabbed bottles of water from the fridge.

Ari gratefully accepted one from Hudson's outstretched hand. "Thanks." She drank down half the bottle. "Of course, I picked the hottest day of the year to move." Ari leveled her gaze on Hudson. Moisture glistened on her neck and traveled down the center of her chest. Her tattered T-shirt was soaked. Dark crescents formed under her breasts, and she couldn't pull her focus away before noticing Hudson's nipples pressing against the fabric. Heat coursed up her neck to her cheeks and their eyes locked. Before she found the strength to turn away, Hudson wiped her lips with the back of her hand. Ari glanced down again. The edge of the fabric rose above her navel, revealing the rippling muscles she remembered from the shower.

Hudson set the bottle on the counter without breaking eye contact. "It's definitely hot."

There was no way she was going to trust her voice. She had to think quickly. She rushed over and slapped at Hudson's stomach.

"Ow." Hudson's hand went to the spot. "What the hell was that for?"

"Sorry," she giggled. "I saw a spider crawling on you."

Hudson looked around on the floor. "I don't see anything." She looked up. "Are you sure you saw a spider?"

Ari bit her lip and nodded. "It was definitely a bug. It had legs."

Hudson checked the floor again.

She did a serious hunt of her own. "Well, it was there. It probably crawled under something." Hudson stared at her and pursed her lips. She had all she could do not to laugh at the look on Hudson's face when she'd smacked her.

She shrugged. "It's gone now so you don't have to worry. I saved you." She splayed her hands like she was doing magic.

"Thank you for saving my life. I'm sure I was in mortal danger."

"Silly, you weren't in mortal danger unless you're allergic. My God, are you allergic? Maybe I should check to make sure it didn't bite you." She moved closer, leaning over while pretending to look for a mark. She was totally faking concern, since there'd never been a spider, but if she had any chance of convincing Hudson otherwise, she had to make it look good.

Hudson's hand slid over her abdomen. "Ari, relax. I'm not allergic and I'm sure nothing bit me." She drank the rest of her water and tossed the bottle into the recycle bin.

Happy to move on to another topic, Ari asked, "Have you picked colors for upstairs?"

"Yes. That reminds me, I have a receipt for you in my car."

She rolled her eyes in mock exasperation. "Great."

Hudson frowned. "I could cover the cost if—"

Ari touched her arm. "I agreed to pay for supplies. I keep my word. I'm catching on to this teasing thing."

Hudson looked down and shuffled her feet. "Things change." Hudson's breath caught in her chest.

Ari squeezed her hand. "Hey, what's going on?"

She swallowed. "Ghosts."

"Must be some pretty relentless ghosts." Ari nudged her shoulder. "Let's go get some fresh air and you can give me that receipt."

CHAPTER THIRTEEN

Hudson wiped the paint splatters from her arms while admiring her work. All that was left were the faucets in the kitchen and bathroom, and she could move in. After bagging up used newspaper, paintbrushes, rollers, and a bunch of other stuff, she headed out to the trash barrels Ari had bought and stored along the side of the house. A short honk of a car horn brought her head up. Ari waved out her window as she pulled into the driveway.

"Hi. I didn't want to scare you by whipping in the driveway," Ari said with a mischievous grin.

"So you thought honking wouldn't?"

Ari leaned against her car. "Maybe, but at least I wouldn't be running you over."

"True enough." Hudson scrubbed at a stubborn streak of paint on the back of her hand with the wet rag. Ari reached out and brushed her cheek. The unexpected touch made her freeze. As many reasons she found to not allow her feelings for Ari to surface, she found just as many to stop fighting them. Ari was smart, funny, beautiful, and ambitious. But it was the last one that scared her the most. Pam had been ambitious. *Stop. Stop comparing Ari to Pam.* It wasn't fair to Ari and it didn't do her any good either. The past, for whatever it was worth, was over. It was time—past time—to move on. And she would keep telling herself that until she believed it.

"You missed a spot." Ari took the rag from her hand and gently wiped at it. "There. All clean."

Hudson knew Ari had a good heart. The only question was if she dared to trust it. She thought about how vulnerable she was when she took someone at face value.

"Earth to Hudson?" Ari's voice interrupted her internal reflection.

"Sorry," she mumbled.

"It wasn't those pesky ghosts again, was it? Because if it was, I would consider doing a cleansing before you move in."

"It wasn't ghosts, so we're good. I was thinking about when I could bring my things."

Ari reached into the backseat and pulled out bulging gym bags. She slung a couple over one shoulder and hefted the others. "Does that mean it's done?"

"Pretty much. Just the faucets left to install. I can do them before I head out." She reached for a couple of the bags.

"Thanks," Ari said. "I'd love to see it."

Hudson dropped the bags just inside the door. "Would you mind waiting until I'm moved in?" She knew it was silly. Ari was her landlord. But she wanted Ari to not see just the space, but her things in the space. Right now, it was an empty shell, reminiscent of her life. This was the fresh start she'd been searching for and wanted Ari to be a part of it.

"Of course."

Hudson nodded. "I need to do some shopping. I didn't bring a lot with me when…" Her breath caught in her chest. The reason she had next to nothing was because her ex had kept almost everything they'd purchased together. The word "ex" was a revelation unto itself. Maybe she really was moving on since she'd started thinking about Pam as an ex. She shook her head to clear the images.

"I want some new furniture for my new place."

"You work hard, Hudson. You deserve nice things in your home." Ari grabbed two of her bags and headed to her bedroom.

"Where do you want these?" she asked.

"In the den," Ari said over her shoulder.

Hudson set the bags on the floor next to the futon. The room had turned out better than she'd hoped. Ari's secretary desk looked like it had been made for the space and the vintage library bookcase was the perfect match. Light streamed in, casting a soft glow over the oak hardwood floors, and she was glad she'd had them sanded, stained, and polished.

"The room looks great."

"It was fun. This is the first time in my life I've been able to do what I wanted." Ari admired the pictures she'd hung, amazed at how good they looked. "Would you like to stay for coffee? I made blueberry muffins last night."

"You know it's not fair to coerce me with food. I have no willpower."

"Does that mean yes?"

Hudson looked at her watch. "Sure. Let me run up and put in one of the faucets while the coffee brews, then I won't feel like I'm goofing off."

"Honestly? That's the last thing you have to worry about," Ari teased her. When she headed to the back door, she stopped her. "No need to go around. You can use this door." Ari pointed to the one connecting the first floor with the apartment.

"I don't mind. It's not an emergency." She didn't want Ari to be concerned about her using it even though she didn't lock the door at the top of the stairs. "Give me fifteen."

Ari set her cup down. "I can't understand why I haven't gotten the bill from the floor guys. I need to know how much wiggle room I have." She had a budget to stick to, and having outstanding bills made it hard to plan. When she looked up, Hudson had a guilty expression.

"Uh…yeah, about that. You won't be seeing one." Hudson parted her lips and placed a small piece of muffin in her mouth. She swallowed hard enough to cause a click.

"What do you mean?"

"I paid for the final refinishing." Hudson sat back and pointed to the plate of muffins. "These are really good."

"You did what?" Ari asked. *Why would she pay for the floors in my home?*

Hudson leaned forward. "It's my way of showing you how much I appreciate you offering me the apartment and letting me have my way with decorating." She splayed her hands in the air. "Surprise!"

"I thought we had an agreement? Or did you knock yourself in the head and develop amnesia?"

Hudson smirked. "We did, and we still do. Does that mean I can't show my appreciation?"

"No, but…" Ari began.

Hudson's hand closed over hers. "Please?"

Ari studied the pleading green-tinged gray eyes staring back at her. Hudson had done so much already she was about to argue the point but, like her, Hudson didn't seem the type to take advantage, and she admired her for that. Hudson squeezed her hand again.

"Okay, for this one time. There better not be another." She put her hand over their joined ones. "Promise me?"

"All good."

Ari tugged. "Promise?"

"Gee, you drive a hard bargain, woman." Hudson rolled her eyes. "Promise." She glanced at the clock over the sink. "I hate to eat and run, but I need to finish upstairs before calling it a day." She took her cup and plate to the sink, and then turned back, rubbing her stomach. "If you keep inviting me to sample your cooking I'm going to need to work out more."

"I doubt it. From what I can tell there's not an ounce of fat on you." Ari cringed. *I can't believe I said that.*

"Good to know my efforts pay off," Hudson said. She hesitated as though she wanted to say more. "Enjoy your night, Ari. I'll see you tomorrow."

Ari dropped her cup in the sink with such force it was a miracle it didn't shatter. She had no excuse for blurting out how she'd checked out Hudson's body.

"Not like I haven't been caught more than once," she mumbled.

Maybe Hudson knowing she found her attractive wasn't such a bad thing. Ari tried to be a good person and considerate of other people's feelings. Others told her she was pretty even when she was adamant about her many flaws. And although she hadn't done a lot of it since focusing all her energy on opening her business, she did like to have fun.

For the last six years, she'd been convinced she would never find the one thing she didn't have. Love. Her father had stripped away the comfort and reassurances of his love when she was vulnerable and needed it the most. It had taken Kara and Chelsea, her two besties, to convince her she could have everything she wanted in life—including love. She hadn't given it much thought, until recently. Love had always been last in the scheme of things. There had never been anyone like Hudson. She lost all focus whenever they were together and her libido had a mind of its own. No amount of self-chastising had tempered her feelings. If it were not for the instances Hudson pulled back, they probably would have shared more than coffee by now.

Which brought another disturbing point to the forefront. Someone had hurt Hudson. Deep inside. Enough that she recoiled at the mention of emotions and relationships. If it was true she was haunted by ghosts from her past, what kind of a future, if any, did they have? Would Ari be able to prove she was worth trusting? Did she even want to try?

Ari didn't want to think about the what-ifs anymore. She wrapped two of the muffins and put them on a plate. She set them on the side stairs and hoped Hudson would see them when she left for the night. As she fixed the coffee pot for morning, she heard her light footfalls overhead. It was comforting to know there was someone else in the big house, and she was looking forward to hearing it on a regular basis. She'd only been sleeping in her bedroom for a few nights, and it was eerily quiet, making her long for sounds of life. She hadn't been scared, but the lonely feeling was hard to shake.

It was still early and she knew sleep wouldn't come easy. She settled on the couch, her legs tucked under her, and flicked through channels. The warm breeze from the open windows caressed her skin, and she closed her eyes. The creaking of stairs brought her out of the trance and she heard a faint "thank you" before the door shut. The empty space of her heart filled with tenderness. Whatever lay ahead for them, only time would tell. For now, she was content with their friendship. She knew how to handle friendships. It was the only kind of relationship she had experience with. She wasn't sure she wanted more.

Coffee sloshed over the edge of the mug Ari held. A horrific bang had shaken the house.

"What in the hell…?" It sounded like it had come from the garage. She looked out the window. Hudson's SUV was pulled up near the back door and the hatch was open.

Shit. I hope she's not hurt. Her heart pounded as she scrambled toward the back door.

There was Hudson, sitting on a step, wedged between the wall and a huge dresser that was leaning on her shoulder.

"Are you okay?"

"Oh, hi. In case I forgot to tell you, it's moving day." Hudson grunted and the dresser tipped a fraction to the right.

"Don't move. I don't have renter's insurance yet, and I'll be really pissed if you get hurt."

Hudson's chuckle gave her a smidgeon of relief. "What can I do to help?"

"If you can pull it up a couple inches, I can stand and push it from here."

"Hang on." Ari rushed inside and ran up the apartment stairs, praying Hudson's door was unlocked. She almost shouted when it swung in. The top of the dresser blocked all but a triangle of blue cotton.

"Ari?"

"I'm here." Ari could hear the desperation in Hudson's voice. "Okay. I'll count to three." She leaned against the wall for leverage and grabbed the drawer opening. She had no idea if it was as heavy as it looked, but she was determined to get the weight off Hudson. "One, two, three." She groaned and pulled with everything she had.

Below her, Hudson let out a moan before the dresser straightened and then leveled out. "I've got it." Hudson peered around the edge.

"What's the plan?"

"Can you guide it while I push?" Hudson asked.

Ari adjusted her footing, her arms and back straining from the odd angle, but she refused to let it slide back down. "Ready when you are."

It wasn't long before the dresser rested on the landing. Ari felt a wave of relief.

Hudson looked embarrassed. "Thanks. I lost track of how many steps there were and stumbled." Her cheeks were flushed.

Ari's first concern was Hudson, but she couldn't check for injuries with the dresser between them.

"Let's get this inside."

"There's a moving blanket in the kitchen. Can you tuck it under the edge? I don't want to scratch the wood floors," Hudson said.

She folded it on the floor and shoved it under when Hudson tipped the end of the dresser. They pushed it to the bedroom and stood it upright. Hudson wiped her face with the edge of her T-shirt, her stomach muscles heaving. Ari turned her head, afraid she'd give away what she was thinking. She tapped her fingers on top of the dresser.

"Are you done trying stunts for today?"

Hudson nodded and laughed. The sound of laughter, a pleasant distraction. She wished she heard it more.

"For today anyway. I wanted to start sleeping here tonight. The movers are coming tomorrow with the rest from storage."

Ari stepped closer, her hands running up Hudson's arms. Muscles twitched beneath her fingertips. She licked her lips as Hudson's full mouth came into view. They looked incredibly soft. Fighting the increasing desire to touch them, kiss them, and feel them, Ari pushed her away. "Turn around."

Hudson resisted. "Why?"

"Because the dresser was on your shoulder and I want to be sure you're not hurt."

"I'm fine."

Ari pursed her lips.

Sighing, Hudson faced away. Ari lifted the edge of the T-shirt, looking at Hudson's back for any signs of trauma. The higher the material rose, the more skin became exposed. Ari marveled at her finely sculptured back, parts of which were still hidden under a sports bra.

"Cross your arms in front." She moved out of the light and gasped. Hudson's right shoulder had a large welt and displayed an angry red mark that would soon turn into a bruise. She was afraid there was more damage than she could see.

"What?" Hudson asked.

"You have a big knot that's starting to bruise." Ari lightly palpated the area and Hudson pulled away. "Does that hurt?"

"It's tender. I'm sure it's fine." Hudson rotated her shoulder and then her arm. "See. All good."

Hudson turned back around. "Thank you." She brushed Ari's cheek with her fingertips. Her thumb traveled along the jawline, where it lingered. Ari sucked in a ragged breath.

Hudson leaned in and then suddenly backed away, as though she had gotten too close to a flame. "I have to finish unloading." She fled out the door.

Ari touched her lips. *Did Hudson just almost kiss me?* She had been convinced she was going to. Just before their lips met, she saw the terror in Hudson's eyes, but there had also been a silent plea in them. What had frightened her? Had she been too willing? Did Hudson have second thoughts and the brush of their lips only happened by accident? Was the ghost back to haunt her, and if so, would Hudson ever be able to overcome the obvious battle of wills?

Shaking her head, she let out a shaky sigh. The heat of the moment was over for the time being and there wasn't anything she could do or say to bring it back.

The skin was silky smooth beneath Hudson's fingers. She glanced at the slightly parted pink lips and fell into Ari's questioning eyes. She wanted to kiss her so badly. The two warring sides, her heart and mind, fought for control. She wanted to love and to be loved again. Terror gripped her heart, squeezing so hard she knew she would die if she didn't *do* something. Say something. The opportunity was slipping away. These were the times of fairy tales. The stuff dreams were made of. Pushing aside all reasoning, she leaned closer and looked at Ari's waiting lips one more time. At the last possible second, she lost her nerve, and the resulting barely-there kiss was feeble. It was the best she could do.

Ari's eyes had fluttered for a second, and when Hudson chickened out, she was left standing there blinking, a look of confusion clearly visible on her face.

And once more, Hudson had fled.

She sat in the open hatch trying to settle her churning stomach. She'd been so close to kissing Ari the way she'd wanted to, she could almost taste the sweetness of her mouth. Then she remembered the thrill of another first kiss, and panic won over reason. *Why? Why can't I just stop worrying and kiss her?* How would Ari react to the near kiss? Hell, *she* was confused by her actions. She could only imagine what Ari must be thinking. Maybe Ari thought she was crazy. Maybe she *was* crazy. Maybe she needed professional help. Closing her eyes, she pictured Ari's perfectly kissable lips.

"I'm a fool."

"No, you aren't. You're scared. Big difference."

Hudson opened her eyes to find Ari standing in front of her. Heat rose in her chest. "Ari," she whispered.

Ari took her hand and turned it palm up before placing a tender kiss in the center. "I think I know what spooks you."

Hudson opened her mouth to explain, but nothing came out. Instead tears fell from her eyes. She didn't want Ari to see her like this. There had been a time when she'd been a confident, self-assured woman. At ease in every situation. She was desperate to find that part of her again.

"You don't have to tell me. I just want you to know I'm not that person." Ari pulled her to her feet.

Ari's green eyes showed flecks of gold and her gaze held Hudson's. She saw concern in them, but she also saw raw need—and desire. The desire for her. Then it happened. Ari's mouth covered hers, her lips soft, yet firm. They slid back and forth before her tongue traced the edges, asking for entry. Her lips parted and Ari slipped inside, gently exploring, her intent clear. This wasn't the fleeting almost-kiss she'd clumsily avoided a few minutes ago. This kiss was passionate without demanding more. It was a promise of things to come—if and when she let them. God, how she wanted to let them. She pulled Ari closer. Their bodies pressed together, and Ari's arms circled her neck. The kiss deepened and blood roared in her ears. All rational thought left, and she concentrated on the feel of Ari's lips and tongue and body.

Ari broke away gasping for breath. Hudson's mouth had been as soft as she'd imagined. Her skin tingled. She took Hudson's hand from her hip and brought it to her lips, kissing each tip before holding it against her cheek.

"I've been waiting to do that since we first met. I couldn't wait any longer." Ari wasn't about to apologize. There was no reason two consenting adults couldn't share a kiss. Or two. She wanted there to be two, and three, and four. Until they became too many to count. A shudder ran along her spine, her body's reaction to the awakening of so many repressed cravings. Particularly the knot between her thighs that grew when she'd slid her tongue inside Hudson's warm mouth. She needed to slow down. The last thing she wanted to do was spook Hudson back into her cocoon by being overly aggressive.

"I'm glad you did. One of us had to have the nerve, and I'm pretty sure you know it wasn't going to be me." Hudson smiled and ran a thumb over Ari's bottom lip.

"About upstairs. You can't leave a gal hanging like that," she teased her.

Hudson's head fell back and she looked skyward as her hands held Ari's shoulders. "I know, I know. Like I said, I'm a fool." Hudson pulled her into her arms and tightly hugged her, as though wanting to scatter any doubt Ari might have about how she felt.

Ari winked when she stepped back. "Come on. Let's get the rest of your things inside."

Hudson lay awake listening to the relative silence of the new neighborhood. The memory of Ari's lips made her mouth tingle. The thought of more than a kiss, more than a light brush of fingertips, thrilled her. She wouldn't let her anxiety about the kiss mar the moment. It felt too good. The sound of peepers in the distance lulled her and she drew her pillow against her before drifting off.

The day before, she'd said her good-byes to Cathy and Jill. They'd laughed and cried, promising to keep in touch, though she wasn't sure they would. Jill was entertaining job offers and likely to move out of the area. Cathy's boyfriend had proposed. Life constantly changed. No one knew that better than she did.

She stood with her hands on her hips. Everything in the apartment was hers. This was a home. This was a space she could really call her own and be at ease in it. She opened the kitchen window and stopped. The scent of fresh baked goods wafted into the apartment and she didn't need to guess where it was coming from. Her stomach rumbled in response. She hadn't eaten in hours, and the enticing aroma from below reminded her how empty it was. She thought about using the connecting door to follow her nose. Before she knew it, the doorknob was in her hand. Curiosity got the better of her and she yanked it open, about to launch down the stairs and demand some of whatever Ari was making. Instead, she ran into a very startled Ari.

Ari lost her balance and stumbled backward. She would have had a nasty fall if Hudson hadn't grabbed her around the waist and pulled her against her. The impact caused the container Ari held to tumble to the floor.

Her lips twitched. "We have to stop meeting like this. People will talk." She took a reluctant step back and retrieved the container.

Ari smoothed her clothes and brushed a stray lock of hair from her face. Her cheeks were rosy.

"Meeting? I'd say it was more like an all-out collision." Ari laughed.

"No witness, so I guess it's your word against mine."

"I guess so."

"Here." Hudson held out the still warm container.

Ari shook her head. "I was bringing them to you," Ari said. "What were you rushing out the door for anyway?"

"I opened the window and smelled something delicious and knew it had to be you." She grimaced at the obvious slip. "Cooking…your cooking."

"Uh-huh. Next time yell down first before we kill each other. Anyway, it's a new recipe and I wanted your opinion. I think there's something missing, but I don't know what."

Lifting the lid released the scent of cinnamon and blueberries. Nestled inside were three scones coated with an opaque icing. Her stomach growled loudly enough for Ari to hear.

"You probably heard my stomach downstairs and felt sorry for me."

Giving her shoulder a shove, Ari chuckled. "No, but I bet I could have. Let me know what you think of them." She became shy and glanced up through her eyelashes. "I didn't mean to barge in."

"You didn't. I barged out and nearly knocked you over." Ari turned to leave and she wanted to find a reason, any reason, for her to stay.

"Want that tour?"

Ari's eyes sparkled. "I'd love it."

A little while later, Ari placed a glass of sun tea in front of Hudson and sat across from her. "The décor is beautiful. It's definitely you."

At first, she'd been surprised by the bold accent walls in each room. Chartreuse in the bathroom. Sea blue in the bedroom. Sunny yellow in the kitchen, and what Hudson called "Paprika" in the main living area. The rest of the apartment had been painted a soft white. Hudson had picked up the accent colors in rugs, pillows, and decorations. All without overdoing it. A variety of prints and photos of all sizes that fit together in a sensible pattern hung on the walls. A black-and-white print with a bright tennis ball. A young woman with blue eyes. A puppy with a red collar. All framed in ebony wood with white matting. Hudson's taste and style sense showed through in ways Ari would have never imagined.

Hudson's face colored. "Thanks. It feels like home, and I haven't felt that way in a long time."

Ari watched a sea of emotion wash over Hudson's otherwise handsome face and wondered if the reason was the tortured memories left behind by a former lover. She wished she could make them go away. For good. Hudson deserved happiness. *Can I handle the growing attraction between us? Do I have to choose between my business and love?*

There were a lot of people out there who had it all, so why not her? Her head hurt with the pressure she felt to succeed. She knew the success of her business was in her hands. But there were no guarantees in love. Still, Hudson was the first woman she'd even thought about having a relationship with. Didn't that mean it was time for her to get on with her life and stop worrying about what her parents thought? Hudson's voice brought her back to the present as she walked with Hudson to the connecting door.

"Thanks for the break." The expression on Hudson's face revealed her natural sincerity. "There are still boxes to unpack and they're not going to do it themselves." Hudson stood in the doorway. "And just a friendly warning…" She paused.

"Yes?"

"If you're going to bake every day, you might want to lock the door, otherwise I might be begging for samples."

Ari's cheeks heated. "I have no intention of locking the door and you don't have to beg. I'm happy to have you as my taste tester, and I value your opinion." Ari grinned. "Maybe you'll want to buy into the business some day?"

Hudson shook her head. "Not a chance. That baby is all yours. But I'll gladly sample whatever comes out of your kitchen. You know—for quality control."

"Sure. Quality control. Whatever you say." Hudson was engaging and funny when she let her guard down. "The only thing I ask is for a rating on everything. Deal?"

"Hell, yes, it's a deal." Hudson bolted up the stairs.

Ari quietly shut the door and leaned against it. This could work. All she had to do was convince *both* of them it was possible.

Chapter Fourteen

The flashing message indicator on Ari's phone caught her attention. She wiped her hands on her apron and swiped the screen. The text displayed *two*. Her lips pressed together, she typed back, *Why not a one?*

It didn't take long to get a response. *Not enough of them to confirm.*

Shaking her head, she pulled open the door and yelled. "There's a few more if it will help my score." She closed it with a bang. As she put two scones on a plate at the end of the island, she heard Hudson clamor down the stairs, and then a rapid succession of knocks sounded.

"Come in."

Hudson skidded to a stop in front of the waiting pastries, a travel mug clasped in her left hand. "I only need one more, but two is better." She broke off a large chunk, and shoved it into her mouth. She rolled her eyes, smiling around stuffed cheeks. "These are really good," she mumbled through the mouthful before washing it down with a swig of coffee, then taking another bite.

"So why only a two?"

The devilish grin spread across Hudson's face. "Because I was hoping you'd want to give me more." She licked her lips, catching the crumbs that clung to them.

Ari watched the tip of Hudson's tongue as it followed the curve of her lips. They were full and sexy. She glanced lower. The flat plane of her stomach led to the subtle flare of her hips and the denim strained across her muscular thighs. Ari's clit twitched and she inhaled sharply before looking up to meet Hudson's knowing leer. She went back to the dirty dishes in the sink. *Something's gotta give soon.* She'd had to take care of her sexual needs the last few nights. It had taken the edge off, but wasn't nearly as satisfying as sharing physical pleasure with another woman. Confronting her runaway libido was easier than meeting Hudson's gaze. "And now that you've had a fourth," she leaned closer in exaggeration, "and a fifth?"

Hudson maintained eye contact for a long time before speaking. "Aces. All the way." She stepped next to Ari and placed the empty plate in the sink.

The space between them heated. Hudson was mere inches away and the warmth emanating from her body caressed Ari's skin. *I'm going to die if I don't touch her soon.*

"Thank you. I'm glad you liked them." She moved away, doing her best to not show her need, and took a large container out of the refrigerator before holding it out to Hudson. "Dinner, for whenever."

Hudson hefted the meal. "Ari, you don't have to cook for me, you know. I have a kitchen."

"Yeah, yeah. I know. I've always had a hard time cooking for one, so don't be surprised if there are more of those." There was probably enough for at least two dinners, if not more. "Now get out of here. I need to do some research on insulated food carriers for my car." She shooed her with a wave of her hand.

Hudson leaned in and kissed her on the cheek. "*Thank you.* I could easily become spoiled and fat."

"Ha! I doubt that, but if you keep eating desserts for breakfast I can't promise you won't. Now get."

❖

The small plot of dirt was hard-packed with sparse patches of grass. Big shade trees kept the sun from reaching most of it, and where it did, the weeds greedily took over. Hudson bent and yanked them out by the roots, throwing them into a growing pile. This was supposed to be her day to relax, but tension filled her shoulders. Her mind raced. She wasn't able to concentrate on setting up Ari's books and was too restless to sit still. The dojo was closed for the next few days because Master Jin was at a martial arts workshop. Her best option was delving into physical activity. Not knowing what else to do, she decided to tackle the backyard.

Drips of perspiration ran into her eyes, and her shoulders ached after an hour of raking, digging, and pulling at tough weeds. A small cooler sat on the dilapidated picnic table and she reached for water, wondering if the table would collapse if she sat on it. She drank deeply and absently looked over at the neighboring yards while replaying in her mind what she couldn't forget.

She wished she'd had the nerve to kiss Ari again and hoped the one they'd shared wasn't their last. Ari was different from many of the women she'd dated over the years. Nothing about her showed pretense. She was genuine in everything she did. The last thing Hudson wanted to do was fall into bed without knowing there'd be more. The knowledge that their relationship might be moving toward intimacy scared and excited her. Over the last month, hopes of finding love had crept into the realm of possibility. But the thought of giving what was left of her heart terrified her. *What if it doesn't work?* As scared as she was at the prospect, she wanted someone to share her life with. She was tired of pretending it didn't matter to her.

Hudson picked up the shovel and surveyed her accomplishment on the sorely neglected space. Another hour and the soil would be ready for whatever Ari decided to do with it. It was too late in the season to start vegetables, but they could still plant grass and flowers. Somewhere she had a book on building outdoor furniture. It would be a great housewarming gift for both of them to enjoy.

❖

Ari's feet ached. Work had been insane, running from one department to another trying to fix all the computer-generated errors—the reason she and a few other co-workers were doing overtime on the weekend. She couldn't wait to soak in the old-fashioned claw foot tub Hudson had managed to salvage during the renovations. A glass of wine, soft jazz playing in the background, and lounging until the water cooled. *Heaven on earth.*

It was just after six, and the day's heat had receded to a tolerable level. She pulled up in the driveway and grabbed her bags from the passenger seat. It was too hot to cook, so deli selections and fresh ciabatta rolls, along with an exotic pasta salad, would serve as dinner. She stacked the packages in one arm and picked up her purse and files with the other. She made it to the bottom step before everything started to slip from her grasp.

"Shit." She readjusted the load and papers slid out of the folder, scattering in the light breeze. She looked at the mess at her feet. "Great. Just great."

"Need help?"

Ari jumped at the sound of a voice and dropped the rest of her things on the ground. "Christ! Don't do that." Her hand flew to her chest. Hudson's face showed amusement, and she laughed in spite of the mess. "Where the hell did you come from? Thin air?"

Hudson thumbed over her shoulder before bending to pick up what Ari had dropped. "The yard. I needed something to do while the dojo is closed."

"You don't have to do that."

"Don't be silly. I can't just stand here while you pick up everything."

"I meant the yard. I don't expect you to do *everything* around here. You've already gone above and beyond our agreement." Ari reached for the jumbled bags. They stood at the same time, and Hudson held a sheaf of slightly wrinkled papers.

"It's not a big deal." Hudson shrugged. "I didn't have any plans anyway."

Ari touched her arm. "Hey, what's wrong?"

Hudson turned to face the sky as if to gather her thoughts. "Ah, you know. Sometimes you feel down in the dumps. No particular reason." Another shrug and she took a bulging bag from Ari. "Let me help you inside."

"Okay." Ari opened the door to the landing. Hudson stood in the doorway.

"I've got dirt caked in my shoes."

Ari took the bag from Hudson. "Thank you."

"Sure." Hudson's eyes were downcast.

"Want to join me for dinner?"

Hudson turned back and shoved her hands in her pockets. "Don't you want to have some time to yourself?"

It was obvious Hudson was trying to act like she was okay; Ari was pretty sure she was anything but. "I have plenty of alone time. It's too hot to cook, so I picked up salad and stuff for sandwiches. Nothing fancy." When Hudson hesitated, she went on. "We can fix plates and go sit on the front porch. Maybe have a couple of beers. I could use an evening of R and R."

Hudson's face lost its somberness. "Okay. I have some kettle chips and a kick-ass guacamole that I made."

"Great." She glanced at the clock on the stove. "How does seven sound?" That would give her about thirty minutes or so for herself. Hudson looked like she could use some company and she wasn't about to turn her back on her. The bath could wait for another night.

"Would you mind making it seven thirty? I have to finish putting stuff away in the garage, and you definitely want me showered before we eat. I stink." She pulled a bandana from her pocket and wiped her face.

"See you then." *Maybe there's time for a bath after all.*

❖

Hudson took a long pull of the ice-cold beer and set it down next to her empty plate. "Thanks." They'd been sitting in companionable silence for a little while, giving her time to gather her thoughts.

Ari lifted her head from the back of the chair and opened one eye. "For what?"

She searched Ari's face for any indication she regretted the invite. "The dinner invitation." She met Ari's gaze. All she saw was kindness reflected back at her. "I want to apologize for earlier."

"You're welcome, and there's nothing to apologize for." Ari rubbed a thumb across the back of her hand sending a delightful shiver along her nerves. "I enjoy your company." It seemed Ari had no intention of letting go. "Even if you weren't in a funk, I would have asked you to join me."

She remained silent. Lately, it seemed as though she was taking advantage of Ari's compassionate nature and she didn't want the trend to become a habit.

"So are you done?" Ari broke the uncomfortable lull in the conversation.

Hudson's head leaned to one side. She had no idea what Ari was talking about.

Ari waved her hand in the air. "Interior designer. Bookkeeper. Gardener." A smile wrinkled the corners of her eyes. "The only way I can afford to pay you is with food."

She couldn't hold back the laughter. Ari made her laugh. A lot.

"That's a wonderful sound." Ari pressed a hand to the side of her face. "And a beautiful smile. You should do both more often."

She'd never been good at taking compliments. Ari made her feel like she was special. That she was deserving of all good things, along with realizing she deserved another chance to find the kind of love her parents had.

Ari leaned closer. Her breath caressed Hudson's cheek. "You. Are. Beautiful."

Before she knew what was happening Ari's lips covered hers. Ari's mouth was tender, pressing softly, moving slowly over hers. She traced Ari's bottom lip with the tip of her tongue. Ari gasped, giving her entrance. Their tongues explored each other's mouth. She memorized the taste of her. The warmth. The heat between them. Ari wound her fingers into the hair at her neck, sending a bolt of electricity that traveled all the way to her toes. This time she didn't question what was happening because she wanted to feel every bit of Ari's passion. She'd lived too long without feeling anything.

The old saying was true. Time stood still and the street noises faded away. The only thing she was certain of was the pounding of her heart and her building desire. Her body craved the touch of another. She not only wanted it. She needed it. Now if she could only convince her head.

Ari pulled back and gazed with such intensity Hudson felt as though she could see into her soul.

"I've wanted to kiss you like that since the first one." Ari slowly drew her thumbs along Hudson's jawline.

She took a shuddery breath. "I've been fighting the same urge."

"I'm glad you feel it, too." Ari stood and took her hand, leading her inside. Once they were next to her bed, Ari faced her. "I don't want to talk anymore."

The breath stilled in Hudson's chest as second thoughts crept in.

Ari's finger touched her lips. "Just feel."

Those two simple words made her body pulse with excitement. Ari kicked off her shoes and turned down the bedding.

This is it. I'm scared and I want to touch her so much. Her mind raced in a million directions.

"Just feel."

Ari's hands slid up and down Hudson's sides before lifting the edge of her shirt, exposing her stomach. Her muscles twitched in anticipation as Ari lowered her head and placed light kisses along the ridges of her abdomen. Her knees trembled. If Ari didn't stop, it wouldn't be long before she crumbled to the floor. Ari glanced up, her eyes burning like hot coals, and backed her against the bed until she was sitting. Hudson wanted to say something. Anything. But she could barely breathe, let alone form coherent words. Her hands, thankfully, knew what they wanted to do, and she pulled Ari closer.

Hudson nuzzled her mouth against the tender flesh rising above Ari's blouse. She would go crazy if she couldn't touch the hard peaks pressing against the fabric, the stiff points rubbing against her face.

"Lift," Hudson whispered.

A blue lace bra held Ari's breasts captive, but not for long.

Hudson unsnapped the clasp, releasing them. Cupping the perfect shapes in her hands, she brought them to her mouth, sucking on a nipple and running her tongue around it, making it even harder.

Ari's head fell back. "Feels so good," she moaned and snaked her fingers through Hudson's hair, pulling her closer.

If this was any indication of what was to come, she would not be able to draw out their lovemaking. Hudson's tongue and teeth nipped and flicked while she massaged handfuls of flesh. A quick turn and Ari was on the bed. Hudson straddled her hips without making contact. She reached between them and pulled Ari's zipper down, one set of teeth at a time.

Damn. "Hudson?" Ari panted.

Hudson's heavy-lidded eyes darkened to the color of obsidian. Desire wasn't the only thing swirling in their depths. Hunger rose to the surface and the power of her gaze excited Ari like nothing in her life ever had. Hudson answered her by focusing on Ari's other nipple. It tightened to the point of pleasurable pain. A pain she wasn't accustomed to. Her former liaisons were efficient couplings with no need to prolong the act. Tonight. Here. With Hudson, she wanted to feed the animalistic craving. Every surge of lust and longing. It wasn't enough to seek and give physical pleasure alone. Hudson returned to her other breast, pulling the flesh deep into her mouth. If Hudson didn't touch her where she needed soon, she'd damn well do it herself.

"What do you want?" Hudson asked between licks.

"Touch me before I explode."

After kissing her way to Ari's quivering stomach, Hudson made quick work of getting her shorts off and tossed them across the room.

"Like this?" Hudson kissed the inside of her thigh at the junction of her pelvic bone. Hard enough not to tickle, but not nearly enough to satisfy her quivering clitoris. The throbbing in her breasts was nothing compared to the constant pounding between her thighs. A gush of her essence soaked her panties.

Ari hissed. "More," she begged. She tried to make contact with any part of Hudson's body. She no longer cared where. Arm. Leg. Hand. Mouth. Anything and everything, as long as she got some pressure on her swollen center. Hudson kneeled and pulled off her shirt, her pointed nipples poking through the fabric of her tank top. Hudson surprised her when she paused and ran her thumbs over the tight knots before peeling away the final barrier. Hudson's breasts were high and beautifully shaped, with dark brown areolas and mouthwatering nipples. She leaned over and lavished kisses across Ari's panty line before capturing her mouth again.

Ari pressed her lips together against Hudson's seeking tongue, wanting to deny Hudson entrance for making her wait. It wasn't long before she gave in, reveling in the feel of her mouth. Hudson broke away and her breath heated Ari's flesh as she trailed down her body, pulling the material off as she went. Her chest heaved in response and her breath froze when Hudson's fiery glance traveled over her flushed body like the kiss of a campfire. The intensity in the look did more to excite her than any touch so far. It traveled to her very core. Hudson settled between her legs and wrapped her arms around them. Her fingertips gently slid along Ari's folds. She was so close to where Ari needed her, she whimpered.

She grabbed a handful of Hudson's hair and pulled hard enough to get her attention. "If you don't touch me soon, I'm going to do it myself," she said. She moved her other hand over her sex. She'd never been more serious in her life. Hudson caught it and moved it to the bed.

"I'd like to watch you do that sometime—but not now." Hudson blew a warm breath over Ari's hot folds before pressing her mouth against the soaked center. She licked the swollen flesh and Ari fell back on the bed. The scope of her universe shrunk to the hardened point of pleasure, now in Hudson's mouth, as she stroked the throbbing knot with the tip of her tongue. Ari's stomach muscles tightened and her legs fell open, giving Hudson more access. Hudson's finger slid inside.

"Mmm, you're so wet."

Hudson moved in and out in time with the strokes of her tongue before adding another finger, filling her more. Ari's hips picked up the rhythm in counterpoint, driving her deeper each time she buried her fingers inside. She pressed her lips to a quivering thigh.

"You're so beautiful, Ari. Come for me."

"Oh, God, yes. Please," Ari whimpered.

"Tell me what you need." Hudson's desire to please Ari became paramount, and she ignored her own throbbing sex.

Ari writhed in the sheets. "Your tongue. More of your tongue," she gasped.

Hudson deepened her strokes and licked and sucked with more pressure until she felt the inner walls tighten.

"Now, baby, now."

Hudson pulled her fingers out and pressed her tongue inside, her thumb making tight circles over Ari's extended clitoris. Ari arched off the bed and froze in space, before wracking spasms overtook her. Hudson licked every inch of her slick center, coaxing more and more from her. Each contraction of Ari's sex coated her chin in the silken moisture of her pleasure.

"Oh...baby. Yes."

Moans of satisfaction came out in staccato as Ari gasped. When her body began to settle, Ari pushed on the top of Hudson's head and tried to move away.

"Stop, please. No more," Ari begged her. "I…I can't."

Hudson cupped Ari's sex with gentle pressure to help calm her flesh. She moved up the bed and pulled Ari's limp body against her naked chest. Ari sighed and snuggled closer.

"That was incredible," Ari whispered as her gaze locked with Hudson's.

"Yes, it was." She kissed Ari's forehead, then closed her eyes and drew her hands over Ari's back, enjoying how good she felt in her arms. *The last time I felt this content I was…*Her eyes popped open. *No.* She didn't want to go there. Not now. Not when there was a glimmer of hope she might have found a woman who could make her feel again.

"What's wrong?" Ari asked.

This wasn't the time to have second thoughts. She would only end up hurting Ari for letting her mind wander to thoughts of another time and place. "What do you mean?" Ari's hand came to rest between her breasts and she drew in a sharp breath.

"Your whole body went stiff." Ari got on her elbow and searched her face.

Hudson was about to deny anything was wrong but stopped. Hiding her emotional ghosts from Ari was not the way to treat the person you just made love to.

"I was thinking how good it felt to hold you."

"And that's a bad thing?" Ari asked.

She traced Ari's chin. "It's a very good thing."

Ari took her wrist and held it. "But?"

She let out a sigh. "It made me think about the last time I'd felt content and *that* was a bad thing." Disappointment weighed heavy in her heart. The revelation would most likely drive Ari away and she had no one to blame but herself. Why she couldn't let the errant thoughts of Pam fade away, she had no idea. Still, she needed to be honest with Ari if they had any chance of a future.

Thinking they might actually have a future had been a constant during the last few weeks.

"I told you no thinking." Ari tugged at the leg of her shorts. "Why do you have these on?"

"I got caught up in the moment and never took them off."

Ari straddled her thighs. "I can fix that," she said and ran her fingers inside the waistband, moving the tips of her nails over skin and bones. Her muscles contracted under Ari's touch before Ari popped the button, slid the zipper down, and peeled the two sides open.

"Lift." Ari maneuvered the shorts down her thighs, scratching lightly down her legs and making gooseflesh. She snaked her hands inside the loose legs of her black boxers, coming dangerously close to Hudson's turgid folds before gathering the material and pulling downward. A small corner of her tattoo was revealed, and Ari sucked in a breath.

"You have ink," Ari said in a surprised tone.

She touched the area. "Yes. It was a present to me."

Ari leaned closer.

"What is it?"

Hudson rose to her elbows. "The Chinese symbol for strength. It was something I desperately needed." She thought back to the darkness of the days following the breakup. She'd never felt so alone. Even after the fiasco in high school, she'd managed to lift her head and move on. Of course, her parents had been there to lend her encouragement and give pep talks about the pitfalls of young love and the ignorance of her first crush. She remembered their words while walking to school every day of her senior year. And they were right. There had been only a few of her classmates around to witness the scene, and no one teased her. If anything, she'd gained some respect, which gave her the confidence to be who she'd always been on the inside. Since her liking girls was no longer a secret she hid from everyone, she could be who she was on the outside, too.

"It suits you." Ari pressed her lips to the mark before revealing her neatly trimmed triangle of dark hair and ran her fingers through the soft curls. She tipped her pelvis to meet the touch. She was wet from making love to Ari and her body hummed with need. Blood rushed beneath her skin and the heat brought sweat to the surface. She watched Ari smooth her hands over her thighs. Their eyes met and Ari climbed along her body. Their slippery centers made contact, and she couldn't suppress the moan when Ari's wetness covered her.

"Your body is amazing," Ari said, leaning in to capture her mouth.

She pulled Ari down on top of her, holding on to her ass, and creating some much-needed pressure against her throbbing, swollen clitoris. She opened her mouth to Ari's insistent tongue and enjoyed the sweet taste.

"What do you want?" Ari's fingertip traced the ridge of her collarbone.

"I want to come for you." Being able to tell Ari what she needed felt good.

"Oh, yes. I want to make you come hard, baby."

She spread her thighs and Ari settled between them; her thumbs caressed her swollen folds. Hudson looked along her body and saw that her center glistened with evidence of excitement. Ari gathered the slick fluid on the tip of her finger and spread it over the outer folds before circling the hardening knot at her center. "Ari…" she gasped.

The scent of Hudson's sex rose to greet Ari and she inhaled deeply. The ruby red folds of her sex made Ari's mouth water.

Hudson wound her fingers through Ari's long strands of hair and gently tugged her head closer to the heat source.

"Oh, God…"

She coated her fingers and slid two inside, making Hudson rise off the bed. She stroked in and out driving deeper each time she entered her hot opening. Ari curled her tongue and cupped the underside of Hudson's rock-hard clit. She alternated licking and sucking, pressing her fingers all the way inside. Hudson's hips rose and fell in time with her strokes, and she could feel her approaching orgasm. Hudson's pants filled the brief lapses between gasps.

"Come for me, baby." She sucked harder, then flicked her tongue back and forth over the knot of nerves. Hudson's body went rigid. She slid deeper inside, turning her hand. The moan that rose from Hudson's throat was followed by the walls of her sex locking Ari inside.

Liquid heat coursed through every fiber of Hudson's being. It had been a long time since she'd felt this connected to a woman. She'd gotten good at being a detached participant in the act of physical release. If she thought about the implications of what she felt, she'd ruin the moment for both of them, so she pushed it away. Ari had told her to just feel. And now Ari's skillful tongue was playing over the most sensitive parts of her body until she was twitching like a live wire. *God, I need to come soon.* The impending orgasm became so intense she couldn't think. She embraced the sensations and let go of all thought. Waves of pleasure built in every cell.

Ari kept her at the edge of the precipice until she begged for release.

"Please," she whimpered.

She stiffened and the walls of her sex pulled Ari's fingers deeper inside as she neared orgasm. Ari closed her lips around her straining clit and gently sucked, coaxing her to let go. She arched against Ari's mouth, a long, low moan escaping as the walls of her vagina pulsed, sending shock waves down her legs. Ari licked the juices from her until she collapsed back on the bed in a heap. Her breathing began to return to normal. Ari kissed the inside of her thigh and slowly pulled out to gently massage her still throbbing mound.

Hudson sighed in satisfaction. "You're amazing." She pulled Ari up alongside her body, and Ari dragged the sheet over them, snuggling into the crook of her arm, and traced the ridges of her collarbone.

"I'm glad you think so." Ari placed a light kiss above her breast and met her gaze.

She knew, even with all her insecurities about the future, Ari wanted more than just sex. It would be up to her to show Ari she could let go of the ghosts of past loves.

Chapter Fifteen

"It's peaceful out here," Hudson said.

"It is."

She should have stayed upstairs. Ari most likely did not want her company after the way she'd left Ari's bed and surely didn't want to hear the reason for her abrupt departure. A lump formed in her throat. Maybe she should just make another excuse and disappear.

Ari rose from the wicker chair. "I'll be right back." Ari opened the screen door and went into the house.

Hudson drew her hand across her face, lost in memories and the awkwardness between them. The neighbors waved as they slowly drove by. The only sounds were from songbirds in the trees and the rustle of leaves from the breeze. Her time alone on the porch gave her a chance to mull over the last few days. After making love, she'd panicked, unsure what it meant for the future, and she'd left Ari's bed a short time later. The word "future" scared her most of all. For more than a year, the decisions she'd made affected only her. As much as she enjoyed spending time with Ari, and as amazing as they'd been together in bed, it made her nervous to think she might be giving real consideration to the relationship moving forward. She hadn't given Ari a chance to share her thoughts. For all she knew, they'd had a pleasant evening of mutual pleasure and that was all. Maybe she was worried about nothing. Certainly, if she'd had an opinion, Ari would have talked to her. Ari wasn't the type to beat around the bush. No, Ari only had one thing on her mind, and that was making a go of her business. She didn't have time to think about anything else.

Still, the little sleep she'd gotten in her cold bed had only confirmed how guilty she felt. Ari wasn't one of her casual pickups. She'd fought the urge to return and apologize, but what could she say that wouldn't make the situation worse? Her body and mind were exhausted. Hudson sat back and closed her eyes.

Ari wiped off the wooden tray she'd found at a garage sale. It was intricately carved with a floral pattern and polished to a high gloss. It was special, like the time she spent with Hudson. The memory made her smile. She reached into the refrigerator and pulled out several items. She sliced cheeses and arranged green and red globe grapes in a decorative pattern on the center of the plate. She added a basket of crackers, a bottle of wine, and two goblets. Once everything was on the tray, she stopped and took a breath, looking through the house toward the front door. Hudson was out there. They'd been quiet, not saying much. Most likely both of them lost in thought. They needed to talk about the other night, but she wasn't sure how to approach the subject. She hadn't been prepared for Hudson's quick departure, and it had left her feeling empty. She knew Hudson fought against the memory of her ex and the abrupt end to their relationship. Had Hudson learned from the experience? Was she capable of moving on, and if so, was that what Ari wanted? Or was she biting off more than she could chew?

And hadn't she sworn off getting involved because there wasn't room for success in business *and* success in an intimate relationship?

She was about to push open the screen when she saw Hudson. Her eyes were closed and her chest moved in and out in a slow rhythm. Her face didn't hold the earlier tension Ari had noticed. She looked at peace, and Ari liked what she saw. As quietly as possible, she stepped onto the porch and set the tray down on the small table, then poured the wine. Curling up in her chair, she took the opportunity to admire Hudson's striking features. Her eyebrows were narrow and dark enough to draw attention to her almond-shaped eyes. Her cheekbones were exquisitely sculpted and her chin lent character to her androgynous appearance without masking her femininity. In her relaxed state, the cute dimples that appeared when Hudson smiled mischievously were mere shadows. The tank top did little to hide her perfectly shaped modest breasts, and she couldn't help remembering how the hardened point of her nipples felt in her mouth. Her center heated in response to the memory, and she hoped there would be a chance to feel them again.

Hudson's eyes fluttered and she stretched her arms over her head, making her top rise up, exposing her well-defined abs.

Ari's center clutched at the sight. This time she didn't turn away.

A sheepish grin broke out on Hudson's handsome face. For a fleeting moment, the dimples reappeared.

"Sorry. I can't believe I nodded off." Hudson rubbed her face and shook out the cobwebs.

"No apology needed. I had a really nice view." Hudson's cheeks colored. Ari held out a glass of wine. "A penny for your thoughts."

Hudson swirled the contents and sipped before meeting Ari's gaze. "Life is unpredictable."

"That's about the only thing that *is* predictable." She didn't know if now was a good time to talk business, but at least it was a topic Hudson was comfortable with, and it looked as though she could use the distraction. She couldn't avoid discussing their lovemaking followed by her fumbling departure, but if given a little time, she hoped Hudson would be the one to bring it up. "What are you doing tomorrow?"

"I'd like to put some flowers in and spread grass seed. It's supposed to rain over the next couple of days. What did you have in mind?" Hudson asked.

Ari leaned forward. "Well, you know how I wanted to create a menu?"

"Uh-huh."

"So, I was thinking…"

Hudson had been shocked when Ari asked her to try her hand at designing advertising materials for the catering business. She looked through her sketches and made a few finishing touches, pleased with the end results. It wasn't that her designs were spectacular, but they *were* good. Even more so since she hadn't done anything like it since college. A big part of her excitement came from knowing Ari valued her artistic eye. From a young child, she'd always surprised teachers with her color choices. Her bold strokes, in an otherwise standard palette, were the things that garnered praise.

The house and apartment had been her biggest decorative undertaking so far and she'd loved every minute of it. Admittedly, she hated seeing the project end. It had filled the void of lonely nights and wayward thoughts of Ari while she'd spent every free minute on the house project. Not that she hadn't continued to think about her in more than a professional manner, but she was able to let it run in the background while she concentrated on details of the renovations. She had wanted to be sure they fell in line with Ari's vision.

Until the night they'd made love. When everything changed. When Ari had left no doubt about her attraction for her.

She had been sure Ari would ask why she'd suddenly left the bed, grabbed her clothes, and hurried upstairs. Panic had set in, and she hadn't been able to control the overwhelming feeling that she was headed down the same path she'd traveled with

Pam. She knew it wasn't fair to Ari and wanted to call and tell Ari the real reason for her abrupt departure, but it was a lame excuse. Instead Hudson acted as if nothing had happened. Doing so wasn't any better, but at least she'd avoided talking about her own insecurities.

She knew she had to face what they'd shared sooner or later. The thought of talking about its implications made her cringe. What if Ari expected a commitment, or worse, what if she believed sleeping together meant they were a couple now? She wasn't ready to take that step. She wasn't even able to process that she'd slept with Ari knowing she could never be a one-night stand.

It was time to face the music. Hudson tucked her laptop under her arm, picked up the sketches, and grabbed a bottle of wine from the refrigerator. She knocked on the door at the bottom of the stairs.

"Come in." Ari stood at the stove, a cookie sheet in her mitted hand.

"Hi. I come bearing gifts." She opened the bottle and went for glasses.

Ari stood with a hand on her hip. "I told you not to knock. Remember?"

She nodded, not ready to make eye contact yet. "I know, but boundaries and all…"

Groaning, Ari tossed the mitt on the counter and stood beside her. "I think it's a little late for boundaries, don't you?"

Her stomach tightened in response. They needed to air things out. *No time like the present.* She handed Ari a glass, their fingers accidentally brushing. Visions of their lovemaking ran through her mind, but she was determined to do the right thing. Ari deserved an explanation. She clasped Ari's hand, and led her to the couch, pulling Ari down next to her.

"About the other night," she began. "I really enjoyed our time together and I hope you did, too."

Ari held her gaze for a long time. "I did, but I don't think that's what you really want to talk about."

Hudson bit her lip. It wasn't like her to hedge the truth, but Ari was different. She didn't want to hurt her or lose her friendship, and being honest about what she was feeling might cause one or the other.

"Yeah, well, here's the thing. You know my last relationship ended badly. I thought things were fine, and when they weren't—I wasn't prepared to deal with it."

Ari watched her intently. She wasn't sure if that was a good thing or not. She was having a hard time coming up with the words she wanted to say. Ari reached out and touched her face.

"Stop. You're making this much harder than it needs to be. I told you I wanted you to just feel and not think. I meant it." Ari paused. "I'm not saying I want a casual thing with you. I think you know me better than that. But I *am* willing to take this…attraction we have slowly to see where it will lead. You don't want another broken heart, right?"

"It would crush me," Hudson said.

"And I've never believed I could have a business *and* a relationship. That it had to be one or the other." Ari waved a hand in the air. "But people do it all the time. So maybe it's possible for me, too. I don't know, yet. What I *do* know is how much I enjoy your company. Seeing you on a regular basis makes me happy."

"I like spending time with you, too, Ari. We—click."

"Yes, we do." Ari took a sip and set the glass down. "Physically being with you took me to a place I'd never been even though I'm not a virgin."

"That's good because I don't think a virgin would have been able to do what you did to me." Hudson held her gaze.

Ari blushed and a nervous giggle escaped. This was harder than she thought it would be. "I've never had a real relationship, let alone a memorable physical connection." She could do this. She needed to tell Hudson how much their connection meant without pressuring her into saying words she might not be willing to admit right now. "I'd like to go there again. With you. When you're ready." She pressed her lips to Hudson's before pulling back. "I think we should let things happen without overthinking the future. Life's short and I've worked too hard for too long without taking the time to enjoy it."

Hudson was surprised and a little shocked to hear Ari share some of her doubts. Even more shocking was her feeling of disappointment. She'd expected Ari to argue about the reasons they were great together. How much they enjoyed spending time together. And the sex. Well, the sex was mind-blowing. She hoped for both of them. She refocused. Ari was waiting for a response. She wanted to give her one without ruining whatever chance they might have at making this work.

"So you're really okay with going slow?"

Ari nodded. "I think it's best for both of us. For now."

For now. What did that mean? A week, a month, a year? How long was enough time to see if what they had together worked only as it was right now—casual—or if it could grow into something more? Something permanent. She shook her head. Ari was right. She was overthinking it. They'd been friends for six months and slept together once. That didn't make it a relationship, but it was the start. She took a shaky breath. They were okay. And so was she.

"Come on. I have appetizers for you to taste and then you can show me your ideas."

Ari stood and walked away. The view made her salivate. Ari had a beautiful ass. She wasn't sure if or when they'd be together again, but if they were, she planned on not missing a single inch of Ari's delectable flesh.

CHAPTER SIXTEEN

A few days ago, Ari had watched Hudson's expression as she explained how color and lighting affected the room's overall feel. How texture was just as important when creating a mood. She hadn't understood all of what Hudson talked about, but she did enjoy the surprised look on Hudson's face when she'd asked her to design a logo and help with promotional items.

"So, what do you think?" Ari had asked while she'd waited for Hudson to answer.

"Why me?" Hudson asked.

"I trust your sense of style." Ari waved her hand at the kitchen. "You did this and it's perfect."

"Are you sure you don't want a professional? I know how important your business is to you." Hudson had tried her best to dissuade Ari, without success, and finally gave in. "Only if you're sure."

Ari had sensed Hudson's enthusiasm at the prospect of putting her talent to use. She would have done anything to keep the sparkle in Hudson's eyes. "I'm sure."

"Ari?"

Hudson looked at her with questioning eyes, bringing Ari back to the present. Creases between her brows marked her otherwise flawless features.

"Sorry. I drifted for a little bit, but I'm back now. Let me look at your designs." Ari carefully took in the details of each page. She tapped the nearest sketch. "I like this one." It read *Ari's Epicurean Delights* in a stylish print with flair. "What's this font called?"

"Monotype Corsiva. It's one of my favorites."

Hudson's eyes danced. Ari wasn't sure if it was from her liking the artwork or having the chance to talk about her hidden talent. Her interpretation of Ari's vision was spot-on. She had an eye for design, and Ari couldn't understand why she wasn't making the most of her true talent.

"Why aren't you doing this for a living?" she asked.

Hudson paled and shook her head. "It's just a pastime." She turned away and shuffled the sketches in a nervous gesture.

Ari reached out and stilled her hands. "It could be more. You're capable of anything you want, but you already know that."

Hudson met her gaze with a sadness Ari read as doubt. "I used to think so."

"And now?"

Shrugging, Hudson picked up her wine and finished it. "Things change."

Ari wasn't ready to get up. She'd worked until one in the morning, and her back had been screaming by the time she sat down after the last customer left the Station. She wasn't going to keep this pace up much longer. The business, not the funds to sustain it, would soon be taking on a much bigger chunk of her time. She'd give up the restaurant job first.

"Huh," she said out loud. Once the decision was made, she felt relieved.

She threw the covers back and sat up with a groan. It was just after six. She had time for a quick cup of coffee and a shower before heading out to her day job.

She padded to the kitchen, poured and fixed her coffee, then blew across the surface of the steamy liquid. After a tentative sip, she sighed and closed her eyes. When she opened them, the shelf of cookbooks called to her. *Menus.* She had to make time to pull together sample catering menus for different occasions. Items she could make in large quantities if needed. Should the business grow quickly, she would likely need a sous chef or assistant. Lately, she didn't have time for much, including Hudson. Seeing her on a daily basis had been a pleasure, but with the completion of the house there weren't as many reasons to get together. That needed to change. Soon.

Ari held the sheet of paper up near the window and let the rays of sunlight bring the colors to life. Her original concept had been simple. She asked Hudson to design a flyer introducing her catering business, contact information, and the events she specialized in. She thought it best to start with smaller functions like birthdays, cocktail receptions, wedding rehearsals, baby showers, and the like. Down the road, she'd take on more formal events like weddings and corporate functions, but she'd need staff for those.

The flyer was alive with color, the font, easy to read. Cream paper with accents of lime green and pale orange caught the eye, making it stand out among similar advertisements. For a modest amount, she was now the proud owner of two thousand *Ari's Epicurean Delights* flyers.

She danced around the kitchen. *It's happening. It really is happening.* She picked up her cell, intent on calling someone to share her excitement with, and then she heard the sound of a car in the driveway. She rushed out the back door and down the three stairs leading to the shared rear entrance. With a full head of steam, she threw open the door and nearly bowled Hudson over with her enthusiasm.

"They're here! They're here!" She threw her arms around Hudson's neck and kissed her cheek. Hudson grabbed her by the waist to keep them both upright. When she set her back down, Hudson tried to read what Ari was waving around.

"What's here?"

"The flyers." She waved the wrinkled paper up for Hudson to see. "Well, the rest are nice and flat. Aren't they beautiful?"

Hudson studied the paper for a long time after she'd smoothed it out on the doorjamb and held it up to the dappled light. "Everything is spelled correctly and the colors are very close to the ones I…we picked out." She handed it back.

Ari punched her playfully in the arm. "Are you kidding? They're gorgeous! Just like you."

"I wouldn't go that far, but they *are* nice."

"Stop being modest. You were right. The colors work and I like the paper." She had boxes of napkins, magnets, and business cards to inspect, too.

"So what's next?" Hudson bent to pick up the gym bag that had landed at her feet.

Ari leaned against the doorway. "Good question." She needed to get the flyers out to her target customers. Hudson had been instrumental in researching neighborhoods that could afford, and might actually use, her services.

They'd created a Web site together, and Hudson had shown her how to track the hits that the site received. Then she uploaded catering menus for functions with fifteen to fifty attendees. It was a lofty number, but she could always advertise for a part-time helper when the time came. She was also going to run a small ad in the community newspaper.

"We…" She shook her head. The business wasn't Hudson's responsibility; it was hers. "I need to distribute the flyers and make sure the pantry has all the staples if someone books a party."

Hudson took her hand. "Not if—when. If you want to walk them around this afternoon, I have time to help. I just need to shower and change."

Ari hadn't paid any attention to the fact Hudson was in workout clothes and perspiring. "Oh, my God, I'm sorry. I didn't even notice how you were dressed. You should have said something."

Hudson shrugged before heading toward the stairs. "I seem to have a knack for being invisible. I'll be down in a little while."

Ari recoiled from the stinging remark. She hadn't missed how Hudson was dressed on purpose. Ari *did* feel bad for not having noticed. She'd been too caught up in her own excitement to see anything else.

Steam filled the shower stall, insulating Hudson from the world beyond the glass enclosure. She hung her head as hot needles of water drove into her tired muscles. She welcomed the onslaught. Ari hadn't meant anything by her comment, but she still felt raw at times. As if she had a fresh cut in an awkward place that refused to heal. She'd glanced through her mail this morning and found a letter from Pam's lawyer stating her ex had no intention of giving her half the value of the house or its contents. The last thing on her mind when they broke up was her legal rights to material possessions, but now that she had more than just a bedroom to furnish, she'd like them back, especially the furniture and heirlooms from her family. A month ago, she'd admitted to walking away without thinking it through, and Mom D. had taken up the "what's fair is fair" cause, telling her just because things hadn't worked out didn't mean Hudson didn't deserve her share. So Hudson wrote a letter to Pam asking for the items that meant the most to her.

Now Pam was refusing to give them up—and had told her through a lawyer no less. The last thing she wanted was the situation to become uglier.

The news had soured her mood. She thought Pam had put the petty quibbling behind her. The shame of making a mess of her life reared its ugly head. Her bad mood wasn't Ari's fault. It was hers. Once again, she'd let Pam take control of the situation, and her recent upbeat attitude had soured. Shaking her head, she grabbed the sponge and soap. She wasn't going there. Not tonight. Not again. Tomorrow morning, she would call her mother for the name of her lawyer. She was done playing nice. Her money and sweat equity had gone into the home Pam was now living in. She'd be damned if the woman would get everything she wanted, and then some, from their broken relationship. A relationship Hudson had invested in.

Hudson smoothed lotion on her skin before pulling on her favorite shorts and T-shirt. The cotton material felt cool against her skin. Her gaze traveled to the mirror and the woman reflected in it. She looked tired, but she didn't have time to dwell on things she had no control over. Pam could do whatever the hell she wanted, but this time she'd better be ready for a fight.

With a heavy sigh, she headed downstairs and hoped to avoid any further humiliation. She owed Ari another apology.

She rapped her knuckles against the door louder than she intended and heard a gasp from the other side, followed by, "Shit." The door swung in with a jerk.

"You scared the crap out of me." Ari looked pissed, her hands on her hips. "Will you please stop knocking?"

"Sorry. I'll try to remember next time."

Ari's face softened. "It's okay. I was going to come up anyway."

Hudson held up her hand. "Please. Let me do this." She met Ari's questioning eyes. "I overreacted. You didn't do anything wrong and I shouldn't be so sensitive."

"And I need to keep some things inside my head," Ari said, tapping a finger against her temple. She moved forward and placed a hand on her chest. "Are you all right?"

"Yeah, I just…" She paused and shook her head. "No. Not really."

Ari pulled her farther inside and shut the door, guiding her to a chair. "Do you want to talk about what has you so upset?"

She was pretty sure Ari knew it had to do with Pam. Maybe that was what bothered her most. It seemed every time she moved in the right direction, something from her past yanked her backward.

"I keep asking myself why it happened."

"You mean the breakup?" Ari asked.

"Yeah, but not just the breakup. Why didn't I see things between Pam and I weren't going well?" She met Ari's patient gaze. "I knew something was wrong; I just didn't want to face it."

"I can't think of a single reason why a woman would not want to be with you."

Her laugh was harsh. "Yeah, right. That's why I got dumped." She couldn't stand her self-pitying attitude and stood to leave, but Ari kept a grip on her.

"I don't know anything about your past. I don't know much about your and Pam's relationship, either. But I do know you're a kind, caring person and I'm very happy we're friends. I'm hopeful what we have and what we've shared is growing stronger."

The tenderness of Ari's simple declaration brought tears to her eyes. Her vision blurred as she fought for control.

"Then why do I feel so..." She didn't have the words to express what she felt. Her heart was heavy. Try as she might to make sense of it all, she felt encompassed by her loss and all it entailed. Maybe she had taken things for granted, like having someone to come home to. Someone to share the details of her day with and hear about theirs. The simple things. In some ways, she already shared many of those same moments with Ari.

Maybe her life wasn't in such a bad place after all. The weight in her chest lessened a bit. "You know what?"

Ari shook her head.

"Life is as good as I make it, and I'm done making it a downer. Let's see that list of addresses. It's time to let people know how talented you are."

❖

Ari watched Hudson leave. She still appeared sad, and there were tension lines in her face, but at least she had a better understanding of the cause of Hudson's mood. The knowledge helped explain the times Hudson closed up and withdrew. She did it to hide her true feelings from the world. *She* wanted to be part of Hudson's world. Not just *a* part—a big part.

Staring into her coffee, she thought about the pros and cons of pushing for a deeper relationship between them. She'd be lying to herself if she didn't admit her initial attraction had been purely physical. Hudson was handsomely beautiful with a gorgeous smile and a killer body. All rolled into one damn alluring package. Once she'd gotten to know her better, the person on the inside was just as appealing. But damn, she was beginning to lose her patience. Hudson wasn't the only woman to ever be crushed from a breakup. If she couldn't recover from what happened well over a year ago, what did that say about their future? The pressure of the business was bound to affect them both. How would Hudson handle seeing less of Ari if the business flourished? What would she do then?

For the first time in Ari's life, something—correction—*someone,* had pulled her attention away from her career. What did that say about her changing priorities? She needed to take it slow, for both their sakes. She wasn't about to throw her hard work out the window, but she couldn't imagine making the journey without Hudson by her side.

She pulled the box of flyers closer and picked one up. Again. They'd decided to put off handing them out until tomorrow. She might even get a chance to talk with residents. Meeting them in person would give a face to the business and add a nice touch. Making personal connections was good business savvy.

Stretching, she glanced at the clock. Where had the time gone? She set her cup in the sink and vowed to get up early enough to make her lunch. If she'd been tight with her purse strings before, it was damn near sewn shut now. Giggling, she headed for her bedroom and stopped at the door leading upstairs.

"Good night, Hudson. I hope your demons leave you in peace."

❖

Hudson strolled along the sidewalk at an easy pace and watched young children playing in front yards. Their parents kept close tabs on them even though traffic was almost nonexistent. Her spirits were better than yesterday, and Ari was doing everything she could to keep things light. She was grateful for her friendship and support. Her life had changed for the better since they'd met. Fate had brought them together, and she took it as a good sign. Perhaps Master Jin had been right all along. Balance came from within, and she was finding her fulcrum. Could Ari be the crucial element in the grand scheme of her life? Was she willing to take a fateful step into the unknown, or was she destined to be forever off-kilter with her emotions? As unpredictable as the weather. She was grounded whenever they were together. Her footing solid and her resolve clearer. Ari was interested in more than friendship and so was she, even if it was what she feared the most. Ari's touch pulled her back to the here and now.

"You haven't heard a word I've said, have you?" Ari asked gently.

Hudson stopped and faced her. "I'm sorry. I'm being rude and you deserve my full attention." She held up her stack of flyers. "This is important to you and it's important to me, too."

"I *know* it's important to you, otherwise you wouldn't be here. I'm sure there are plenty of other things you could be doing, but you chose to be here—with me. I just want to make sure you stay here and don't go wandering off." Ari tapped the sheet on top of her stack indicating the streets they were targeting. "You do the other side for three blocks and I'll do this one." Ari turned her in the right direction.

Ari climbed the first staircase and called over her shoulder. "Don't get hit by a car. I don't want to have to finish on my own."

Hudson waved her off. Before she stepped into the street, she looked both ways, and then yelled back, "Got it!"

CHAPTER SEVENTEEN

Hudson watched the corners of Ari's mouth lift and couldn't miss the twinkle in her eyes. The more they were together, the more she appreciated Ari's beauty. Her heart beat a little faster and her center clenched. Her only regret was not having met Ari sooner, but she knew better. Situations took shape the way they were meant to. *One step at a time.*

"What are you thinking about?" Ari asked.

"You."

"What about me?" Ari scooted her chair around.

She glanced at Ari's mouth before meeting her eyes again. "How beautiful you are." Ari's cheeks flushed and Hudson's pulse sped up. "And how much I enjoy seeing you happy."

"Aren't you the charmer?"

She shook her head. "I mean it. Thank you for letting me be part of your dream come true." Hudson cherished the way Ari made her feel like she was part of Ari's dream come true. She would have liked to sweep her off her feet, carry her inside, and make love to her. Unfortunately, moments like those were meant for couples, and she didn't consider them a couple after one physical encounter. Perhaps they should talk about dating, but that was for another conversation. This was Ari's time to shine, and she didn't want to do anything to break the spell.

Ari took a breath and leaned forward. "It's because of you I've gotten this far. I don't know what I would have done if you hadn't stepped in and helped with everything."

"I have no doubt you would have managed. All of your saving and planning led up to today and it's just the beginning. You're amazing." Her nipples tightened and desire flooded her senses. About to spoil the atmosphere with selfish longing, she stood and stepped back. Space would be her ally for the time being.

"I should go. We both have to work tomorrow. Thanks again." Hudson cringed for her cut-and-run attitude, but this time it was for a different reason.

Ari stood. "Stay with me."

Hudson heard the longing in Ari's voice. If she didn't turn around, if she didn't see Ari's face, she'd be able to keep going and make another excuse; let the lies tumble from her lips. But she couldn't. Every fiber of her being wanted to be with Ari.

"I don't know if I should." She came back and took Ari's hands in hers. "I don't want the special times we share to always lead to the bedroom."

"They don't have to. Let's cuddle on the couch and watch a movie. I don't want to celebrate alone. I'd like to celebrate with you." Ari stepped into her arms.

Hudson moaned. Ari's warm body molded to hers, and she smoothed her hands up and down Ari's back. "You're not going to make this easy, are you?" She planted a kiss on the top of Ari's head.

Leaning back, Ari looked up. "Do you want easy?"

She thought about the question. A few months ago, easy was about all she could handle: clear, precise, and uncomplicated. She didn't fit that mold anymore. Her needs were changing, and while she hadn't figured out what that meant, it felt good to be going in a new direction.

"No. I want pleasant. Enjoyable. Fun. I want to help you celebrate."

Ari gave her a playful shove toward the living room. "Great. You pick the movie. I'll make popcorn and grab a couple beers."

❖

Ari lay in bed listening to the cricket clicks coming from the backyard. It was late and she should be asleep, but the images playing in her mind wouldn't go away. She and Hudson had laughed at the movie until they cried. Their hands brushed in the bowl of popcorn more than once. Sexual tension still teased her flesh. She needed release. Closing her eyes, she moved her hand to her wet center and slid a finger between the slick folds.

"Jesus," she whispered.

Hudson's body heat had caressed her skin like a lover's touch across the short distance between them. She'd thought about tackling her before Hudson's words reminded her just spending time together was intimate. She didn't *need* physical contact, no matter how much she craved it, but she couldn't deny she wanted it. Picturing Hudson's muscled arm flexing as she reached in the bowl had sent her yearning up another notch. Her clitoris thumped against her fingertip. Staring at the ceiling, she pictured the source of her hunger sprawled naked above her. Hudson had filled her, taken her, and awakened her dormant sex drive. All she had done for months were work, save, eat, and sleep. Sex hadn't been important to her daily existence. One night with Hudson had changed her opinion. One touch lit the fire inside, burning hot enough to scorch her nerves. Hudson was above her, out of reach. Regret weighed her down. Ari shouldn't have let her slip away, but it was too soon for either of them to start spending nights together on a regular basis.

Her legs fell open to her stroking touch and she dipped inside, filling the emptiness in her body. She bucked against the thrust and drove deeper. Her heavy breathing filled the room. Release couldn't come soon enough. She added another finger and stroked the hard knot in tighter circles with her other hand. Ari cried out as she came. The bed shook from the violence of her spasms.

When she opened her eyes, sadness washed over her. Hudson wasn't with her, where she belonged. She'd barely managed to school her reaction when Hudson mentioned not wanting to end up in bed. She hadn't wanted her to see the disappointment on her face. Not with Hudson still unsure about where they were headed. The void in her heart, however, wasn't as easy to hide. The goal-driven person she used to be was becoming an ideal-driven one. She was coming to realize her worth was not based on her financial success. Up until now, she'd built her entire life around proving to her parents she had not wasted her time in culinary school. Since meeting Hudson, she wasn't sure that was true anymore. What good was her success if she didn't have anyone to share it with? Wasn't it time she gave in to her human nature and find a person she could love and would love her back? *Was it too much to ask?*

She shoved all the questions away, while she tucked the covers around her, content with images of Hudson as she drifted toward sleep.

"Ms. Hudson," Katie asked, "are you feeling okay?"

"I'm fine, Katie."

Physically, she was great. Mentally, she was a mess. The push-me-pull-you dilemma centered around her past and Pam, battled with her longing to find the type of love her parents shared. She hadn't been able to sleep since she and Ari were together for movie night. She tried to ignore her body's hunger for Ari's touch without success. Last night she'd masturbated in hopes of quelling her urges. Nothing helped. The orgasm was organic but unfulfilling. Not since her last months with Pam had she felt so empty. Ari had ruined her, leaving her to covet the intensity she felt when they'd shared their bodies. They shared more during those precious hours than she had with any other woman her entire life. Ari saw her at her most vulnerable. Their coupling wasn't only physically satisfying. They meshed on a spiritual level.

The feeling was beyond her personal experience. The beauty of the unplanned encounter scared her and was one of the reasons she resisted another fateful encounter. But maybe if she gave in her fears would subside, and she could spend her time being productive rather than distracted by thoughts of Ari. Her body. Her sideways glances. Her passion for cooking. Her fierceness in bed. A loud splash next to her woke her from her daydream.

"So, are you ready or what?" Katie, the energetic student, kicked water into a whirlpool around Hudson, making her laugh.

"I could do with a few more like you to keep me on task." Hudson blew her whistle and the rest of the group jumped in the water. "Okay, get in your lanes."

She managed to focus for the remainder of the class and hoped the trend would continue through her day.

By late afternoon, Hudson was done. After her last swim class, she headed to the dojo to vanquish what remained of her pent-up energy. Master Jin put her through a rigorous set of postures before engaging her in a sparring match. It left her emotionally drained and physically exhausted. A long, hot shower and a quick meal were all she thought about. Her stomach growled after being neglected most of the day. She made it as far as the first floor landing before her plan went out the window.

"There you are." Ari took the gym bag from her and pulled her inside.

"Ari, I'd love to chat, but…"

"Oh, I can see you're tired." Ari poured her a tall glass of iced tea and set it in front of her. "I won't keep you."

Grateful for the quenching drink, she downed it, and then licked her lips. Ari made the best raspberry iced tea she'd ever tasted. "Good. I don't know how long I'll be upright."

Ari held up a datebook. The page for the next month displayed several neatly printed entries.

"What am I looking at?"

Closing the book, Ari looked her over. "I've done it again, haven't I?"

She didn't know what Ari was talking about, which wasn't a surprise considering the state she was in.

"You came home exhausted and I'm bombarding you. I'm sorry."

Ari did look sorry, and Hudson regretted her inability to grasp what was so important. "It's okay. Tell me what it means." She pointed to the datebook.

"No, it's not, but if you insist." Ari's eyes sparkled. It was easy to see she was excited.

Even though she was bone-tired, Hudson wanted to be excited for her. Ari's animated expression drew her in and made Ari more attractive than her outward beauty alone.

"Two catering orders. Can you believe it?" Ari rested her chin on her palms. Her attempt at tamping down her enthusiasm was adorable.

"I'm not surprised at all. It's what you've worked so hard for." She stood and pulled Ari to her feet to hug her. *Damn. She feels good.* Ari trembled in her arms. She pulled back to create space between them.

"Hey, what's this?" Hudson thumbed away the two wet trails from Ari's cheeks.

A sob escaped Ari's lips before she answered. "I had my doubts. First my father telling me it wasn't worth my time, and then the loan denial..." Her voice trailed off into another sob. "There's no one I'd rather share this minute with than you." Ari attempted to smile despite the tears.

A hard knot of emotion formed in her chest. "I'm honored you chose me." She forgot how tired she was. How annoyed she'd been when Ari dragged her inside. All she wanted to do was convince Ari how remarkable she was. It was time Ari enjoyed her success, no matter how small.

"May I take you on a date to celebrate?"

Ari cast her eyes to their joined hands. "You don't have to do that."

"You're right, I don't have to, but I want to. I want to be part of the celebration for how much you've achieved. And I intend to keep saying you have every reason to be proud of what you've accomplished." The walls of her emotional prison were changing. Ari was proof that not all women were out to use her for selfish reasons.

"Is this a date-date, or a friend date?" Ari's eyes bored inside, reaching her soul.

"Dating is a big step for me." Hudson fought the fear gripping her heart. Ari waited for an answer. "Yes, a date-date. If that's okay."

"It's very okay." Ari took a deep breath before holding Hudson at arm's length, wrinkling her nose. "You are going to shower first, right?"

Hudson's clothes were wrinkled and were becoming stiff as they dried. She was a mess. "What? You don't like the butch attire?"

Ari stepped closer, her mouth at Hudson's ear. "I very much like the butch attire, and I plan on showing you how much with a very special dessert later."

The desire she'd managed to tamp down throughout the day was back in full force. *So much for physical exhaustion.* Grabbing her bag, she headed for the door.

"Give me forty-five minutes to show you a different butch look."

Ari fumbled with the necklace clasp. She shouldn't be nervous. She'd been with Hudson dozens of times and, aside from the first few, she'd never been as anxious as she was tonight. *Maybe it was the catering calls.* It would be easy to blame the jitters on her worries about making ends meet. That would have explained a lot. But that wasn't the real reason. Even though she'd admitted it was a big step, Hudson had asked her on a date. Hudson had no way of knowing it was a big step for both of them. Ari didn't date. Oh, she had the occasional dinner companion.

They were nice. Safe. Temporary. They didn't demand much in the way of time, energy, or emotional investment. Just how she liked it. At least, that's how she used to feel. Hudson made her feel differently about what she'd pictured her life would be like down the road. Hudson wanted a full life, but was scared to try again. Ari believed she had a full life, but she'd been foolish to think she didn't want a partner to share it with.

What would a future with Hudson look like? Would there be room for careers, a social life, and possibly children? Did Hudson even want children? Did she? Without having any interest in a partner, she hadn't given much thought to having a family, but along with other aspects of her life, change was coming. Her intuition told her a meaningful life meant growth and challenges, and she stood on the brink. Dating meant commitment. Commitment meant planning the future, and the future meant long-term. Would Hudson overcome her anxiety and find a way to let down her defenses, willingly entering a relationship on which to build a meaningful future?

And would she be willing to sacrifice some of her former notions about having to choose between her dream business and sharing a dream life with another person by her side?

The clock on the dresser glared at her. Hudson would be down soon. She needed to remember to relax and have fun. Tonight wasn't a test she had to pass. It was about two mutually attracted women enjoying each other's company with the possibility of amazing sex. *I can do this.* She smoothed the summer dress over her hips and slipped her feet into sandals. She sprayed cologne in the air, and then walked through it. She paused to glance in the mirror and admire the woman looking back.

The hostess led Hudson and Ari to a table for two tucked into a quiet corner of the eclectic restaurant located in the arts district of the city. It was early for the dinner crowd and she'd worried if it was a mistake taking a chef out for dinner, but she'd always found the food delicious and hoped Ari did, too. An expensive bottle of wine was already on the table, and she was glad she'd thought to order ahead.

Hudson's heart beat loud in her ears. She'd argued with herself while she dressed. There wasn't any reason to not date Ari, except in her mind. She needed to stop making excuses. So what if she'd been hurt. There were millions of people on the planet who had been hurt, and most of them went on to love again. She could, too. *I won't die from a broken heart.* It was true. She hadn't died. Even when she thought dying would at least end the torment, it hadn't come to that, and it never would. If her two mothers saw how insecure she was being, they would tan her ass. They'd never worried about the effects a spanking would have on her mental health. Fortunately, she learned at a young age she much preferred praise and hugs over a swat on the behind for misbehaving. They gave her all the love and support she needed to have a happy, fulfilling life. If she didn't take a chance with Ari, she'd be wasting all the sacrifices they'd made to give her the tools she needed to find her own happiness. Ari was kind, warm, and giving. She was also stubborn, independent, and tenacious. Not to mention beautiful with an infectious laugh.

"What are you smiling about?" Ari asked.

"How life can change in a heartbeat."

Ari set her wine glass down. "Tell me."

She leaned forward. "You are an amazing woman."

"Thank you," Ari said. "But what does that have to do with life changing?"

Hudson held Ari's gaze. "A few months ago, you didn't know me, and today here we are on a date." She waved her hand between them. "Like I said, an interesting turn of events. Don't you agree?"

"I'm not sure where this is going."

"Exactly," she said. "You had no idea we would develop an attraction for each other and become not only friends, but lovers." *Wow. Did I just call us lovers?*

Ari's hand trembled as she reached for her glass and Hudson caught it. Their eyes locked. Hudson let go and waited.

"I have a confession to make. I was attracted to you before I asked you to be a tenant."

Hudson felt disappointment clench her gut. Ari must have noticed her reaction and rushed on.

"I didn't know we'd become romantically involved. I asked you to move in because I trusted my instincts. They told me you were a good person. You proved that when you said you would help with the house and the business."

Hudson's summation that Ari had been attracted to her was confirmed. Did that mean Ari's intentions were less noble than she'd originally thought? She hadn't been totally honest with Ari either, and that had to change.

"I have a confession, too."

Ari's eyebrows rose.

"I'm not who I appeared to be."

Ari sat back, her hands dropping to her lap. "What are you saying?"

"My parents did a great job raising a happy, independent child. I grew up knowing life was meant to be a thrill ride. You take chances, get knocked down, brush yourself off, and get right back up. You haven't seen much of *that* Hudson. The person I am on the inside has been in hiding for a while, and I'd like to let her out."

"I'm not sure what to say. I know you've been through a rough time since Pam, but is there more?"

She placed her hand on the table hoping Ari's would join hers. When it did, she ran her thumb over the smooth skin and continued. "It's true I've had a trust issue, but that's not who I am. I'm open and candid. I don't hold back, and when I love, my love is fierce—a force to be reckoned with. Have you seen that person?"

"Not really."

"That's what I mean. In a big way, you're responsible." Ari blanched and tried to pull her hand back, but Hudson held on.

"It's a good thing, Ari. You helped me realize not all women are manipulative. Not all women see my kindness as something to be exploited. You set clear boundaries at the beginning, and I appreciated your understanding how I felt."

Ari snorted. "I think those boundaries are kind of out the window at this point." She glanced at their clasped hands.

Hudson chuckled. "There's no regret here." She remembered how she'd bolted from Ari's bed and had to ask. "Do you have any?"

It was Ari's turn to squeeze their joined hands. "Not for a minute."

"Good." Satisfied she'd made it clear how determined she was to be more like her former self, Hudson picked up the menu. "Shall we continue the celebration?"

The door swung open, and Ari almost fell inside she was laughing so hard. Hudson caught her by the waist and leaned against the doorframe.

"I can't believe you said that." Ari couldn't stop giggling.

"I did." Hudson started laughing again.

On the way home, Hudson had told her about her little confrontation at the restaurant. She'd gone to the restroom and received a disapproving glare from another patron. She hadn't been sure if it was her androgynous looks or the clothes she wore, but either way she couldn't ignore the insult. She'd caught the woman's stare in the mirror.

"Like what you see?"

The woman had wrinkled her nose in obvious disgust. "How dare you dress like a man?"

Hudson told Ari a few months ago she probably would have left without saying anything. But not today. Ari thought Hudson had responded with the perfect comeback: "The same way you put on makeup to look like Mimi."

The flustered woman had hurried out. Hudson was barely able to sit through coffee without making a spectacle, and she nearly lost it when the woman walked by their table.

Hudson pulled Ari closer and gazed at her mouth.

"You've certainly found your voice," Ari said.

"She was rude and deserved it." Hudson brushed her lips over Ari's satin smooth ones. "Is that a problem?"

"No."

Hudson pressed her thigh against Ari's center and firmly kissed her, tracing the shape of her lips with the tip of her tongue. Hudson took her time exploring.

"Do you want to keep making out in the hall or would you like to get comfortable?" She fingered the edges of Hudson's tie.

"I'm pretty comfortable right here."

"I'm not sure if I like this new smartass attitude." She took Hudson's hand and unlocked her door. Once inside, she set the dead bolt and pressed Hudson against the wall, tossing her keys and handbag aside. The heat from Hudson's body felt like being too close to a flame. Her skin wasn't the only thing burning. The places Hudson's hands touched her were scorched. Nerve tracks tingled along her arms and legs. Ari's mind raced with what she wanted to do to Hudson, but it was all happening too fast even for her. Her pulse pounded at her temples. Hudson's tongue found hers and danced along its edge. She couldn't think, let alone breathe, and she pulled away.

Hudson whimpered. "I want you."

She tipped her head, indicating Hudson should follow. She was too turned on to trust her voice.

They stood in the bathroom, and Ari turned on the shower before she faced Hudson, trembling at the sight of her. Hudson leaned against the doorway, hands in the pockets of her trousers and giving the illusion of a bulge. The image shot a streak of lightning through Ari. Hudson's legs were crossed at the ankles. For all of her casual stance, Ari didn't miss the heat burning in Hudson's eyes as her gaze traveled down Ari's body before returning to her face.

Hudson slowly unknotted her tie and pulled it from her collar in one fluid motion before letting it fall to the floor and stepping closer. Her nimble fingers made quick work of the buttons on her shirt, and then slowly pulled the fabric from her pants. Watching the scene unfold was an agonizing torture Ari willingly endured. Hudson slipped her feet from her shoes and unbuckled her pants. Ari consciously licked her lips as she reached back to find the zipper of her dress. Hudson shook her head.

"No. Mine to remove." Hudson's tone was firm. "Turn around, please," she said in a gentler voice.

Ari had no idea what to expect. This was a much different Hudson than she'd seen during their previous intimacies. Warm hands rested on shoulders and moved down the length of her arms. A little tug started the zipper downward. Soft, moist lips touched the exposed skin. Hudson's hands moved inside the material to cup her breasts; her hardened nipples pressed against the firm flesh of Hudson's palms.

"You feel so good. We should have had dessert first."

Hudson's hot breath brushed against her neck. A gush of arousal dampened Ari's panties. Hudson kneaded her breasts and kissed the edge of her ear.

"Are you ready for your shower?"

She held Hudson's arm. "I don't know if my legs will hold me." Her eyes closed and she focused on Hudson's seductive touch.

Hudson slid the dress down her arms and removed her bra. "They don't have to. I'll hold you."

"Hudson…" Ari whispered.

"Mmm, I like the way you say my name."

Hudson smoothed her palms down Ari's legs, dragging her panties along the way. Ari turned around and saw undisguised desire reflected back at her, caressing her exposed flesh. Hudson led them into the warm spray of the shower, and then pulled Ari against her. With an arm wrapped around her waist, Hudson slid the other to her mound and cupped her, squeezing the flesh and sending a jolt of electricity through her body. The guttural noise from her throat was unrecognizable. Hudson's lips assaulted her earlobe, neck, and shoulder. She yelped at the nip to her flesh.

"Did I hurt you?" Hudson's hands continued to roam over every inch of her body, tweaking her stiff nipples.

"You surprised me." She reached back and found the neatly trimmed triangle of soft, curly hair. Hudson backed away.

"I want this to be about you. All about you."

Hudson faced her and found her mouth, her pointed tongue snaking between Ari's lips. Hudson explored every crevasse, deepening the kiss to the point she couldn't breathe. She raised Ari's leg and placed it on the bench, then kissed her until she was kneeling between Ari's parted thighs. Hudson licked from her opening to her clitoris and back, each stroke sending a shockwave that threatened to buckle her knees. She found the thick head of hair, and she guided Hudson's mouth to her sensitive nub. She was close to climaxing, waiting no longer an option. Hudson pressed harder, her tongue hitting the spot where she needed it most, and she trembled.

"Hudson," Ari moaned.

Their eyes met and she couldn't miss the yearning she saw. The shifting shades of gray were like a stormy sea. She looked on, helpless, yet wanting the waves of Hudson's desire to bring release. Her clitoris turned to granite and the quivering in her belly traveled with lightning speed through her hot center, exploding in fireworks behind her eyes. She fought the urge to close them. She wanted Hudson to see what she did to her, but her control was slipping away. Crying out, her head arched back, and she gave her body over to her.

Hudson lapped the sweet juices flowing from Ari as she cried out. Her body shook as the orgasm coursed through her and Ari's face was transformed from beautiful to stunning. A pink flush traveled up from her breasts to her cheeks, as though sun-kissed. Her chest heaved, and Hudson was mesmerized. She held Ari's thighs to keep her from falling.

"Baby, I need to sit." Ari's trembling hand landed on her shoulder, urging her up.

The water had cooled, and she turned it off before grabbing a towel to gently wipe the droplets from Ari's flushed body while supporting her weight, then eased her down on a stool.

"You are incredible," Ari whispered.

Her heart swelled. Making love to Ari was easy. Even though they'd only been together in a physical sense a couple of times, their intuition for each other's needs came naturally. She'd like to believe their future held the same certainty, but only time would tell. She met Ari's gaze.

"I love making love to you." Her voice cracked. The truth of her confession sucked the air from the room.

Ari touched her face. "Come to bed with me."

The longing in Ari's eyes sent a flame of fire through her. She was wet and needed Ari's touch. Ari stretched out beside her and kissed along her shoulder to her mouth. Ari stroked her tongue over Hudson's lips before pushing inside. The kiss ended too soon and Hudson moaned in frustration.

"I…want…to…taste…you," Ari said between kisses.

Hudson's clit twitched. She'd had Ari's talented tongue on her hot center before, and the memory brought another flood that coated her thighs.

Kissing her breast, ribs, stomach, and hip, Ari covered the trail to her center with hot breaths and a wet tongue, eliciting a lengthy groan. The pounding of her clit blocked her ability to speak. She lifted her pelvis in anticipation, seeking the pleasure Ari's mouth would bring. Her body jerked at the first stroke of Ari's tongue.

"You taste like syrup." Ari lightly licked a circle around the head of her clit. Once. Twice.

Hudson strained upward. "More," she pleaded.

Ari's hands traveled over her stomach to the pebbled knots of her breasts. She fingered each one and gently tugged, sending a shock wave downward. Ari tongued her opening, spreading the hot fluid over her swollen folds. She nipped along her thigh down to her ankle and repeated the ministrations on the other side before inching up to straddle her hips. She bucked, hoping to send a message to Ari. Her entire body was on fire.

"What are you doing?" she gasped.

Leaning closer, Ari blew on her nipple, making it tighten painfully.

"Giving you pleasure," Ari said before her mouth covered Hudson's and explored it with her tongue, the essence of her flavor still on Ari's lips.

Pulling away, Ari smiled. "Don't you like it?"

She closed her eyes and inhaled. She had to concentrate to form coherent words. "It's torture."

Ari reached behind her and pressed a finger against Hudson's clit before sliding inside. Ari rode her hips in rhythm with the strokes. She grasped Ari's hips and synchronized their grinding to deepen the thrusts, but every time she felt the tension in her belly build, Ari moved to a different beat, interrupting her progress.

"A nice kind of torture, right?"

Ari filled her and then withdrew completely to spread the liquid coating her fingers over her throbbing knot of nerves. "Please," she groaned. "Please let me come."

Ari wanted to please Hudson more than anyone she'd ever been with. Hudson's beautiful body made it easy. That didn't mean she wanted it to be quick. Drawing out Hudson's arousal to the point of begging, made her own folds wetter. Hudson's plea for release made her clit pound in response. Ari drove deeper into the hot tunnel, reaching the sensitive ridge and twisting her hand. The inner walls threatened to lock her inside before she focused all her attention on the clit that was impossibly hard beneath her fingertips.

"Come for me, baby."

She watched Hudson's face while the hands on her hips gripped harder as Hudson rose against the pressure of her fingertips. A slow flush began at her ridged abs and traveled between her breasts. Hudson bucked hard and cried out, nearly throwing Ari off. The small knot pounded against her palm and she slid back inside to feel the spasms of Hudson's orgasm. Her sudden entry caused another climax, and Hudson's entire body shook with another set of waves. She was beauty in motion. Ari waited until her heaving chest slowed and the jerking movements quieted. Withdrawing, she leaned over and covered Hudson's mouth with butterfly kisses.

"God, you are beautiful."

Hudson's eyes fluttered as her mouth moved into a languid grin. "I'll bet you say that to all the women you torture."

Hudson pulled Ari on top of her, and she spread her body over Hudson's, relishing the warmth against her cooler skin. Their swollen lips touched tenderly, without the earlier urgency. Satiated, Ari curled against Hudson's side, tucked under her arm, and sighed. She pulled the covers over them and rested her hand in the center of Hudson's chest, her thumb lightly brushing the curve of her breast. Hudson stroked her back, drawing a circular pattern. It was the last thing she remembered.

Ari stretched along Hudson's body. Somehow, she'd ended up almost completely on top of her. She inhaled the scent that was uniquely Hudson's, tinged with the not unpleasant linger of sex.

"Are you awake?" she whispered.

"Uh-huh." Hudson's hand slid down to cup her ass. She gave it a gentle squeeze. "I didn't think I was that tired."

She reached up to cup Hudson's face. "I don't think it was fatigue."

Laughing, Hudson met her gaze. "I think you're right."

Ari snuggled close, enjoying the ease with which they'd apparently both fallen asleep.

"I could stay here forever."

Hudson stiffened beneath her and she regretted thinking out loud. Maybe it was too soon. Maybe Hudson's heart wasn't as invested in moving forward as hers was. Maybe she was the only one who thought she was falling in love. Even though she had nothing to compare her feelings to, romance novels described it as a feeling of euphoria. Of total bliss. The emotions she felt when she was with Hudson were indescribable, and falling in love was the best description for her current state. She needed to do damage control before Hudson bolted again. Rising on her elbow, she met Hudson's stormy eyes.

"What's wrong?"

"Nothing."

"Why don't I believe you?" Ari sat up.

"It's not you or anything you did. It's me. All me." Hudson broke eye contact, staring off into the distance like she was looking for answers. "I haven't wanted to think about forever. Until you."

"That sounds nice, but the doubt is a little disconcerting." She didn't want to discourage any progress they'd made, but she wasn't going to tolerate Hudson's insecurities forever and she needed to know what Hudson was thinking. "So why *are* you comparing me to Pam?" She couldn't help the edge in her voice. She didn't know how Hudson felt because she'd never been in love and she wasn't prepared to have it all come to an end. What she did know was that she didn't want that kind of an ending for them, which didn't make any sense since their relationship had only just begun.

Hudson's face paled. "I don't know. You're nothing like her."

Ari turned away, her eyes brimming with tears. She wasn't sure if she could fight a ghost. She wasn't sure if she wanted to. The only thing she did know was that Hudson filled a void in her she hadn't even known existed. Something inside her had shattered and the splinters scraped away the layers formed by self-preservation. What did it mean to stay whole if it meant a life empty and alone?

Hudson's fingertip guided her chin to face her, and she took Ari's hands in hers. "I know it's crazy. I know it's irrational. But I swear I'm not making excuses. You are a wonderful person and I think we can be great together…" Hudson stopped and pursed her lips, "in more ways than we already are. I don't want to question my feelings, but it happens."

Ari took Hudson's hand and placed it over her heart. "I trust what's in here. I listen to what it's telling me, and it's telling me we can make a wonderful life together." She waited a beat. "Am I wrong?" She needed to know if she had to pull back. Step away. Stop falling for Hudson, even if her heart told her otherwise.

"No, you're not wrong. I am."

She hesitated even while knowing she had to push on. "Then why do we keep ending up here?"

Hudson shook her head. "I don't know. If you can't wait," Hudson's voice cracked, "I'll understand."

"I didn't say I wouldn't wait. I just wish you could believe in the confident woman I saw earlier. She was magnificent." Ari trailed her thumb along Hudson's strong jaw and felt it tremble.

"Let's get up and watch TV. I think we both could use the distraction."

CHAPTER EIGHTEEN

Hudson watched Ari dozing next to her. Their lovemaking had been as spectacular as the first time. Full of steamy hot desire and passionate kisses. That was until she'd soured the mood. She'd reacted defensively to Ari's innocent statement and regretted where her mind had traveled. When Ari said "forever" she couldn't help thinking, "Nothing lasts forever." And even though Ari listened to Hudson's explanation, she'd been hurt. A shadow had clouded her beautiful features. And when she'd turned away to hide it, Hudson feared she was slipping away. The pain she caused lingered when Ari had finally faced her. Tears pooled in her red-rimmed eyes, obscuring the hazel color Hudson had come to read so well. Much like her own pain, Ari's had been palpable and she had caused it.

"Idiot," she grumbled.

Here was the woman of her dreams. One who didn't hide her feelings. And in return, Hudson had sent a very clear vibe of "don't go there." But why? Wasn't the fairy tale of a happy-ever-after ending—the same kind of relationship her mothers had shown her was possible—the same thing she'd always wanted? Against all odds, her parents had sought each other out and professed forbidden love. They'd even dared to have children—and still, their love endured. What secrets did their love hold? How had they managed to sustain their relationship through times of uncertainty and heartache? As a child, she'd rarely heard more than occasional heated words. She also remembered sounds of passion when, as a teenager, she'd sneak home, thinking they were asleep.

And still, a life of fulfillment and love eluded her. She had managed to think she could embrace the fairy tale for a little while tonight, but her bravado had vanished in the blink of an eye—replaced by the all too familiar fear of commitment. Ari deserved a partner who would stand by her, be strong with her, love her, and take chances. Hudson was failing miserably.

She'd be pacing right now if she didn't think she'd wake Ari. Their shoulders touched. Ari's face was at peace. How could she fix whatever was broken inside her? What would it take to push her forward? She *did* want a lifetime, not of perfection, but of perfect balance. With someone who loved her. Was it too much to ask? She let her head fall against the back of the couch, stared at the ceiling, and sighed.

"Hey," Ari said.

"Hi. Sorry I woke you."

Ari sat up and tucked a leg under her, watching Hudson before lightly tapping her forehead. "You've been stewing again."

She couldn't help laughing. "What gave you that idea?"

"Wrinkles."

Hudson gasped in mock exaggeration, attempting to be shocked. "I do not have wrinkles."

"You do when you're thinking."

She mirrored Ari's posture, resting her arm across the back of the cushion, and intertwined their fingers. She loved touching Ari in any way she could.

"Yeah. I was thinking how much of an asshole I am."

Ari frowned. "You aren't an ass. You're confused and scared, and sometimes oversensitive."

"Maybe." Thinking about her mothers made her wonder about Ari's family. "Tell me about your childhood. What are your parents like?"

Ari looked off to the side. "You don't really want to know."

"Sure I do. I want to know everything about you." Even as the words came out, she realized she hadn't shared much with Ari either. Ari took so long that Hudson thought she wasn't going to answer, but she finally shrugged and curled deeper into the corner.

"I'm an only child born to a conservative couple who grew up with prejudiced beliefs."

Ari was facing her, but her eyes glassed over and Hudson knew she was lost in memories.

"I…" Ari faltered, then cleared her throat before going on. "My father didn't want me. I don't think children were ever in his life plan, and being a girl was his biggest disappointment. He went out of his way to let me know how much of a failure I was. How I'd never amount to anything."

She wanted to reassure Ari her father's view of her wasn't how she saw her, but she had a feeling if she interrupted now the story would end. "What about your mom?"

Ari snorted. "She was the typical beaten down, dutiful wife. She never had a backbone. It's a wonder I have any at all." The bitterness in her words was cutting.

Hudson wanted to find a way to put a positive spin on what must have been a contentious childhood. "But you survived." Ari nodded, so she pressed for more. "And you grew strong."

"It's not like I had a choice. I knew the only person I could rely on was me."

"No friends?"

"Chelsea. We were pretty close until the sixth grade. Her dad was offered a job in Kentucky, and they moved away. I was devastated."

She couldn't stand the look of abandonment on Ari's face any longer. "Come here." Hudson backed into the corner of the couch, making room for Ari between her legs. She wrapped her arms around her, reassuring Ari she wasn't going anywhere.

"Better?"

"Yeah. Thanks." Ari rubbed her hands along Hudson's forearms.

"Can you tell me more?"

"There's not much to tell. I kept my grades up so that I didn't have to hear what a failure I was. In high school, Kara and I got to be close. She was a godsend. I wouldn't have survived without her. She is the only person I've ever known who loved me."

The statement caused an intense sense of privilege for the wonderful childhood she'd had surrounded by loving adults and a bevy of close friends. Hudson had no control over the tears that fell. She'd lived with love her whole life and she couldn't imagine living without it. Ari turned in her arms.

"Hey." Ari traced Hudson's lower lip with her thumb, sending a shiver through her. Everything Ari did was intimate, even when there wasn't a hint of sexual intent. Ari touched the essence that was Hudson.

"Baby, don't cry." Ari wiped the tears away. "We'll get through this."

Ari's certainty anchored her to the possibilities that lay ahead. If Hudson was going to love again, Ari was definitely the one, but her mind was a jumble of mixed emotions, and she didn't have the strength to sort them out.

"Come to bed with me."

"I don't know if that's such a good…" she protested.

Ari shook her head. "Just to sleep. I want a night wrapped in your arms and you in mine. I want to wake up beside you in the morning."

Hudson could do this. She could give a night to Ari and maybe she could give her more of them—in time. "Okay."

"Thank you."

"Don't thank me yet." Ari tipped her head in confusion.

"I need my toothbrush and nightclothes."

"Do you want me to come upstairs?" Ari asked.

"No, no. I'll be quick." She placed a chaste kiss on Ari's mouth and made a dash for the stairs.

❖

Ari woke to a warm breath moving across her chest. She had slept well wrapped within Hudson's arms. It had taken a while to go to sleep as she replayed their lovemaking over and over in her mind. It had been more than satisfying. Hudson had a way of taking her to the pinnacle over and over again before letting her reach climax. The feeling had been worth every torturous second, and she'd made sure she'd given Hudson a night to remember. She was well aware that sometimes Hudson cloaked her feelings, but she didn't think it was true while they were in the throes of passion. Ari was able to read all of her emotions then, and each facial expression, each touch, had been with desire, need, and tenderness.

It was Hudson's ingrained hesitation—the moments that clouded her handsome features in dread—that caused Ari the greatest concern. Even if she had no prior experience with love, Ari had no doubt she was falling for the enigmatic Ms. Frost, and there wasn't a damn thing she could do to stop it. The only thing she could do was show Hudson how she felt. For the first time in her life, she was willing to give a relationship equal importance as her business. She remembered her father's words, could hear them as if he were in the room with her.

"You'll never be successful with that foolish cooking thing. It's a waste of time and money. No one will want to marry a failure." His lean, tall frame had towered over her and his face contorted in disgust. The crow's feet that gathered at the corners of his anger-filled eyes had caused her overwhelming feelings of despair.

His words had cut to the quick, but she hadn't let him see how much they hurt. Instead, she'd walked away with her head high after telling him he was wrong. She was stronger than he thought and each sacrifice she'd made was a testament to what she was capable of.

And then there was Hudson's curiosity about her childhood. She hadn't seen it coming, but she had to admit it had been a relief to share a part of her secret with Hudson. There would most likely be more conversations between them of a similar nature. She was curious about Hudson's upbringing and wondered if she had a similar story and if that was the reason she hadn't heard about her family.

But the intimate story had done little to ease her angst. How much of herself was she willing to sacrifice to have a relationship with Hudson? Or maybe it wouldn't be a sacrifice at all. Maybe they could overcome their insecurities together. Every question brought another, and the answer to each one was the same. Only time would tell. But how long she was willing to wait was the biggest one of all.

Hudson stirred; her hand moved down Ari's tank top and stopped at her belly. She felt the heat of her palm and luxuriated in the caress.

"Morning."

"Good morning."

"What time is it?" Hudson stretched, her long arms reaching toward the ceiling.

She glanced at the clock. "A little after eight."

"Holy shit." Hudson sat up, disoriented.

Ari touched her arm. "Hey, it's okay. It's Saturday."

Hudson relaxed against the headboard. "Wow. That was a head rush," she said. "I do have classes today, but not till this afternoon." She rubbed the sleep from her eyes like a young child, and Ari's heart melted a little more.

She placed a gentle kiss on the corner of Hudson's mouth. "I'll turn on the coffee and start breakfast if you don't mind making the bed."

"Mmm…sounds like a deal."

The aroma of coffee filled the kitchen, and she hummed as she pulled breakfast items from the refrigerator. She dared to imagine more mornings like this with Hudson. Maybe it was foolish on her part, but she couldn't help it. Every time they were together the more she wanted another. There was only one other person who needed to share her sentiment. Hudson sashayed in as if on cue.

"Smells good." She reached around Ari for the carafe and poured coffee. "Want some?"

"Please." Ari whisked the pancake batter. When the griddle was hot, she ladled out four perfect circles and then turned the sausage links. Hudson handed her a mug. She inhaled the rich chicory aroma and blew across the steaming liquid. There was nothing like the first sip of the day. Her eyes closed and she relaxed against the counter, ready to face another day.

"I like seeing you just out of bed," Hudson said. "You're so damn sexy."

"You don't have to say that just because I'm cooking you breakfast." The tease in her voice was an attempt to hide her embarrassment. She knew what she looked like in the morning, and it was anything but sexy. She flipped the pancakes before pulling plates from the cupboard. Warm hands on her shoulders guided her around.

"It's true." Hudson's eyes spoke volumes. She saw the sincerity in them and wished they were always this vulnerable. Hudson's natural charisma intensified when her guard was down. Like now.

"Thanks, but if you don't let me get back to the stove, the pancakes will burn."

Hudson slid her hands down Ari's shoulders and stepped back. "We can't have that." Her voice was serious, but the hint of a grin wasn't lost to Ari.

After the first mouthful, Hudson made satisfied noises and licked her lips, catching bits of food with her tongue. "These are delicious." After the last morsel had been scraped from her plate, she sat back.

"They aren't anything special, but I'm glad you liked them." Ari stood.

"Come home with me."

Ari stopped gathering dishes in mid-motion. "What?"

Hudson brought her plate and mug to the sink. She leaned against the counter. "Come with me to visit my mothers. They live on the Cape in P-town."

Dumbfounded by the sudden invitation, she backed up to the counter across from Hudson and crossed her arms. "Where is this coming from? You've never mentioned your mothers before." Ari wasn't sure what the intention behind the invitation meant. If it was to introduce her to Hudson's family, she knew it was a huge step, and she wanted to be sure Hudson was serious.

"I know I haven't shared much about my life, and I want to start. I think you'd like them, and I know they'd like to meet you."

"They know about me?"

"Well, they know *of* you. I haven't talked to them in about a month, so they don't know we've become—involved."

"Why now?" She looked at the two catering orders hanging on the refrigerator clipboard. The first was a midweek engagement and the second was the following Saturday.

Hudson blew out a breath. "I want to know more about you, and you want to know more about me. Right?"

"Of course."

"What better way than to meet my parents and take a little vacation at the same time." Hudson's eyes pleaded, even if she didn't voice how much she wanted Ari to agree.

"I can't drop everything and go away." Hudson's face fell, and Ari realized how much this trip meant to her.

"When were you thinking?"

"Whatever works for you." Excitement filled Hudson's voice. "I can help with anything you need." Her face beamed like a child expecting her first puppy. How could she say no?

Ari pulled her date book closer and flipped through the next few weeks. She'd blocked off Labor Day weekend a few months ago. It might work. She tapped the page. "Here."

Hudson looked over her shoulder. "That's a busy time on the Cape, but Mom squared will be thrilled." She paused. It was plain she was deep in thought. "If we leave after work on Thursday and head back sometime Sunday, we'll avoid the heavy traffic."

"Mom squared?"

Hudson laughed. "Yeah. A nickname I came up with in grade school."

Three nights away from thinking about the business would be good for her. If catering orders started coming in with any regularity, she wouldn't be taking any vacations for a while. And getting to know more about Hudson and her family was something she'd wanted to ask about but hadn't pushed.

"Okay, but only if I pay my way."

Hudson waved her off. "We'll be staying at my house if you don't mind sleeping with me. I have a queen bed."

"In your parents' house?" The thought of Hudson's mothers knowing they were sleeping together made her a little uneasy.

"Well, yeah." Hudson faced her. "I think they already know I'm a lesbian."

Ari slapped her in the stomach. "Smartass. You know what I mean. Won't you feel funny?"

"I don't think so. I have my own bathroom, so you won't have to streak around naked…unless you want to."

She chewed her lower lip. She hadn't done an overnight at another person's home since grade school. The times with Kara didn't count because she was more like a sister. Still, the anticipation on Hudson's face was hard to ignore. If Hudson was as excited as she appeared, maybe it meant she was gaining confidence, and Ari didn't want to destroy any progress she was making.

"Okay, but I reserve the right to be embarrassed."

"Fair enough." Hudson glanced at the clock as she rinsed their dishes. "I hate to eat and run, but I need to go to the dojo before class."

"I'd love to go sometime."

"To the dojo?"

She nodded. "I've heard you talk about it so much I know it's a big part of your life, and…well," maybe this was a part of her life Hudson wanted to keep apart from Ari. "I'm sorry. It was a silly idea. You go ahead. I've got this," she said and began filling the dishwasher.

Hudson stood next to her. "If you want to follow me in your car, I could still get to the Y in time."

She studied Hudson's face to see if she was just asking her to be nice, but she seemed genuine. "Only if you're sure."

"I am."

Ari closed the dishwasher and glanced at her nightwear. "Can you give me fifteen minutes?"

"Okay. And thank you for agreeing to the trip. It means a lot to me." Hudson's mouth covered Ari's, and the kiss conveyed her appreciation. "I'll meet you outside." Hudson's smile lit up the room.

She'd do whatever she could to keep Hudson smiling, including sleeping in the same bed under her parents' roof. *God help me.*

Hudson pulled next to her in the parking lot then took her hand as they walked up to the entrance.

"This is it." The sign hanging over the door simply read Master Jin's Dojo. The storefront windows had been painted halfway up, giving privacy to those inside while providing lots of natural light. "I'll introduce you to Master Jin, but once I begin my practice, I might not make eye contact again until I'm done."

"If you'd rather not have me there, I'd understand."

Hudson shook her head. "No. I'm glad you're interested. It's just…" She blew out a breath. "I've never brought anyone to my dojo. Ever. But I want to share with you all the things that are important to me." Hudson's lips touched her cheek before she let go of her hand. She faced the door and closed her eyes, pulling in an unbelievably long breath before exhaling for an even longer time.

"Ready?"

The enormity of the moment wasn't lost on Ari. Hudson was about to share a very private activity with her, and she was determined not to do anything to make Hudson regret trusting her.

"Yes."

Ari didn't know what she expected when she walked through the door, but the energy in the room surrounded her like a down comforter on a cold winter night. Hudson's hand rested on the small of her back, and she waited, not sure what to do next. Hudson set her bag on the floor and watched as a small group of adults performed a type of slow-motion dance. The instrumental music playing in the background was just loud enough to be heard. Others, both young and old, knelt along the edge of thick mats that covered the majority of the center space. She wasn't very good at guessing measurements, but she knew it was close to half of a basketball court. When the group ended, they bowed to a short, elderly gentleman, and Ari knew he must be the dojo master. He turned and walked in their direction, although she could have sworn his feet didn't touch the floor, his movement was so fluid. Hudson closed her right hand into a fist and covered it with her left.

"Master." Hudson bowed.

He bowed in return.

"I would like you to meet my…friend, Ari. Ari, this is Master Jin."

Ari was about to reach out to shake his hand, but caught herself at the last minute and did a small bow instead. "Master Jin."

Master Jin met her gaze, and a small smile graced his lips. "Ms. Ari. Have you come to join us today?"

She glanced at Hudson before answering. "Not today, but I would like permission to watch."

Master Jin's eyes sparkled with more than curiosity. He gave the slightest nod and with an open hand gesture, led her to a bench with a thick cushion. She was glad it had a smooth back to lean against. She settled in, noticing Hudson was no longer in the room.

"Thank you."

He moved to the center of the room and invited four of the more than dozen onlookers to the mat. They lined up behind him and closed their eyes, breathing similarly to the way Hudson had before they'd entered the building.

And then she was there.

Hudson knelt on the corner of a mat across the room. Her eyes were closed and her face relaxed. She wore a bright white *gi* with a black belt tied high around her waist. Ari turned back to the group and watched as they repeated the movements several times. When they finished, everyone bowed before returning to the edge of the mat. Others paired off at the far end of the room and engaged in mock combat. There didn't seem to be any force behind the punches and kicks because none landed, but she imagined there was a great deal of energy behind them. Each one could have been a lethal blow. Master Jin didn't make a sound when he faced Hudson, but her eyes opened as though he had spoken. He invited her to join him, and they turned to each other.

Master Jin bowed first, and Hudson followed, their gazes locked. "Begin."

Hudson's body moved in a fluid motion, unlike anything Ari had ever witnessed. Each pose morphed into the next without her knowing where one ended and the next began. Within a few minutes, Hudson had performed a series of leaps, kicks, and punches. Ari couldn't believe Hudson wasn't even breathing heavy from the exertion. Then all movement ceased with a gesture from the master.

They faced each other again, and the sparring began. A rapid succession of blocked kicks and thrown punches followed until Hudson landed on her back with a thud. With lightning speed, she was back on her feet and engaged in the battle. She made contact twice before Master Jin took her to the mat again.

Ari was transfixed. The speed at which things happened while everything seemed to move in slow motion was nothing short of amazing. It was easy to understand how Hudson's body had developed such chiseled musculature. For the entire time, Hudson didn't look at her, and she knew why. Even a second of lost concentration could bring a serious injury. When she fell, each landing was controlled. No energy was wasted in the motions of engagement. When she attacked, she knew how far her body had to move to make contact, although she rarely got the chance. Master Jin avoided most strikes with a simple shift of his weight. Their battle ended as quietly as it began.

Hudson cleaned the mats they'd used and then retreated to a corner, once more closing her eyes for several minutes before walking through the only other door at the end of a short hallway. Ari imagined that was where the lockers and showers were located. She felt a peaceful calm wash over her as the floor participants continued practicing. They were respectful of each other and their master. Most impressive was the sureness of their art. She had a much better understanding of the pull the dojo held. Hudson reappeared a few minutes later. Her hair was wet, and she'd changed into her street clothes.

Master Jin approached Ari, and she stood out of respect.

"I hope you have found what you were looking for." He spoke in a gentle tone, and his eyes softened as Hudson neared.

Ari gazed at Hudson, then faced Master Jin. "I believe I have." This time she did hold out her hand. "Thank you." She'd thought about saying more, but it wasn't necessary. She had no doubt he knew what she meant.

Fist in hand, Hudson bowed to her teacher before guiding Ari to the exit.

She wasn't sure if she should talk. She'd witnessed more than just sparring and blows exchanged. Hudson and her master had engaged in a reverential dance of death that was full of life. And now, as she tried to recall specific details, it all felt surreal. As if it was more a dream than reality. Perhaps it had been. Time had stood still.

Ari took Hudson's hand. "Thank you seems feeble after what you've shared."

Hudson's face reflected serenity. "Thank you for wanting to be a part of it." She gestured to the building. "This is a big part of my life." Hudson cupped her neck and leaned in. Their lips met in a soft kiss.

"Can I see you tonight?" Ari asked.

"I'd like that." Hudson slid her hand over Ari's shoulder and trailed down her arm. "I still have laundry to do. How does seven sound?"

Ari brought Hudson's open palm to her lips. "Until then."

Ari watched Hudson drive off, then looked at her phone. They'd been at the dojo almost two hours. Where had the time gone? No wonder Hudson felt the need to be here as often as she did. It brought things into perspective. She felt centered even though she hadn't participated. The energy that had washed over her left her feeling changed. Cleansed.

Life with Hudson would be filled with many experiences she'd never imagined. If she were ready. If Hudson was willing. Bringing her today should have convinced Ari that Hudson wanted her to be involved in every aspect of her life. Not to mention asking her to go with her to her childhood home to meet her parents.

She started the car and decided to stop at the farmers' market to pick up a few things for dinner. They needed to talk about the trip, and she had to make sure she could handle the booked catering jobs on her own.

Hudson poured a capful of detergent into the swirling water and thought about her earlier turmoil. When Ari had mentioned wanting to go with her to the dojo, her first reaction was to make an excuse why she couldn't go. However, thinking about the philosophy of Asian arts and how all people and events were connected to the greater cosmic realm had changed her mind. The dojo did not "belong" to anyone. It was a vessel for interaction and awareness. It was a gift to her, and she was obligated by those beliefs to share it with everyone who was called to seek a deeper understanding of the Universe. Ari had embraced it, and Hudson liked seeing the awed expression of what she was witnessing. Ari also understood it was a part of her life never witnessed by any former partners. Until today, it had been her refuge and respite from the angst of the world. She'd been concerned that somehow Ari's presence would change those feelings, but she needn't have worried. If anything, Ari had earned another level of trust. If Hudson could share an activity that she considered sacred, and Ari acknowledge how special the sharing was to her, it only solidified what Hudson already knew. Ari was unique, and she would be a fool to let the past keep her from her future.

Checking the clock to see how much time she had before heading downstairs, a thought surfaced.

"Shit." *What the hell was I thinking?* She had to call home. She knew it wouldn't be an issue for her to spend the holiday weekend, but she needed to let her parents know she was bringing Ari. It had been years since she'd brought anyone to meet her folks. Not since before she and Pam moved in together. *Look how well that had gone.* She shrugged off the thought. Ari wasn't Pam. Far from it. They were total opposites, and it wasn't fair to her or Ari to keep comparing them. *So why do I do it?* The cell phone in her hand mocked her. It had been a few weeks since she'd called home. She missed her parents, even more so when self-doubt reared its ugly head. They'd always been her greatest supporters, and she should have relied on them more when she was at her lowest, but she'd wanted to prove they'd raised a strong, independent woman.

"Well, if it isn't my long-lost daughter," her mother's voice was flat.

She rolled her eyes, glad Momma G. couldn't see her. "Hi, Momma, I'm not lost. In fact, I'll be home in a few weeks."

Her mother squealed on the other end, and Hudson pulled the phone from her ear. "Hudson honey, you've made my day."

Hudson heard the smile in her mother's voice. "Good." She pulled in a breath and pushed on. "I'm bringing Ari with me."

"Oh? As a friend?" She waited quietly on the other end.

"Yes. No. I mean, she is a friend, but we've been—seeing each other." Hudson didn't know why she was shy all of sudden. She'd always been able to talk about anything with her mothers, especially Momma G.

"Does that mean you've slept together?"

Hudson looked at the ceiling, hoping to find a delicate way to respond. "Yes."

"Hot damn, it's about time."

"Momma," she warned her.

"Don't you Momma me. I've been worried sick about you. We both have, Hudson. It's not normal for a woman as beautiful and charming as you not to have a lover."

"I'm fine."

"We were beginning to think we needed to take your card away," She said, laughing. The sound warmed Hudson's insides. It was a familiar memory that had filled her childhood home on a daily basis, and one of the many reasons her schoolmates loved being invited for sleepovers.

"I'm going to regret this visit, aren't I?" She ran a hand over her face. She would have to prepare Ari for Momma G.'s warped sense of humor. She would take every opportunity to embarrass Hudson unless Mom D. stepped in to save her.

"Nonsense. Since when can't you take a little ribbing? So when can we expect you?"

From the noise coming over the phone, Hudson pictured the big calendar being taken off the wall. For as long as she could remember, every important date had been kept on the pages of a wall calendar. There were two totes full of them in the attic. Hudson had asked why she kept them and was told memories fade, but what's written lasts forever. Some memories were meant to be forgotten, but others she was grateful someone had kept track of. She could always count on Momma G. to supply the details of the family's events, from her first broken bone to her learner's permit to going away to college. Each was recorded, and they had celebrated every one in a special way.

"The Thursday before Labor Day."

"Let's see, that would be August thirtieth. Got it. Will you be here for dinner?"

"Don't plan on it, Momma. We both have to work and won't get there until nine or ten. We'll grab something on the way." P-town was home to some great restaurants, but they'd probably only make it to a few on this trip. If Ari enjoyed the quaint community, and Hudson would never understand how a person couldn't, they would visit again.

"Earth to Hudson."

"Sorry. I missed that."

"It's okay, honey. I'm sure you have a lot on your mind. This is a good thing, bringing Ari home, isn't it?"

"That's what I'm hoping. Is Mom around?"

"She's out in the garden. Hang on." The telltale squeak of the back screen door made her wonder why they'd never fixed it. It had been like that since they'd moved in.

"Dale, our daughter is on the phone."

Hudson heard her mother yelling. A few minutes later, Mom D.'s voice answered.

"Did she have temporary amnesia?" Mom asked.

"Hush now, she'll hear you."

"Good."

Hudson heard their good-natured quibbling and shook her head, grateful some things never changed.

"Hello?"

The rougher voice of her birth mother brought her more comfort than she'd thought possible. "Hi, Mom, and before you say it, I already know. I need to call more."

"See, you are smart. To what do we owe the honor of hearing from you?" Mom didn't pull any punches when it came to dealing with her children.

"I'm coming for a visit."

"Really? When?"

Hudson repeated all the pertinent details before sharing the most important. "I'm bringing Ari with me."

"Wow. She must be special. It's been ages since you've brought anyone home. I think Pam was the last one."

She expected the mention of her ex's name to make her defensive. When it didn't, she took it as a good sign.

"I know," she said. "I think you'll like Ari. She's warm and friendly." Her mom had never cared for Pam, saying there was something "off" about her.

"Is she pretty?"

Hudson rolled her eyes. "Yes, Mom, she's beautiful."

"Just teasing. I don't care what she looks like as long as she treats you well and you like each other. That's the main thing." Her voice dropped lower. "'Course, there's nothing wrong with having a good-looking woman on your arm. Just icing on the cake."

Mom D. was old-fashioned in many ways, and Hudson believed she would have done well in the Roaring Twenties, even though life had been scary for many in the LGBT community back then.

"Mom, I've gotta go."

Her mother sighed. "Sure. You're a busy woman. I miss you, baby girl."

"I miss you, too, Mom. I promise not to make it so long between calls. Okay?"

"Okay. I love you, Hudson."

"I love you. Tell Momma G. I love her and I'll see you both soon."

"Will do."

Hudson stared at her cell phone. She loved her parents and was grateful for all they'd done. Especially for how they'd raised her and her brother. It hadn't been easy for lesbians to raise children in the eighties, but they'd faired okay by living in Provincetown where everyone was family in one way or another. She wanted to raise her own family in a neighborhood like the one she'd grown up in. Each person shared in their neighbors' well-being, and she knew where her caring nature came from.

The buzzer sounded. She went to flip the laundry and stopped after a few steps. *Huh. That's the first time in ages I've thought about having a family of my own.* She didn't want to be distracted from her plans for the next few hours, so she tucked the thought away. She needed to consider what the idea of a family meant for her and Ari.

CHAPTER NINETEEN

I can't believe you've never been to the Cape." Hudson's shock was apparent in her voice.

"Gee, don't make it sound so villainous. I was a country girl before moving to the city. We never spent money on vacations," Ari said. Not to mention her parents would never have visited the lesbian Mecca of the East Coast.

"I didn't mean to insult you. I'm just surprised." Hudson concentrated on the road until they came to a traffic light, and then she glanced in her direction. "It's beautiful. Once you've been here for a few days you'll understand the attraction."

Ari looked out the passenger window, admiring the quaint houses and the flowers that grew everywhere. "I like the flowers."

"Then you'll love Momma G.'s plants. She's got them in every available nook and cranny. She says it adds to the rustic charm of the house."

Ari wondered how anyone got anywhere. The streets were so narrow that cars could barely pass. Everyone parked along the roads.

"Why are all these cars here?"

"Most of the B&Bs only have room for a few cars, so the town designates spaces on the street. People who come here often aren't fazed. It's just part of the ambiance." The pure joy on Hudson's face made Ari think of a kid in the candy store.

"You really like it here."

Hudson nodded. "A lot. Aside from it being home, P-town has a wonderful sense of community that I've never found anywhere else."

Ari wished she'd grown up having the security of being surrounded by like souls; individuals who cared for, and about, each other. She'd constructed her own world with goals being more important than feeling like she belonged to the human race. The hollowness inside had always been there. She understood Hudson a little better every day. Maybe Ari's idea of what was really important would be tested on this trip.

Traffic waited for pedestrians at every corner. Hudson turned left, and then right onto another long street. Her eyes opened wide. Every building held a shop, restaurant, or hotel. A steady stream of meandering people of every gender type, nationality, and family unit filled the sidewalks, spilling out into the street. Hudson slowed to a crawl; a huge grin graced her handsome features.

"There's nothing like taking a first-timer for a ride on Commercial Street. Isn't it amazing?"

"It's something, all right." She feared a walker was going to be run over, but everyone on the street had the same carefree look. "Is it always like this?"

"No. Sometimes there are so many people you can't move."

She stared out the windshield as they crept along. She couldn't imagine more people than were already in front of them. And beside them. It was like the parting of the Red Sea. As soon as the car passed, the crowd closed in behind them, reclaiming the street.

Hudson patted her leg. "We'll be out of it soon. I need to get back onto Bradford." Hudson deftly maneuvered the car, heading up a steep hill and turning left, then right, then left again. After a few more blocks, the road widened and only a few people were walking. Ari relaxed against the seat.

"I'm glad you're driving. People were way too close back there." She shook her head, still unsure what the attraction was. It appeared to be just another tourist trap. She caught a glimpse of the water to her left and the sand dunes to her right.

"The views are worth it. I'm glad we were able to leave early. Driving through town in the dark just isn't the same," Hudson said before pulling into a narrow driveway running the length of an adorable Cape Cod-style home. The light blue clapboard siding and white trim fit the landscape. A covered porch started at the back door and disappeared around the front. An English garden took up a huge part of the side yard and planters graced the stairs and railings. Every color in the natural world was represented.

Hudson grabbed the two duffle bags from the trunk while she got their backpacks. The sun seemed lower in the sky than at home.

"Is there a place to watch the sunset nearby?" Ari stood at the top of the stairs looking off in the distance.

"On the beach is the best. We can take a sunset dune ride if you'd like." Hudson's face glowed in the golden light before she closed her eyes and took a deep breath. "There's nothing like the salt air."

Ari wasn't sure if it was the salty air, the atmosphere of the town, or that she was away from the whirlwind schedule she kept, but she felt her soul settle. When she opened her eyes, Hudson was in front of her. The look reflected back at her could have meant almost anything except she'd seen it before. Hudson leaned in and she took a step back, looking to see if anyone could see them.

"Hudson, not here," Ari whispered.

One side of Hudson's mouth lifted in a mischievous grin. "*Here* is the perfect place."

She rolled her eyes. "I don't mean 'here' I mean, here. Your parents' home."

Hudson laughed out loud. "Did I mention they're lesbians?" She took a step closer and Ari put up both hands to keep her at a distance.

"Very funny. Can I at least meet them before we make out on the porch?"

"Okay. You win—this time, but I'm not making any promises once you're in my bed." Bending to pick up the discarded bags, she winked. "Hope you're hungry. Momma G. loves to cook for people."

"I'm starv—" she didn't have a chance to finish. The front door opened and a very tall, handsome woman with salt-and-pepper hair and slate gray eyes grabbed Hudson and spun her around as if she were a small child.

"You're home."

Laughing hard, Hudson got her feet under her and kissed her mother on the cheek. Ari couldn't remember the terms Hudson used to distinguish her parents. She needed to pay attention. "Yes, Mom. I'm home." She turned to Ari and pulled her close.

"Mom, this is Ari Marks. Ari, this is Dale. I call her Mom or Mom D."

Ari held out her hand. "It's a pleasure to meet you, Dale. Thank you for letting us invade your lovely home."

Dale took her hand in both of her larger ones and gave a firm yet gentle squeeze. "Manners *and* pretty. How nice for a change."

"Mom." Hudson's tone held a hint of displeasure.

"Sorry. Where are *my* manners?"

"What manners?" another woman chimed in. "You haven't bothered with them since I said I'd live with you." The voice came from a shapely woman Ari guessed to be in her fifties. She stood in the doorway and kissed Hudson on the cheek before extending her hand.

"You must be Ari. I'm Gina and we're delighted you made the trip." Her hand was soft and warm. Her touch had a tender quality. One of the many attributes she found appealing in Hudson.

"Thank you. It's nice to meet you." Ari's mind spun. Hudson's features resembled both of the women, and she wondered how that was possible. "Your flowers are beautiful." Ari waved at the plants.

"I do love getting my hands dirty. Come inside and get settled, then we'll have drinks." Gina held the screen door.

Inside was just as quaint as the exterior. Comfortable furniture in a pale blue checked pattern and white end tables lent itself to the beach atmosphere. Family photos lined the mantel and a collage of babies up to adulthood hung in the hall. They walked to the far end and turned left.

"Here we are." Hudson's face turned a rosy shade. "It's not much, but it's home." She appeared embarrassed by the simplicity of the space.

Ari stepped inside and waited for Hudson to follow before shutting the door. "I think it's lovely." She ran her hand along the antique white chest of drawers. Its well-worn surface was smooth and cool beneath her fingertips. Mementos from Hudson's childhood sat on a shelf in the corner. A swimming trophy. A small plaque for first place in a spelling bee. A framed photo of a younger Gina and Dale with two children.

"May I?" she asked before picking it up. Hudson nodded and she pointed to the young boy. "Your brother?"

"That's him." Hudson looked wistfully at his reflection.

"You okay?"

"I miss him. Most of the time I'm all right with not seeing him, but it's been a while."

"How long?" She placed the frame back on the shelf and took Hudson's hand.

Hudson looked up to the ceiling as if searching her memory. "About four years."

"Wow. That *is* a long time." Their gazes met. Turmoil churned in Hudson's eyes.

"We have the same father. We had fun growing up. Not being able to hear my brother's voice or see him is hard."

"I didn't know." She wondered about the logistics, but left it alone. Hudson must have surmised what she was thinking from the way she was chewing on her lip.

"Curious?"

It was her turn to feel the heat in her cheeks. "Yes, but I don't want to pry."

"You aren't." Hudson led her to the bay window seat. The cushion was thick, comfortable, and most likely handmade. She imagined Hudson as a child, curled up in the corner with the pile of pillows and a book.

"Momma G. donated the egg and Mom D. is my birth mother. They asked one of their best friends if he would be the surrogate father. He agreed. They said it was because his coloring and heritage was similar to Mom's, but I think they couldn't imagine having anyone else as our father. That's how close they were."

"Were? Did they have a falling out?" Ari knew friendships, even long-standing ones, sometimes ended.

"He died about ten years ago." Hudson's demeanor conveyed a deep sorrow.

She wished she hadn't asked. This wasn't how she thought their mini-vacation would start. "I'm so sorry. Did you spend time together?"

A lopsided grin appeared. "Yeah. I mean, not like a parent really. More like an uncle. He lived in Sandwich and worked in Boston. Every other weekend he'd drive over to see us, and when my mothers decided to try for another child, he willingly stepped in again. He taught me a lot about the town's history and the Cape. We fished and played on the beach. Momma G. would cook and we'd tell stories around the dinner table." Hudson was quiet for a few minutes. "I had a great childhood and more love than anyone could want. It was the same with my brother when he came along. Daniel loved us and we loved him."

Ari tried to imagine what growing up in a loving family would have felt like. Without siblings to fill the void, she'd grown independent and relied on her friendship with Chelsea, then Kara, to fill in the gaps. It was the single most important factor behind her unwillingness to create bonds. She had no experience with feeling loved or loving someone else. Giving all her attention to schoolwork, then college studies, gave her a sense of purpose. Her outstanding grades led her to believe working hard was all she had to do to be a successful woman.

"I'm glad you grew up with so many people who loved you. It shows. I'm so glad we met." She hugged Hudson.

"Thanks." Hudson looked around the room once more before she stood. "We should probably make an appearance or they'll think we're having sex."

Ari gasped. "You're terrible. How can I face them now?"

"Didn't take you long to forget how wonderful I am."

❖

"Mom?" Hudson called from the kitchen.

"Out on the porch."

She turned to Ari. "Behave yourself. No kissing."

Ari slapped her ass and laughed.

"There you two are. We were beginning to wonder if you were going to hole up in your room for the weekend," Gina said.

"I thought about it, but Ari…" Hudson stopped teasing when she saw Ari clench her fists at her side. Maybe she was going too far. "Sorry," she muttered.

"No, you're not," Ari whispered.

"There's no reason to be embarrassed around us. We've pretty much heard or done most things you can imagine. I don't think times have changed that much since we were courting." Dale pointed to a small serving cart. "Pour yourselves a drink."

There was an assortment of beverages including mojitos. She reached for the pitcher and turned to Ari. "What's your pleasure?"

Ari pursed her lips, but a corner of her mouth twitched, and there was a gleam in her eyes that relayed she got the innuendo. "That looks good."

She and Ari sat in matching rockers and sipped their cocktails. She missed the simple pleasures of being near the water, not having to think about anything. She'd been away far too long.

"It's good to be home."

Momma G. reached for her hand. "It's good to have you home. I've missed you. I can't say I wasn't worried." She squeezed

Hudson's hand. "Until you and Ari connected." Gina regarded Ari and tilted her head. "Hudson's found a reason to be optimistic about the future. I think you had something to do with that, so thank you."

"I don't think it was me, but thank you for saying so."

Ari looked at her and Hudson's heart picked up speed. Ari had that effect on her most of the time.

"Hudson was a great source of strength for me when I needed it, and we can count on each other for support." Ari looked at Gina and Dale before continuing. "I can see where she gets her best characteristics."

"That's very kind of you to say." Mom D. glanced in Hudson's direction, prompting her to respond.

"We've grown close over the last few months." Her parents smiled. A knowing look crossed between them. She'd be cornered at some point to explain exactly how close they were.

"Well, now that the pleasantries are out of the way, I'm going to put the finishing touches on dinner." Gina headed to the door.

"Can I help?" Ari asked.

Gina winked at Hudson. "I'd appreciate the company."

Hudson knew it was Momma G.'s code for wanting to spend time alone with Ari. Her stomach fluttered with nervous energy. Her mothers could be rather demanding at times when it came to the people in their children's lives. She settled back and relaxed. Ari could handle the interrogation.

"So, what's been happening in your life?" Mom D. asked.

Guess it's my turn to be interrogated.

Ari cut the cucumber into thin slices and Gina mashed potatoes in a pot. They worked in amicable silence, but she knew it wouldn't last. Ari could tell Hudson's parents were protective of her. She would be the same way if she ever had children.

"How did you two meet?" Gina asked as she added milk, then butter to the pot.

She relayed the story as she remembered it, first at the Y, then bumping into Hudson a couple of times. "When I found the house and needed a tenant, I remembered Hudson was looking for a place." Shrugging, she went on. "From the first time I met her, I felt I could trust her, and I went with my gut. It hasn't failed me yet." She made eye contact. "I've grown very fond of your daughter."

Gina stopped what she was doing and faced her, one hand on her hip. "I have a distinct impression you're more than fond." A smile played at the corner of her mouth, much like the one that often formed on Hudson's.

"Yes. I am." She looked at the salad, needing a break from Gina's intense stare. "Hudson—isn't ready for a commitment. I hope that will change."

"We raised her the best we could and we're proud of the woman she's become. What we didn't do was let her fail, and she never wanted to disappoint us. When she and Pam broke up it hit her hard. Real hard. I've never seen her turn tail and run from anything, but that's what she did." Gina went back to mixing the potatoes, sprinkling in chopped chives and a splash of heavy cream. "I asked her why. She said she hoped she and Pam would have the fairy-tale life Dale and I have. Damn near broke my heart." She spooned the mixture into a dish and put on the lid.

Gina turned to face her. "She's stronger than she appears. She just needs to find her way again. I think you're helping her do that." Gina wiped her hands on her apron. "All set there?"

"I think so." Ari had added grape tomatoes and pecans to the bowl. She couldn't wait to dive in. Her stomach grumbled.

"Let's get them in here. Dale gets cranky if she's not fed on a regular basis."

"Please, no more stories, Mom!"

Hudson brought the last of the plates to the sink and rinsed them before putting them in the dishwasher. She and Ari had been entertained throughout dinner by her parents recounting her less than stellar early years when she'd been a klutz and suffered a variety of injuries. Improving her balance and stamina were the main reasons she'd taken up martial arts. It had been one of the best decisions she'd ever made.

"Okay," Dale said. "We'll save some for another time."

Shaking her head, she took Ari's hand. "Want to walk into town?"

"Sure."

"I'm going to put on jeans. It'll turn cool once the sun sets." She knew the weather on the Cape well. The days were often warm, but nights could be downright chilly by the water.

"Good idea," Ari replied.

Hudson kissed her parents on the cheek. "Don't wait up for us."

Momma G. laughed. "Those days are long gone, honey. You two have fun."

"Good night," Ari said. "Thanks again for the delicious meal."

"Glad you enjoyed it. Thanks for your help."

Standing on the top step, Hudson took another deep breath, marveling at the internal peace the ocean air brought. She'd spent a lot of nights sitting on the top step listening to the crickets and gulls, feeling the breeze brush her face, and working out whatever worries or problems were in her head. She'd never struggled with her sexuality; coming out hadn't been an issue, although her mothers had assured her she didn't have to love women because of them. That had made her laugh till she cried. Ari's voice broke through her reminiscing.

"Hey, are you okay?"

She looked into Ari's questioning eyes. "Never better." She shook her head. "That's not entirely true, but I'm getting there." She wrapped her arm around Ari's waist and pulled her close.

"Ready to see my childhood playground?"

"I thought you'd never ask."

❖

"That's decadent." Ari licked her lips. She had no idea what she was in for when Hudson guided her to the flamboyant entrance of Guiltless Pleasures. She'd spent a long time scanning the cases of homemade chocolates, gelato, and pastries. Throwing up her hands in surrender, she'd left the decision to Hudson.

"I know how you feel. It's sacrilege not to stop here at least once whenever I'm home." Hudson scraped every last bit of gelato from her cup before setting it down with a satisfied sigh.

"Good thing we have a bit of a walk ahead of us. I'm stuffed. Again." Ari tossed their containers on the way out and took a sip of her lukewarm coffee. It was still good.

"I guess I got caught up in the atmosphere and didn't realize how far we'd walked."

"I don't mind. It's fun being around all these people." Everyone she passed seemed to be enjoying a leisurely stroll through what she'd learned was the main thoroughfare of P-town proper. Groups of women and men chatted and laughed, stopping for selfies in front of various establishments. The atmosphere gave her a sense of belonging to a greater community. One she hadn't experienced anywhere else. She bumped hips with Hudson. "You were right about this place." She led Hudson around a corner, out of the crowd. "Thank you for asking me to come home with you."

Hudson leaned back against the building, her hands on Ari's hips. "I'm glad you said yes. This place has always felt magical to me. I hope it does for you, too."

Hudson pulled her closer and captured her mouth. The kiss was slow and gentle, and her tongue lightly traced Ari's lips, sending a shiver down her spine. A flare of disappointment coursed through her when they parted.

"No wonder your kisses are magical."

Hudson brushed a wisp of hair from her face. "I want to make love to you."

Familiar longing gripped her and her sex clenched. Visions of Hudson touching her, tasting her, making her wet with a need that flooded her senses. "Take me home, baby."

Chapter Twenty

A ri watched Hudson as she held the mug up to her mouth with both hands and stared across the table. They had tried to be quiet when they got back to the house. Once they were in Hudson's room, they undressed and slid between the soft flannel sheets. They'd talked in hushed voices for a few minutes, followed by slow, tender lovemaking. Ari had covered her mouth to stifle her moans, but from the look on Gina's face, she wasn't sure she'd been successful. "What do you two have planned for today?"

Hudson started and a few drops of coffee splashed from her cup. Ari giggled. She dabbed up the spill and cleared her throat. "I think we might go on a whale watch and then later do a sunset dune tour."

"Oh, I haven't been on that beach at sunset in ages. Have you?" she asked Dale.

Dale rose and placed her dishes in the sink. "Not without you."

"Can we go?" Gina asked.

Dale glanced first at Hudson, then Ari. "Not this time, babe. Let the kids enjoy this trip without us playing chaperone."

Ari picked up her juice and took a gulp. "I don't mind if you want to come along. It's not like we'd be alone. Right?" Ari asked Hudson, who was clearly not enthused about the thought of her parents tagging along.

Gina pushed away from the table. "Of course, dear. You're right." She paused for emphasis. "But I want to hear all about it. Will you be back for dinner?"

"Don't plan on us tonight, Momma, but we'll probably come back for a snack and to rest our feet this afternoon." Hudson drained her mug. "What are you two doing today?"

"School starts up next week. I've got rosters and lesson plans to work on. Maybe weed the gardens later," Dale said.

"What about you, Momma?" Hudson washed the last cup and placed it in the drainer.

"I've got six houses to inspect before we sign contracts, and there's a new garden path at the Caraways' that needs planting. I should figure how many bulbs to order."

Ari sat quietly taking it all in.

"Dale's a teacher at the middle school and I…" she began before Dale came up behind her and wrapped her arms around Gina's waist.

"And Gina does it all. She's a groundskeeper for most of the businesses and some private homes. In the winter, she does maintenance for seasonal owners who are only here for weekends and vacations during the summer."

"You're just saying nice things about me because I promised to bake this weekend." She turned in Dale's arms and gave her a resounding smooch on the cheek.

"It sounds exhausting," Ari said and Hudson chimed in.

"Oh, she'll try to tell you it's not that bad, but when winter comes she's glad for the break, right, Momma?"

Gina sighed. "Sure, who wouldn't be, but I'm not *that* old," she said in mild protest. "Get out from under my feet, now. I've got stuff to do."

"Yes, Momma. Love you," Hudson said.

She placed her hands on the sides of Hudson's face and held her there. "I love you."

Dale patted Hudson's shoulder. "Don't worry about us. Go enjoy the day."

❖

Hudson caught Ari in the camera lens unaware. Her eyes sparkled when the whales were close, and every time they breached the water, she gasped. She was radiant today, as though she was in her natural element out on the water. Hudson felt the same way when she kayaked, but this was different. Her heart sang and her protective outer shell crumbled a bit more. Maybe it was time. Maybe she could tell Ari she was ready to take the next step. Ari told her she'd wait, but she worried she was pushing Ari's patience. Life was short. Too short to have regrets, and she didn't want Ari to be one of them. After they got back home she would tell her what she'd known for a while. She was falling for Ari, and Ari had a right to know their relationship wasn't one-sided.

"Look!" Ari pointed toward the bow.

Hudson caught sight of the calf as it landed in a splash. She was putting on a show for the passengers, and her camera clicked in rapid-fire. She'd been so busy watching Ari she'd missed it breaching the water and hoped there was at least one good shot.

"Did you see it?" Ari grabbed her hand and squeezed.

Ari's excitement traveled through Hudson and struck a chord. A full life included having someone to share moments like these with, and she wanted to share hers with Ari.

"I did. I hope I caught some of the action." She held up the camera.

"That's okay. We saw it together." Ari pulled her down and brushed her lips over Hudson's.

"Ari…" she began, but at the same time the boat's microphone crackled to life, breaking her train of thought and her nerve.

"On the bow side at two o'clock is a pair of adults," the watch director announced.

The blowhole exhalation broke the surface close to the rail, and the backs of two huge whales came into view before diving in front of the boat again. Hudson was happy the animals were entertaining Ari, but the moment of her revelation was lost.

"Wow. Two of them at once." Ari studied her face. "I'm sorry, did you say something?"

Hudson shook her head. "I'm just glad you're enjoying yourself." She pulled Ari closer as they rode the sea.

Ari laid her head on Hudson's chest. "I am."

Hudson's parents listened to the tales of their day. Ari was animated, using her hands to describe how the whales had come up close to the boat. When the story ended, Mom D. leaned forward.

"Hudson, can we talk inside?"

"Sure, Mom." She stood. "I'll be right back."

Ari nodded, looking concerned. "Take your time."

They sat in the breakfast nook and her mother's steady gaze forewarned the talk was going to be serious. Mom moved an envelope between them.

"We received this today from the lawyers."

She stared at the envelope. "The ones I hired?"

"Yes. I'm not sure why it came here. I'm sorry, Hudson. I thought it was about the trusts." She sat back, running a hand through her graying waves. "Pam plans on fighting. She said you walked away and gave up your rights to everything you left behind."

Hudson had every right to ask for what belonged to her whether she walked away or not. But if she were honest, she didn't know if she wanted to fight anymore. Hearing Ari talking with Momma G. gave her another reason to move on.

"It doesn't matter so much anymore, Mom. Let her have the shit."

Her mother tapped the manila envelope again. She had the hardened look Hudson remembered when she had taken a stand and fought for principles important to her and the well-being of her family. She was the rock they all depended on. "There's more."

"What more could she possibly want?" Hudson asked.

"She knows about your trust fund." Mom D. sat back after delivering the news and waited.

Shaking her head, she leaned forward. "How? I never told her. I've never told anyone. You and Momma G. are the only ones who know."

Her mother grasped her forearm and gave a light squeeze. "Who knows. Maybe a private investigator. Everything is out there now, thanks to our cyber age."

Anger welled up inside and acid churned in her stomach. Even though she really wanted back some of the items that had been in her family for generations, they weren't worth the battle. But the trust was hers and hers alone. She hadn't planned on using it until retirement and her plan hadn't changed. Until then, no one touched it. In fact, it was a stipulation from her grandparents. She could access up to fifty percent of it if she married, otherwise it remained in trust until she reached fifty-five years of age.

"She's not getting a damned penny. Not now, not ever. What do we need to do?"

Twenty minutes later, she stepped onto the porch. She was still pissed as hell, but she and Dale had a plan. She just needed to calm down before attempting to be social.

"I'm going to take a walk."

"Great. Where to?" Ari rose and looked up expectantly.

Hudson took both Ari's hands in hers and held them to her chest. "I'm sorry, baby. I need to go alone."

Ari tipped her head and studied her, her brows knit close together. "Are you okay?"

"No, but I will be." She brushed her lips over Ari's incredibly soft mouth. "I'll be back in a little while. My parents will keep you busy until then."

Ari pulled her into a warm embrace and whispered in her ear. "I'll be here."

❖

Ari watched Hudson descend the steps and head down the driveway, wondering if she should have said more, done more. It was clear Hudson was distraught, and she hated seeing her that way. Maybe if she knew what the problem was she could help.

"Can I ask what happened?"

Dale and Gina exchanged knowing looks. Gina nodded at Dale.

"Come, sit down. We'll have iced tea and fill in the gaps."

"I take it you know about Pam?" Dale asked.

"I know she and Hudson were together for a while before they broke up and that's when Hudson moved to Albany. And she wasn't emotionally in a good place for a quite a while." Ari glanced at the door and hoped Hudson would let her help with whatever was going on when she returned. "I know she's upset when she takes off like this."

"Oh, trust me, she's a lot better, and I know you being in her life has made a world of difference." Gina patted her hand. "She's finding her way through you."

Chewing her lower lip, she pushed away her nerves and asked the burning question. "Is that a good thing?" she asked.

"It's a very good thing." Dale's eyes twinkled with some unspoken knowledge.

"Good, because I'm falling for your daughter in a big way."

"Yes, dear, we know."

Ari glanced between them as they shared a grin. "How?"

"It's as plain as the nose on your face." Gina laughed. "For both of you."

"Huh," she said. "Hudson hasn't…" She hesitated. She didn't want to betray Hudson's trust after they'd come so far.

"Don't worry. I know she's treading lightly. It might take her a bit, but she'll come around. I know she cares for you. She's just trying to convince herself falling in love is worth the risk of being hurt again. It's like that for most people." Dale looked at her tenderly. "Wouldn't you agree?"

Ari could feel her face heat up. "Yes." Her voice cracked when she admitted she'd thought the same thing, although for her it wasn't so much risking being hurt as much as the thought of failing at running her business *and* at love.

"Anyway," Gina continued, "when she left Pam, all she took were her clothes. We kind of pushed her to get back the family heirlooms that were meant to be hers. Only it's backfired." Gina wrung her hands. Her eyes dropped to the sweating glass in front of her.

"Now, babe, don't you think for one minute this is our fault. It has nothing to do with us, and everything to do with Pam," Dale stated.

Her confusion must have shown. Dale went on to explain.

"We gave Hudson the name of our lawyer. A person who we knew would stand up to Pam and follow through on Hudson's wishes. Unfortunately, Pam found out there was more to get out of our daughter."

"I'm sorry; I don't know what you mean."

"Hudson has a trust fund and Pam knows about it. That's why Hudson's upset. Pam wants part of it."

She sat back, dumbfounded. She had no idea about the trust fund. Why would she? They hadn't known each other that long, and apparently, Hudson had kept the news from Pam, too. She wasn't angry with Hudson. Her protective feelings for Hudson stirred her anger. An emotion she rarely entertained.

"She can't do that, can she?"

Dale shook her head. "No. Even Hudson can't access it until she's older, but that doesn't mean Pam isn't going to try. I never did like that uppity woman." Dale's fists clenched.

"You know she only visited us once the whole time they were together? She thought she was too good for the likes of us," Gina said.

Dale grasped Gina's hand between hers and gave a little squeeze.

Ari tried to make sense of the info dump. Her head spun as she sorted through the main points. Pam intended to keep everything. Hudson had a trust fund. Pam wanted a piece of the pie.

"Thank you for telling me. What can I do to help Hudson?"

Gina spoke first. "Be there for her. Let her know you care. Be patient. I don't know what the news will do to her."

"And let her come to you. Sometimes she gets quiet with unsettling news. Sometimes it gets her hackles up. Never know which one it will be until she lets on," Dale said.

Gina harrumphed. "I wonder who she gets that from."

Hudson sat on the jetty and let the setting sun soak into her bones. The heat and wind chafed her skin, but her soul gained strength from the place she'd always found solace as a child. The jetty was the last place a person would want to be in stormy weather, but she'd been raised here, and even in the midst of sea surges, she would venture out, thrilled as the water crashed on the rocks and sprayed her face with foamy salt water.

It was here she came to work out dilemmas, and this was one. *Pam wants another piece of me.* She laughed without joy. *That's right up her alley.* Take, take, and take some more. Hudson had given her whatever she'd wanted, including her freedom. Whatever she thought would keep Pam in love with her. No. It was time to be honest. Past time. She gave Pam everything so she'd stay and hoped she'd change her mind about never having a family. Hell, she was even willing to be the birth mother as long as Pam would invest in their family.

"I knew," she mumbled into the wind.

Yes, she had known Pam would never be that parent. The most she could have hoped for was her agreeing to let Hudson stay home and raise their children until they were school age. But she wouldn't have taken an active role. It wasn't in her DNA. Hudson didn't want to admit she'd made a crucial error in judgment when it came to Pam. Sure they made a handsome couple and moved in affluent social circles. Pam knew how to play people to get what she wanted and Hudson had been a casualty of the chessboard.

Hudson was the exact opposite, much like her parents. The simple things brought her the most joy. That was the way she'd been raised. How had she fallen on such dark times? Shaking her head, she walked to the farthest point and looked out at the gently rolling sea. She might never understand the reasons she'd settled, but that didn't mean she couldn't change course from here on out.

Her grandparents had been of hardy stock. They had loved her as only grandparents could and wanted only the best for her and her brother. It was the reason they'd set up the trust funds when Dale had refused to be named as their heir. After a heated argument, Dale had accepted—on one condition. The trust would be split in two and given to her children. Hudson and Sid stood to inherit a small fortune when they turned fifty-five. It was meant as a retirement fund, or if either should marry, they could access part of the money at that time. Grandpa and Nana meant for her to enjoy life without financial worry, and she'd be damned if Pam would have any part of her future.

The sun would kiss the horizon soon, and she knew Ari would be worried. It was time she told the woman who had found a way into her heart what was going on and what her plans were. She also had to tell Ari she loved her. The thought still made her anxious. *One crisis at a time.* For the immediate future, she needed to talk with her lawyers and prepare for the battle that was coming. Maybe she could find an hour or two to spend at her hometown dojo. She would need to center her energy for the days ahead.

CHAPTER TWENTY-ONE

Hudson leaned in and kissed Ari softly when she got back. The scent of the ocean clung to her skin, and Ari longed to take her in her arms and make love to her. She wanted to show her gentleness and devotion she'd never given to any other woman. *God, I really do love her.*

"Are you okay?"

"Yes." Hudson sat beside her on the top step and bumped shoulders. "We're going to miss it." She lifted her chin toward the setting sun they couldn't quite see.

"There'll be more." Ari looked at Hudson's profile. She didn't want to have doubts, but she was human. "There *will* be more, right?"

Hudson's gaze held hers and the shield Hudson normally had up dropped, letting her see inside. For the first time since they'd met, she knew how Hudson really felt and she shivered with the knowledge. Then Hudson pulled her to her feet, took her hand, and walked toward the end of the garden.

"Step up here." Hudson didn't let go of her hand as she balanced on the wrought iron bench and pointed left. "Look."

Off in the distance she could see a small portion of sun and a tiny sliver of the ocean. The reflection coated the water with a fiery shade of orange and cast its glow upward into streaks of clouds. Hudson wrapped an arm around her waist and pulled her tight.

"It's the best I can do for now."

Ari was sure she was talking about much more than the sunset. Hudson was asking for patience, but there was also a promise of more. Not just sunsets, but of their future. She believed in the unspoken pledge. She had to or else her heart would suffer a major blow. After admitting to Dale and Gina her feelings about their daughter, she embraced what she'd been hesitant to say out loud. She loved Hudson. Probably had for some time, and she was certain Hudson felt the same. Why neither of them could say it out loud, she wasn't sure.

"I…" Hudson began before looking skyward. "You know how much I care for you, at least I hope you do. I wish I could tell you the words you want to hear…."

Ari pressed her fingertips to Hudson's lips. "It's okay. I can wait to hear it. I know it's in here." She placed her hand over Hudson's heart. "The words will come when they're ready." She stood on tiptoes and replaced her fingers with her lips. A tear spilled over and ran down Hudson's cheek. She brushed it away.

"I'm still a fool," Hudson said.

Ari smiled. "If you insist."

Hudson playfully slapped her ass. "Hey, you weren't supposed to agree."

"Too late to take it back." Ari stepped down from the bench. "I'm hungry."

Hudson stepped beside her. "Food is the last thing on my mind, but I guess I could treat you to dinner. Let's head to town."

"So, what's your game plan?" Ari placed the last grilled shrimp in her mouth. She washed it down with a crisp Pinot Grigio and waited.

"I'm going to fight her. She has no right to my inheritance. I don't care what it costs in legal fees. She's picked the wrong time to go for the kill."

She'd told Hudson about the conversation with her parents and that she wanted to help.

"I appreciate you being a shoulder to lean on, but this is my battle. I should have known she'd pull something backhanded. Finding out about the trust wasn't on my radar. Of course, my radar's been askew for a while." Hudson's eyes flashed with anger, but it quickly faded. "She's pissed me off, Ari. I'm not letting her have her way. Not this time."

"It's good to see you standing up for yourself. Just remember my offer is for the duration." She had her own battle going on. The two sides of her brain were at war. One side hoped Hudson would lean on her for support. The other, now that Hudson had come to terms with the situation, wanted her to be strong and stand on her own. To find the determination to confront Pam until the conflict was resolved. She was sure Hudson would come through as the victor. She just hoped it didn't cost her any more emotional pain. If her spirit was crushed again, she wasn't sure Hudson would be able to bounce back. She hoped the person she'd met months ago no longer existed. For both their sakes.

"I know." Hudson pushed her plate away. "Coffee?"

Grinning, she shook her head. "You know what I want?"

Hudson blushed in response to the innuendo.

"Well, that too, but I was talking about something else."

Hudson swallowed hard. "What?"

"Let's go to Guiltless Pleasures and have one of those sinful hot chocolates for dessert." She'd been too full from the gelato last night, but the thought of dark chocolate melting into steamed milk had her licking her lips. Hudson watched the swipe of her tongue as it traveled from one corner of her mouth to the other.

"Jesus, you make me crazy."

"In a good way, I hope."

"Oh yeah," Hudson stood and gathered Ari against her. "In a very good way."

❖

Hudson lowered onto Ari's naked body, reveling in the feel of the soft, smooth skin against hers. Leaning on an elbow, she brushed the hair from Ari's face and kissed her. Hudson moved her mouth in gentle patterns over Ari's lips as she tasted the remnants of chocolate. The more she'd watched Ari lick the foamy richness from her lips, the more turned on she had become. By the time they left the café her Jockeys were soaked. As they strolled back, she'd had all she could do not to pull Ari into a dark alley and take her.

"What are you thinking?" Ari asked when the kiss ended.

"How hot you've made me," she said, nipping at Ari's chin before sliding down to take a pointed nipple in her mouth. It grew harder as she sucked. She ran her teeth around the base with enough pressure to make Ari gasp and arch into her. The other nipple tightened and she circled her tongue around the rosy area before capturing Ari's lips once more. Ari lightly raked her nails along her back, sending a fresh wave of heat along her spine. Her sex beat with desire while she explored Ari's hot mouth.

"I want you." She looked into Ari's hooded eyes, hoping to see the need she felt. She wasn't disappointed. Sliding along Ari's heated skin, she placed kisses in areas she knew were sensitive, making Ari squirm.

"Please," Ari whimpered.

She settled between her milky thighs and kissed and nipped the tender flesh. She paused at her center and blew a warm breath over the glistening folds. Ari shivered and groaned.

"You're enjoying torturing me, aren't you?"

Hudson pointed her tongue and touched the tip of Ari's clitoris, making her jump and gather the bedding beneath her in clenched fists. As much as she wanted to dive into the sweetness, her intent was to draw out their lovemaking. She moved her mouth to the other thigh. Ari snaked her fingers into her hair and pulled until their eyes met.

"I'm begging you. Don't make me wait any longer." Hot need burned in Ari's eyes and she trembled under Hudson's stare before letting go and falling back on the bed.

She abandoned her notion of traveling the length of Ari's leg and turned to the core of sex pulsing in front of her. Hudson inhaled the scent of desire and licked the sweet folds from Ari's opening to her throbbing bundle of nerves and back down. Light strokes set the rhythm before she took the hardened nub between her lips and sucked. She tongued the knot in tight circles, never losing contact with the point of pleasure. Ari's sex clenched. Once. Twice. Her thighs began to shake and her tummy muscles tightened. When Ari's climax neared, she slid her fingers inside and stroked the hard knot over and over again. Ari arched against her, color rising along her glistening body. Hudson slid in and out, her fingers coated in the thick juices of Ari's succulent sex.

"Oh God," Ari gasped before her body went rigid, locking Hudson's fingers inside.

She lapped at the liquid heat flowing from Ari as her body convulsed in time with her orgasm. Hudson loved watching her come. Loved knowing she could give her pleasure. Yes, she loved her, but still couldn't bring herself to say the words. She kissed the throbbing flesh once more and moved beside Ari, taking her into her arms. Ari laid her head over her pounding heart.

"You make me feel so good."

Hudson kissed the top of her head and rubbed her back. "That makes me happy." Entwining their legs, she sighed in contentment.

"I'm only staying here a minute. I want to make love to you." Ari's eyes fluttered as she spoke.

"Shh. Go to sleep, baby." Although her sex throbbed, her need to hold Ari was stronger.

"But, don't you want me to...?"

"Right now, all I need is for you to be in my arms."

Ari snuggled closer. "If you're sure?"

I've never been surer. "I am."

❖

Ari glanced over and noticed the tension in Hudson's jaw. She'd been quiet on the ride home and Ari couldn't help wondering what she was thinking. They'd had a wonderful weekend except for the part about the trust fund. It hadn't stopped them from taking walks on the beach, shopping in town, and making love. If this trip was any indication of what their life could look like, she was all in.

"Hey."

Hudson met her glance. "Hmm?"

"I was wondering why you're so quiet." Ari tried to read Hudson's face, but from the side there weren't many clues. She'd need to see her eyes to really know what she was thinking.

"A lot's happened in a short time." Hudson changed lanes and pointed to the rest stop sign. "Want to get a snack and stretch our legs?"

She wondered if it was a stall tactic or if Hudson really needed the break. "Sure."

"Good. We can talk without me having to concentrate on traffic."

Ari didn't know what Hudson wanted to say, but it seemed important enough to have her full attention. She hoped for the best and prepared for the worse. When Hudson took her hand, and shared a grin, it didn't quite reach her eyes, but she forced one in return.

"I've had an amazing weekend. Thank you for making the trip with me." Hudson broke off a piece of her Danish and popped it in her mouth. "My mothers think you're wonderful." She reached across the table and squeezed her hand. "So do I."

"Is there a 'but' coming?" She swallowed a gulp of juice. It was hard making it go down around the lump in her throat.

Hudson shook her head. "No 'but.' I've been thinking how I would have never imagined feeling like I do right now."

She held Hudson's gaze. "How do you feel?"

"Grateful. For meeting you, for the offer of a place of my own, for our friendship." She looked down at the abandoned food for a minute before she continued. "For the relationship we have and the romance we share."

Ari waited, knowing there was more Hudson needed to say and not wanting to interrupt.

"I won't lie and tell you I don't get scared when I think about where our relationship is going, but I've come to realize I'm more afraid of not loving again. Life's short. It gets shorter every day and..." she glanced around, watching the people hurrying around them, "I don't want to be one of those people." Hudson pointed to a woman dragging her struggling child toward the restroom. "Life isn't meant to be raced through."

"I'm not sure what you're saying exactly, but I trust you." She reached to cup her cheek; her thumb stroked the soft fuzz.

Hudson turned her face and kissed her palm. "I'm not sure either, but I think I had a point to make." She grinned. "I just wanted you to know the future is looking much brighter than I would have ever imagined and I want you there."

"That's the last of it." Hudson dropped an armful of packages onto the island. "Exactly what did you buy?" She surveyed the sea of bags. She'd never seen so many in one place at one time.

"Never mind. I had fun." Ari searched in a shopping bag and pulled out a long-handled cooking utensil. "I've been looking for one of these forever," she exclaimed.

"Uh-huh."

"Oh you. You didn't buy anything because you've been to those shops dozens—no, probably hundreds of times. Give me a break." Ari placed her hands on her hips.

Hudson laughed. "As long as you don't ask me to help put it all away, I'm good." She peeked in the open bag, and Ari slapped her on the ass. "Besides, I did buy something."

"What?" Ari smirked and wrinkled her nose.

She pulled a small wrapped box from her back pocket. "This."

Ari moved closer. "It's wrapped beautifully. What is it?"

"It's for you."

"Me?" She looked over at the pile, knowing nothing she'd purchased was for Hudson. She felt terrible. "I didn't get you anything."

Hudson lifted her chin with a finger. "That's okay. I saw this and it reminded me of you."

Ari looked between the small square box in her hand and Hudson.

"Well, are you going to open it or just look at it?" It was her turn to put her hands on her hips.

Ari set it on the countertop and drew one end of the petite green ribbon, then carefully pulled the tape away. Inside, on a layer of white cotton, lay a charm bracelet. Attached to it was a tiny silver whisk.

"It's so delicate." She hugged Hudson and kissed her. "It's perfect."

"Here, let's see if it fits."

Ari held out her wrist and watched Hudson's nimble fingers latch the tiny clasp. The silver chain fit tight enough that she wouldn't lose it. Wrapping her arms around Hudson, she melted against her.

"Thank you." She wanted to say more. Like how much she adored the woman in her arms. How much she fantasized about their future, dreams to be made into reality, and the love they shared. She had no doubt Hudson loved her. She felt it in her touch, her kisses. Saw it in her eyes. Despite all she knew, Hudson had yet to say the words, and until she did, Ari was reluctant to confess her feelings out loud for fear she'd push Hudson away.

Hudson stepped back and held her by the shoulders. "I'm glad you like it." Her eyes shimmered and Ari saw the emotions coursing through the gray depths. Abruptly, Hudson shoved her hands in her pockets and glanced everywhere but at Ari's face. She held her tongue, knowing Hudson was fighting to say something that scared her. *Maybe this is it. Maybe she'll actually say the words I need to hear.*

Finally, Hudson looked back up. "I should go unpack. Do laundry."

Disappointment clutched her heart. Perhaps she'd been wrong. Maybe Hudson would never be able to tell her she loved her. She swallowed hard and nodded. "Okay. I probably should unpack, too, and put all this stuff away." She turned away not wanting Hudson to see the anguish threatening to shred her soul apart. The back door opened and she peered into the nearest bag, unable to see while tears pooled in her eyes.

"Ari?"

"What?" She winced at the tone of her voice. She hadn't meant to sound as sharp as she did. It was too late to take it back.

"Uh…" Hudson hesitated.

Clearly, Hudson heard the annoyance in her voice.

"I was going to ask if you wanted to order in later."

Ari took a deep breath and let her frustration ebb away. Hudson had been clear about her intentions, but she hadn't made any promises she couldn't keep. It was her own fault she was feeling let down. She forced the tears back, refusing to use them against Hudson.

"Okay. Come down when you're ready, and we'll pick a menu."

Hudson walked up behind her, turned her, and cupped her face in the palm of her hand. Her mouth closed over Ari's. The kiss built in intensity and their tongues caressed and explored in a slow tango. When she pulled away, Ari swayed and her eyes slowly opened.

"I don't want our time together to end," Hudson said.

It was hard to read the meaning in Hudson's words. Did she mean today? Tomorrow? Forever? Why couldn't she say what was visible on her face? What would it take to make Hudson sure enough to let go of the one thing she feared more than being alone? Being in love. Ari shuddered, dreading their future hopes might never turn into reality.

"It doesn't have to."

Hudson let out a long breath. Its warmth caressed her face. "I know." Her voice cracked, and she cleared her throat. Her lips parted and closed again. Ari knew she was holding back.

"I'll see you in a couple hours."

"I'll be here."

The door closed and she sat down, fingering the silk scarf she'd bought. The variegated grays reminded her of the many shades of Hudson's eyes.

"I'm not giving up on you," she said out loud to the empty kitchen. After their weekend together, she was more determined than ever to help Hudson find her way out of the emotional chains that still bound her.

Hudson dropped her bags by the door and plopped into the nearest chair.

"Fuck," she said.

Hadn't she had a conversation this morning with her parents about this very thing? They'd encouraged her to tell Ari she loved her. To not waste any more time fighting the feeling. She'd confessed her fears of being hurt again. Their words echoed in her head.

"You do know the old saying is true, right?" Momma G. had asked. She looked at Mom D. who nodded in agreement.

"It *is* better to have loved and lost, than never to have loved again."

She knew they were right. Everything they'd ever taught her spoke of the worth of taking risks, in all aspects of life. Failure is a skewed view of an attempt at a goal. What was her goal? She had it all mapped out at one time, but the foundation she'd built had crumbled and she hadn't had the strength to shore it up again. Instead, she'd run from the rubble.

"Coward," she said. She ran her fingers through her hair and flopped back. She'd made a mess of her life and now her relationship with Ari was paying for it. Ari deserved more, and if she didn't want to lose the woman she loved, she'd better get her act together. She pushed off the chair and groaned. She had a dinner date. Maybe between now and then she'd find a way to tell Ari the truth.

CHAPTER TWENTY-TWO

H i, Dale. It's Ari."

"Hi, sweetie. It's good to hear from you."

She bit her lip. She'd been fighting the urge to call Hudson's parents all week, but she needed sound advice. Not something she'd likely get from her own. Her silence didn't go unnoticed.

"Everything okay?"

"Yes. Well, yes and no." Gathering her courage, she pushed on. "Uh…you know I love your daughter, right?" She sounded like a child and grimaced.

Dale chuckled. "It's pretty obvious, but that's not the reason for your call, is it?"

Damn. Hudson had told her how intuitive her mothers were, and she'd seen it firsthand. *No point in beating around the bush at this point.*

"Closure."

"What?" Dale's confusion came through the phone.

It was her turn to chuckle. "I'm sorry. What I mean is I think Hudson needs to find a way to have closure with Pam. I'd like to help her." There was silence at the other end, and she worried she'd overstepped her boundaries. "I need your advice."

❖

"Damn it, Ari." Hudson fumed. "You know I can't do this. Why would you even ask?" Her earlier calm turned to uncertainty.

"Wait. Please don't go before I can explain."

"No. Never again. This…this is why I didn't want to get involved, and I was right. Relationships always lead to pain. I'm done, Ari." She stormed up the stairs, slamming the door on the pain and, virtually, on Ari.

"What the fuck?" she said. Pacing the confines of her apartment and knowing Ari was downstairs listening to her rant did nothing to help her mood. She grabbed her wallet and keys and fled. Her tires screeched as she sped out the driveway. She didn't know where she was going, but she needed to get distance between them. Her anger simmered, threatening to boil over the top. She pulled over to the curb and slammed the car into park. She dropped her head against the headrest as she gripped the wheel hard enough to turn her knuckles white.

When Ari had called up to her saying she needed to talk, she thought it had something to do with the business. In the past few weeks, Ari had received close to a dozen contracts and it wouldn't be long before she was going to need help. What she'd gotten instead had felt like a punch to the gut.

"I think the reason you can't tell me how you really feel is that you never had closure with Pam."

"Ari, I don't think—" she'd begun before Ari cut her off.

"I've arranged for you and Pam to meet."

She jumped to her feet. "You did what?" She slammed her hands on the island, jarring the dishes. "You had no right." Her anger had burned white-hot and she hadn't given Ari a chance to say a word.

She rubbed her eyes. Why would Ari have gone behind her back and set her up to see Pam? She never wanted to have to deal with her again. She was leaving it up to her lawyer to do that. She straightened up and blinked. Maybe that was it. Maybe Ari believed she'd never dealt with the breakup in a constructive way. While it was true she'd run from admitting there'd been issues between her and Pam, she'd dealt with it ending. Hadn't she?

"Shit."

The answer wasn't pretty. She'd run without looking back. Maybe Ari was right after all. Maybe the reason she couldn't tell Ari she loved her was because she'd never told Pam she *didn't* love her. Compared to what she had with Ari, it was possible she'd never really loved Pam. Or at least, not as much as she thought she did. Maybe she'd settled for a less than loving relationship thinking they'd work at it. That way she could just go on believing she had the life she'd always wanted. A life like her parents had. She'd never taken the time to ask if her dreams would mesh with Pam's. She just assumed they would. After all, they were together. Didn't being together mean they saw the same things for their future?

She'd been wrong to storm out and not give Ari a chance to explain. She had the feeling she hadn't acted alone. How would she have been able to find Pam, let alone contact her? Her parents had a part in it. She wanted to be angry with everyone. She wanted to tell them to mind their own business. This was her life, and she got to decide the path she'd follow. Only she hadn't done such a great job at it, and there hadn't been any monumental dreams she'd followed. How had she missed taking control and doing something constructive with her life? And she hadn't done one thing that revolved around her future since moving away.

Looking around, she got her bearings and headed to a neighborhood bar. A place she could be just another face in the crowd with no one counting on her or expecting her to be reasonable.

Hudson stood at the bar and ordered. She'd thought about having a beer, but knew if she went down that path, she'd be taking a taxi home. Scotch in hand, she settled in a small booth and pretended to watch the football game. She needed to own up to her mistakes, and it made her stomach queasy. She'd made poor choices, but spending time with Ari and making love with her wasn't in that category. Ari was like a breath of fresh air compared to the few women she'd slept with since Pam. Her mind wandered back to their first meeting and how much she'd enjoyed talking with her, even if Ari had appeared a bit clumsy. It seemed like ages ago. What if she'd ruined her chances with Ari? What if her childish reaction was all the proof Ari needed to end their relationship before she was in too deep? Hudson groaned. Once again, when life hadn't gone the way she wanted, she'd cut and run.

She lifted her glass to the television screen. "Way to go."

Ari listened to the footfalls overhead. Hudson paced upstairs, obviously upset at what she'd done. The back door banged, followed by the sound of tires screeching on the pavement. Had she gone too far? Dale and Gina had been cautious in their encouragement of what might be construed as a drastic measure, but they hadn't dissuaded her either.

Dale told her she'd proudly passed on her stubborn streak to her daughter, which went hand-in-hand with rarely asking for help, even when she was desperate. Ari knew they were well aware of how much Hudson was struggling to free her heart from the past. She'd told them she didn't doubt Hudson's love, even if she couldn't bring herself to say the words out loud. Ari said she thought not having closure with Pam was the reason. They asked what she wanted to do and listened to the plan she'd come up with. After voicing their concerns about how it could end disastrously, they agreed to help. She was taking a risk, but neither she nor Hudson could keep going in circles. Something had to give. She was either going to force Hudson to step into the future, or shut the door forever. She had gone with her gut instincts.

"Now what do I do?"

She thought about calling Hudson's parents again, but she'd involved them enough. There was no sense turning Hudson against them. It had been her idea and it was her responsibility to see it through, if she could. She sat at the kitchen table and gathered her upcoming orders, date book, recipes, and supply list. With one ear tuned to the driveway, she dove into work, hoping the distraction would give her time to sort out what she wanted to tell Hudson. If she would listen to her at this point was anyone's guess.

❖

Hudson slowed to a crawl, not wanting to alert Ari she'd returned. Her anger had abated a couple of hours ago. After nursing her club soda, she'd gone for an intense session with Master Jin. He knew her mood the minute she hit the door. Instead of telling her to meditate, he'd put her through a demanding routine, and it had taken all her concentration to complete. The few times her mind had wandered, she'd ended up on the mat with him staring down at her before backing away and engaging her again.

Now that she could think without seething with anger, she realized Ari had most likely been right in asking her to confront Pam. She couldn't move forward with one foot in the past. It was an admission she loathed making. After everything she'd put Ari through, including her inability to make a commitment or tell her she *did* love her, would Ari even want to hear what she had to say?

She crept up the back stairs. There hadn't been any sound coming from the first floor, but she was sure Ari was awake. She turned the key, pushed open the door, and stopped. Ari was curled up in the corner of her couch and sound asleep. Even in slumber her beautiful face showed signs of worry, her brows knit. Hudson set her bag on the floor and knelt beside her, brushing strands of hair from her face. Ari's eyes fluttered open.

"Hi." Ari's gaze held hers.

"Hi. What are you doing here?" Hudson stroked her arm, loving the feel of Ari's skin.

Ari sat up. "I know I shouldn't have invaded your space. I was worried and after you didn't answer your cell…" She hesitated. "I didn't think you'd talk to me unless I waited for you."

She went to the counter and picked up her phone. It blinked. Four missed calls and two messages. They were all from Ari.

"I didn't have it with me. I'm so sorry you were worried."

"Where did you go?" Ari took a breath. "Never mind. It's none of my business." She got up to leave.

"Don't go. Please? We need to talk." Hudson hesitated, and then went on. "I've made a mistake. Quite a few of them."

Ari's face softened. "We all make mistakes. We're human." Closing the space between them, Ari tugged her hand. "But you're right. We do need to talk." Ari led her to the couch and tucked a leg under her so they were facing, their hands still connected.

Hudson watched Ari's face, her lips pursed in a thin line. She looked back up and held Hudson's questioning gaze, still wondering if she'd destroyed her chance of a future together. Ari didn't make her wait long.

"I had no business contacting Pam, and I am so sorry I dragged your parents into it. Whatever my intentions were, that doesn't give me any right to tell you how to handle your situation." Ari ran a thumb over her knuckles. "I thought maybe it would be a chance for closure, and then maybe you'd be able to…" Ari broke eye contact, her eyes glancing at their joined hands. "Anyway, I'm sorry, Hudson. I only wanted to help."

"You were right."

Ari stared open-mouthed before snapping her jaw shut. "What did you say?"

"You were right. I ran away because it was too difficult for me to face, or at least that's what I believed. I never told Pam how I felt other than to deny it was over. I didn't see it coming because I couldn't admit my vision for the perfect relationship with a perfect life and a perfect family wasn't ever going to happen between her and me. It felt too much like a failure to admit the spark between us was based on the physical relationship we had, not the emotional ties we shared."

"I know I pushed you."

"It's because you did that I can see all of it now. Relationships don't *fail*. *I* didn't fail. Sometimes they work out, sometimes not. I'm not above being human and making errors in judgment and neither is Pam. She wanted a high-pay, high-stress career, and the fame and notoriety that went with it. That was her dream, but it wasn't mine. She had the guts to tell me it wouldn't work between us. I can't blame her for being honest. Neither of us verbalized what we wanted once we were sharing a bed on a permanent basis. I think we took it for granted that we wanted the same things without ever having talked about what was important to each of us." She paused, hoping that she was expressing herself clearly. "At the beginning, we were having such a good time nothing else mattered." She pressed her hand to Ari's cheek. "It all matters with you."

Ari's hand covered hers. "Does that mean you're not mad at me?"

Covering her soft lips with her mouth, she hoped Ari could feel the passion inside of her. She ran her thumb along her cheek as she withdrew.

"So, tell me about this meeting I'm supposed to have with Pam."

"Okay, so I got to thinking…" Ari began. Her eyes sparkled with enthusiasm as she talked.

I can do this. I can do this if it means there's going to be a future us.

Chapter Twenty-three

Hudson wiped her hands on her pants again and took a deep breath. She glanced at the clock on the dashboard and turned off the ignition. *Let's do this.* She had no idea if Pam was inside. She'd never been prompt when they were together, thinking it was unsophisticated to show up on time. Pam had a knack for making people wonder if she'd show, waiting to make her grand entrance. She entered and waited for her eyes to adjust to the dimly lit interior and was surprised when she spotted Pam already seated, a partial glass of wine on the table.

"Hello, Pam."

Pam's eyes met hers, and she seemed genuinely glad she was there. "Hudson."

Pam stood and pulled her into a warm embrace, taking Hudson off guard. She'd never been publicly demonstrative, unless it was to impress someone.

"It's good to see you. Please." Pam gestured to the chair across from her and sat. "I wasn't sure what you were drinking these days. I was here a bit early." Pam pointed to her wine.

"It's nice to see you, too." Hudson studied her face. Although it had been almost two years since she'd last seen her, Pam seemed older. There were a few more lines around her eyes, and she'd lost weight, bordering on anemic. Hudson gestured to the waiter.

"We'll have a bottle of whatever my companion is drinking."

"Are you trying to get me drunk?" Pam said, poking fun at her.

Hudson held her tongue. She didn't want their meeting to be antagonistic, even though she hoped it was the last time they'd ever see each other. She was about to recount their last encounter before realizing it wasn't necessary. Tonight was about the future. Not hers and Pam's, but hers and Ari's.

"You seem different. Is everything okay?" Although they'd parted with angry words, she still cared for the woman that she'd spent part of her life with.

"It's kind of you to ask." Pam's cheeks pinked. She was clearly uncomfortable. "My dream job has turned into a nightmare, and my latest ex was cheating on me for the last six months." She finished off her wine and forced a smile. "Other than that, life is great."

"I'm sorry to hear about both. You were so excited about the promotion."

"Yes, well…things change." Pam leaned forward. "Speaking of change, Ari seems like a wonderful person."

"Yes, she is."

"She loves you." Pam sat back. "Hasn't she told you? Oh my, did I let the cat out of the bag?"

"Well…no, it's just…" Hudson had to take a minute to recover. She'd been pretty sure Ari loved her, but for it to be that obvious to Pam made her head spin.

"You and I had issues because we never said what was on our mind. I know we had our differences, but I never thought you deserved the purgatory you put yourself in when we split," Pam said without malice.

Hudson was confused. When she'd moved away, she had the impression Pam couldn't care less. That she was happy Hudson was out of her life. Now it appeared as though Pam was doing a one-eighty, and she wasn't sure she could trust what she was hearing.

"I'm not following you."

Pam poured more wine and took a sip.

"That happened a lot." She swallowed and went on. "Here's the thing. We were good together, but we weren't good *for* each other. You did your thing, I did mine, but aside from sex…which by the way was mind-blowing, at least for me…we never…" She paused and stared ahead, as though needing to find the right word.

"Meshed?"

"Yes!" she exclaimed, drawing the attention of nearby diners. She looked at them and mouthed "sorry" and Hudson had to laugh. She liked this Pam. This stranger across from her was demonstrative and funny, and a little outrageous. Not at all like the stuffy, snobbish woman she remembered.

"What's happened to you? You aren't anything like I remember."

"You want the truth?" Pam asked.

"Yes."

"I was a rich bitch. I put on a show and knew I could get anything I wanted. All I had to do was demand it, expect it, or pay for it."

"Are you broke?" She didn't mean to pry, but she needed to understand what had caused Pam's miraculous transformation.

Pam laughed so hard she almost spit her wine. "Lord, no." She met Hudson's gaze and held it. "I'm still rich. I've just decided I don't have to be a bitch to get what I want. All I have to do is ask for it."

Hudson ate while she considered her next question. She'd come here for a reason and she couldn't leave without knowing.

"Then why wouldn't you give me my things? Why threaten me with wanting my trust fund?"

Pam waved her off. "You really don't know, do you?"

She shook her head, totally confused.

"I wanted to see you again. I thought you'd show up at the door demanding your things—take what was yours and end all the drama. That didn't happen. Then out of the blue you send a lawyer after me. I got pissed. I dug a little deeper, thinking I needed something more to get you face-to-face, and the trust fund served the purpose." She motioned between them. "Here we are."

"So you *don't* want my inheritance?"

"Hell no. I pay enough damn taxes." She giggled. "But seriously, that's yours and no court in the world would give it to me." Pam must have recognized the distress she'd caused. "I had no intention of going through with it. It was a bluff and you called it."

Hudson sat back, letting everything Pam said sink in. If only she'd faced her one more time, this past couple of years could have been spent healing and moving on. Instead, she'd managed to sink into depression. All because she didn't want to hear what Pam had to say. She felt even more of a coward than she had before. But she could change the course of her life going forward. Everything was in her hands; all she had to do was move on without fear. She knew what she wanted. She knew who she wanted to spend it with. Nothing was impossible.

"You've certainly taken the wind out of my sails. I came here expecting a clash of wills, and instead, I find myself liking you more than when we were together." She winced at the crude admission. Embarrassed, she felt her face heat. "I'm sorry. That was uncalled for."

"Pshaw. You're not the first person to tell me how I come across. I'd like to think I've changed for the better."

Hudson reached for her and stroked the back of her hand. "If you don't mind me saying, I can tell how much you have."

"Thank you." Pam became quiet and Hudson believed she'd offended her again. Pam finally met her gaze, her eyes shimmering with unshed tears. "I'm sorry I broke your spirit. I know how much you wanted a family, but that was never in my future. Still isn't." Pam leaned closer. "Can you forgive me?"

"Yes, if you'll forgive me for assuming we were on the same page."

Pam put her other hand over the top of their joined ones. "I never blamed you for our troubles."

❖

Her cell phone's loud tone brought Ari to a stop. She'd been binge cleaning ever since Hudson left to meet Pam. Every time she finished a task, she'd look at the clock and wonder how things were going before moving on to the next project. The house hadn't been this clean since she'd moved in. She picked up the phone knowing it was Hudson and dreading what she might tell her. Maybe they'd talked about how much they'd enjoyed each other's company and perhaps they should try to make it work. Maybe Pam had threatened to take Hudson for a proverbial ride until she was so beat down she'd do anything Pam asked. No. A few months ago, that might have been the outcome, but Hudson had regained her confidence, and Ari was sure she would stand up for herself. Still, when faced with fight or flight, Hudson had a history. She took a deep breath and prepared for the worst.

"Hello?"

"Hi," Hudson said. "I'm glad you're still up. Can I come and talk with you?"

Her heart sank. She dreaded whatever Hudson had to tell her, but just like when she was a child, she'd rather have the bandage ripped off than slowly peeled away. Swallowing hard, she tried to sound poised.

"Okay." She felt anything but. "Would you like coffee?"

"Sounds good. I'll be there in about ten."

She closed her eyes. There wasn't anything in Hudson's tone to give away the reason she wanted to talk, but her chest filled with dread. "See you then."

Her hands shook as she filled the carafe, spilling it down the side. Leaning on the counter, she gulped in air, feeling like she couldn't breathe. She had it bad for Hudson and that wasn't going to change no matter what the outcome of her and Pam's meeting. If it was bad news, she'd deal with it. It's what her parents had taught her when she'd had no choice. Coping was the one characteristic they forced her to master, and master it she had.

Ari didn't want to seem too anxious. Hudson's evening had to have been emotional whether it had been amicable or contentious. She opened the door and stepped back. Hudson met her gaze and held it before stepping in and wrapped her arms around Ari. She covered Ari's lips with her warm mouth. The kiss turned into a slow, gentle burn, kindling the heat in her groin. She didn't want to have a visceral reaction, but when it came to Hudson, she had little control over her body. Hudson backed away.

She held her breath. She thought it was a good-bye kiss until she saw relief on her face.

"Things went okay?"

Hudson nodded. "The kiss was my feeble attempt to thank you for giving me the push I needed to find closure with Pam." Hudson stepped closer. "Pam doesn't want anything. All she wanted was to say good-bye. Wish me well." Hudson's eyes filled with tears. "I never gave her the opportunity to tell me. I walked away and carried the hurt with me until tonight." She let out a breath. "I promise not to let that happen to us."

"Us?" Dare she hope this meant what she thought?

Hudson took her hand and led her down the hall to her bedroom. They stood facing each other, and Hudson's hands moved to the buttons of her blouse. One button flicked open, then the next. Their gaze never wavered. Hudson slid the material off her shoulders, leaned over, and kissed the flesh of her neck, collarbone, and chest. She shivered with delight. The sensual nature of Hudson's deliberate, slow movements sent her pulse racing. She heard her heart pound in her ears. Hudson hadn't even touched her yet. Her sex clutched with longing. She watched Hudson's long fingers unbutton her jeans and the zipper moved downward at a maddening pace. The lack of urgency was infuriating. She needed to be touched, wanted to feel Hudson inside her. When the zipper stopped, a gush of wet flooded her undies.

"Hudson…" She trembled, her legs shaking in anticipation.

Hudson nuzzled her neck. "You smell good," she said, wrapping an arm around Ari's waist. "I can't wait to touch you."

She moaned. "I need…"

Hudson's lips latched onto the pulse point of her neck, sucking the tender flesh. Her legs gave out and Hudson lifted her to the bed, her jeans pooled at her feet. She finished undressing her and stood at the side of the bed. Her eyes filled with adoration.

"You're so beautiful, Ari." Hudson shed her own clothes and lowered herself until their skin melded together.

She caressed Hudson's face and pulled her down until their mouths met once more. Her world exploded into white-hot light. The beauty of the moment wasn't lost in the sensations surrounding her. Tears fell from the corners of her eyes. She'd waited all her life to feel the connection she had with Hudson. No one had ever come close. She'd never *let* anyone this close.

Hudson's lips moved over her chin and down her chest until they reached her nipple. As soon as her lips closed over it, it tightened. She pressed upward, forcing more of her breast into Hudson's mouth.

She lavished attention on one, then the other.

Ari growled. "I need you. Now."

Hudson moved against her flesh. Their eyes had locked before Hudson slid two fingers inside and she gasped when they rubbed the inner ridges. The slow rhythm in and out, alternating with pressing her clit, made her hips jerk. The heat rose in her abdomen, her climax edging closer. Hudson withdrew and spread her quivering thighs wider, her hungry mouth ravishing her swollen flesh. When she pressed her tongue into Ari's opening, she cried out, the orgasm ripping the breath from her chest.

Hudson cradled her in her arms, her body shaking as wave after wave crashed against her. Minutes passed before she could move.

"My God, what you do to me."

Smoothing her hands along Ari's back, Hudson kissed the top of her head. "There's nothing I enjoy more than spending time with you, no matter what we're doing."

The sincerity of her words touched her heart. "We have such a special connection."

"Yes, we do."

She waited for Hudson to say more. When she didn't, she knew it was up to her to draw out what she longed to hear.

❖

Hudson's breath caught in her throat. Her body reacted to the intense pleasure and arched off the bed. She hung on the crest of orgasm for long minutes before falling into the abyss. Crying out Ari's name, she grabbed at the sheets, needing to find an anchor as she tumbled. Ari brought her to the crest again. Breathing hard, she looked along her body to watch Ari lap her juices and saw her satisfaction when their eyes met. Her oversensitive flesh forced her to squirm out of Ari's grasp.

"Where do you think you're going?" Ari climbed along her body and settled over her thighs.

Hudson languidly kissed her. Ari's lips still tasted of her essence. She relaxed into the warmth that enveloped her as they continued to move against each other.

"I'm not going anywhere." She plucked at Ari's nipple with her fingertips.

"Let me feel you."

"I think you already have."

Ari ground her hip against her center and her clitoris twitched from the pressure. Ari stopped moving and leaned back.

"You're so beautiful. Inside and out. I've embraced all the things that make you *you*. I know that there's another piece." Ari placed a hand over Hudson's heart.

"I need to have all of you. Trust me. I've got you, baby, and I'm not going to hurt you. Stop holding back. Please."

The plea reached Ari's eyes.

Hudson palmed Ari's cheek. So it had come to this. Ari was asking for her heart. For months, they'd been moving toward this moment. For months, they'd grown closer and closer. And while the sex had always been fantastic, the last couple times had felt deeply intimate. When they touched, it was more than with their mouths and hands. Their souls touched. Hudson wanted to feel this intimacy with Ari every day.

Her heart had been pushing forward, even when her mind tried to find reasons why it should stay locked away. She'd been avoiding the inevitable even though she knew she wanted to love and be loved again. She didn't know if Ari could feel her inner struggle, but she was determined to stop being a coward. Ari deserved a fulfilling life. She deserved to be loved.

"I never thought I'd want to love again. You've helped me see there's always a chance for love. I know we didn't meet by accident. Fate had other plans for me. For us." She stroked Ari's face. Traced her lips. Felt her heart pound against her chest. "I won't waste another minute. Not this time. I love you, Ari. I'm sorry it took me so long to tell you."

"I've waited so long to hear those words from you. I tried to be patient." Tears filled Ari's eyes.

"No. You were perfect. You *are* perfect."

Ari slowly rolled them, exchanging positions. "I love you, Hudson Frost."

Their lips met and all the doubt she'd had fell away.

EPILOGUE

One Year Later

"You look so handsome." Ari smoothed the shoulder material of Hudson's tux and adjusted her bowtie.

"Don't think I'm going to do this forever. I love helping out, but I'm stretched thin." Hudson finished filling the tray with bacon-wrapped scallops and balanced it on her hand.

Ari was looking forward to the birth of their child. At first, she'd worried it was too soon for them to start a family, but they weren't getting any younger, and she'd assured Hudson there wasn't anything they couldn't handle together. Dale and Gina had heard from Sid and told him to call his sister right away. She'd been excited by the idea of Hudson's brother being the sperm donor. The baby would have characteristics of both her and Hudson. A month later, her eggs had been fertilized, followed by a successful implantation.

Hudson ran her hand over Ari's swollen abdomen. She hadn't thought Ari could be any more beautiful, but pregnancy brought out the beauty she already possessed. She'd moved in with Ari, and they were turning the guest bedroom into a nursery. The full-time accounting job came with benefits so she could provide health insurance for her family. Her parents would come in shifts to help out after the baby was born. She'd asked Ari if she wanted to include her parents, but she'd outright refused, saying she didn't want their negativity ruining their family.

Ari patted her ass and smiled. "I know, darling, and as soon as I'm done with the interviews, I'll have a sous chef, and you can go back to finishing the baby's room. Now go serve the masses. I expect you to share stories of the women who flirt with you."

Hudson brushed her lips over Ari's and smiled. "Okay, but I'm not sharing my tips." She headed out the door and into the bright light of her future.

THE END

About the Author

Renee Roman has lived in Albany, New York, her entire life. Raised with a book in one hand and a dictionary in the other, she credits her mother for nurturing her craving for the written word. Her home is filled with the books she and her wife, Sue, try to find space for. Her second passion is cooking, and she enjoys entertaining friends and family as often as time allows. She even manages to give attention to their two frisky felines. You can find Renee on Facebook, on her website at: www.reneeromanwrites .com, or you can email her at reneeromanwrites@gmail.com.

Books Available from Bold Strokes Books

Between Sand and Stardust by Tina Michele. Are the lifelong bonds of love strong enough to conquer time, distance, and heartache when Haven Thorne and Willa Bennette are given another chance at forever? (978-1-62639-940-2)

Charming the Vicar by Jenny Frame. When magician and atheist Finn Kane seeks refuge in an English village after a spiritual crisis, can local vicar Bridget Claremont restore her faith in life and love? (978-1-63555-029-0)

Data Capture by Jesse J. Thoma. Lola Walker is undercover on the hunt for cybercriminals while trying not to notice the woman who might be perfectly wrong for her for all the right reasons. (978-1-62639-985-3)

Epicurean Delights by Renee Roman. Ariana Marks had no idea a leisure swim would lead to being rescued, in more ways than one, by the charismatic Hudson Frost. (978-1-63555-100-6)

Heart of the Devil by Ali Vali. We know most of Cain and Emma Casey's story, but *Heart of the Devil* will take you back to where it began one fateful night with a tray loaded with beer. (978-1-63555-045-0)

Known Threat by Kara A. McLeod. When Special Agent Ryan O'Connor reluctantly questions who protects the Secret Service, she learns courage truly is found in unlikely places. Agent O'Connor Series #3. (978-1-63555-132-7)

Seer and the Shield by D. Jackson Leigh. Time is running out for the Dragon Horse Army while two unlikely heroines struggle to put aside their attraction and find a way to stop a deadly cult. Dragon Horse War, Book Three. (978-1-63555-170-9)

Sinister Justice by Steve Pickens. When a vigilante targets citizens of Jake Finnigan's hometown, Jake and his partner Sam fall under suspicion themselves as they investigate the murders. (978-1-63555-094-8)

The Universe Between Us by Jane C. Esther. Ana Mitchell must make the hardest choice of her life: the promise of new love Jolie Dann on Earth, or a humanity-saving mission to colonize Mars. (978-1-63555-106-8)

Touch by Kris Bryant. Can one touch heal a heart? (978-1-63555-084-9)

Change in Time by Robyn Nyx. Working in the past is hell on your future. The Extractor series: Book Two. (978-1-62639-880-1)

Love After Hours by Radclyffe. When Gina Antonelli agrees to renovate Carrie Longmire's new house, she doesn't welcome Carrie's overtures at friendship or her own unexpected attraction. A Rivers Community Novel. (978-1-63555-090-0)

Nantucket Rose by CF Frizzell. Maggie Jordan can't wait to convert an historic Nantucket home into a B&B, but doesn't expect to fall for mariner Ellis Chilton, who has more claim to the house than Maggie realizes. (978-1-63555-056-6)

Picture Perfect by Lisa Moreau. Falling in love wasn't supposed to be part of the stakes for Olive and Gabby, rival photographers in the competition of a lifetime. (978-1-62639-975-4)

Set the Stage by Karis Walsh. Actress Emilie Danvers takes the stage again in Ashland, Oregon, little realizing that landscaper Arden Philips is about to offer her a very personal romantic lead role. (978-1-63555-087-0)

Strike a Match by Fiona Riley. When their attempts at matchmaking fizzle out, firefighter Sasha and reluctant millionairess Abby find themselves turning to each other to strike a perfect match. (978-1-62639-999-0)

The Price of Cash by Ashley Bartlett. Cash Braddock is doing her best to keep her business afloat, stay out of jail, and avoid Detective Kallen. It's not working. (978-1-62639-708-8)

Under Her Wing by Ronica Black. At Angel's Wings Rescue, dogs are usually the ones saved, but when quiet Kassandra Haden meets outspoken owner Jayden Beaumont, the two stubborn women just might end up saving each other. (978-1-63555-077-1)

Underwater Vibes by Mickey Brent. When Hélène, a translator in Brussels, Belgium, meets Sylvie, a young Greek photographer and swim coach, unsettling feelings hijack Hélène's mind and body—even her poems. (978-1-63555-002-3)

A More Perfect Union by Carsen Taite. Major Zoey Granger and DC fixer Rook Daniels risk their reputations for a chance at true love while dealing with a scandal that threatens to rock the military. (978-1-62639-754-5)

Arrival by Gun Brooke. The spaceship *Pathfinder* reaches its passengers' new homeworld where danger lurks in the shadows while Pamas Seclan disembarks and finds unexpected love in young science genius Darmiya Do Voy. (978-1-62639-859-7)

Captain's Choice by VK Powell. Architect Kerstin Anthony's life is going to plan until Bennett Carlyle, the first girl she ever kissed, is assigned to her latest and most important project, a police district substation. (978-1-62639-997-6)

Falling Into Her by Erin Zak. Pam Phillips, widow at the age of forty, meets Kathryn Hawthorne, local Chicago celebrity, and it changes her life forever—in ways she hadn't even considered possible. (978-1-63555-092-4)

Hookin' Up by MJ Williamz. Will Leah get what she needs from casual hookups or will she see the love she desires right in front of her? (978-1-63555-051-1)

King of Thieves by Shea Godfrey. When art thief Casey Marinos meets bounty hunter Finnegan Starkweather, the crimes of the past just might set the stage for a payoff worth more than she ever dreamed possible. (978-1-63555-007-8)

Lucy's Chance by Jackie D. As a serial killer haunts the streets, Lucy tries to stitch up old wounds with her first love in the wake of a small town's rapid descent into chaos. (978-1-63555-027-6)

Right Here, Right Now by Georgia Beers. When Alicia Wright moves into the office next door to Lacey Chamberlain's accounting firm, Lacey is about to find out that sometimes the last person you want is exactly the person you need. (978-1-63555-154-9)

Strictly Need to Know by MB Austin. Covert operator Maji Rios will do whatever she must to complete her mission, but saving a gorgeous stranger from Russian mobsters was not in her plans. (978-1-63555-114-3)

Tailor-Made by Yolanda Wallace. Tailor Grace Henderson doesn't date clients, but when she meets gender-bending model Dakota Lane, she's tempted to throw all the rules out the window. (978-1-63555-081-8)

Time Will Tell by M. Ullrich. With the ability to time travel, Eva Caldwell will have to decide between having it all and erasing it all. (978-1-63555-088-7)

A Date to Die by Anne Laughlin. Someone is killing people close to Detective Kay Adler, who must look to her own troubled past for a suspect. There she finds more than one person seeking revenge against her. (978-1-63555-023-8)

Captured Soul by Laydin Michaels. Can Kadence Munroe save the woman she loves from a twisted killer, or will she lose her to a collector of souls? (978-1-62639-915-0)

Dawn's New Day by TJ Thomas. Can Dawn Oliver and Cam Cooper, two women who have loved and lost, open their hearts to love again? (978-1-63555-072-6)

Definite Possibility by Maggie Cummings. Sam Miller is just out for good times, but Lucy Weston makes her realize happily ever after is a definite possibility. (978-1-62639-909-9)

Eyes Like Those by Melissa Brayden. Isabel Chase and Taylor Andrews struggle between love and ambition from the writers' room on one of Hollywood's hottest TV shows. (978-1-63555-012-2)

Heart's Orders by Jaycie Morrison. Helen Tucker and Tee Owens escape hardscrabble lives to careers in the Women's Army Corps, but more than their hearts are at risk as friendship blossoms into love. (978-1-63555-073-3)

Hiding Out by Kay Bigelow. Treat Dandridge is unaware that her life is in danger from the murderer who is hunting the woman she's falling in love with, Mickey Heiden. (978-1-62639-983-9)

Omnipotence Enough by Sophia Kell Hagin. Can the tiny tool that abducted war veteran Jamie Gwynmorgan accidentally acquires help her escape an unknown enemy to reclaim her stolen life and the woman she deeply loves? (978-1-63555-037-5)

Summer's Cove by Aurora Rey. Emerson Lange moved to Provincetown to live in the moment, but when she meets Darcy Belo and her son Liam, her quest for summer romance becomes a family affair. (978-1-62639-971-6)

The Road to Wings by Julie Tizard. Lieutenant Casey Tompkins, Air Force student pilot, has to fly with the toughest instructor, Captain Kathryn "Hard Ass" Hardesty, fly a supersonic jet, and deal with a growing forbidden attraction. (978-1-62639-988-4)

Beauty and the Boss by Ali Vali. Ellis Renois is at the top of the fashion world, but she never expects her summer assistant Charlotte Hamner to tear her heart and her business apart like sharp scissors through cheap material. (978-1-62639-919-8)

Fury's Choice by Brey Willows. When gods walk amongst humans, can two women find a balance between love and faith? (978-1-62639-869-6)

Lessons in Desire by MJ Williamz. Can a summer love stand a four-month hiatus and still burn hot? (978-1-63555-019-1)

Lightning Chasers by Cass Sellars. For Sydney and Parker, being a couple was never what they had planned. Now they have to fight corruption, murder, and enemies hiding in plain sight just to hold on to each other. Lightning Series, Book Two. (978-1-62639-965-5)

Summer Fling by Jean Copeland. Still jaded from a breakup years earlier, Kate struggles to trust falling in love again when a summer fling with sexy young singer Jordan rocks her off her feet. (978-1-62639-981-5)

Take Me There by Julie Cannon. Adrienne and Sloan know it would be career suicide to mix business with pleasure, however tempting it is. But what's the harm? They're both consenting adults. Who would know? (978-1-62639-917-4)

The Girl Who Wasn't Dead by Samantha Boyette. A year ago, someone tried to kill Jenny Lewis. Tonight she's ready to find out who it was. (978-1-62639-950-1)

Unchained Memories by Dena Blake. Can a woman give herself completely when she's left a piece of herself behind? (978-1-62639-993-8)

Walking Through Shadows by Sheri Lewis Wohl. All Molly wanted to do was go backpacking...in her own century. (978-1-62639-968-6)